THE WEATHERHOUSE

Anna (Nan) Shepherd was born in 1893 and died in 1981. Closely attached to Aberdeen and her native Deeside, she graduated from her home university in 1915 and for the next forty-one years worked as a lecturer in English. An enthusiastic gardener and hill-walker, she made many visits to the Cairngorms with students and friends. She also travelled further afield – to Norway, France, Italy, Greece and South Africa – but always returned to the house where she was raised and where she lived almost all of her adult life, in the village of West Cults, three miles from Aberdeen on North Deeside. Shepherd published just three novels, a single collection of poetry, and *The Living Mountain*, her masterpiece of nature writing, in her lifetime, but is remembered as one of the major authors of modern classic Scottish literature. To honour her legacy, in 2016, Nan Shepherd's face was added to the Royal Bank of Scotland five-pound note.

Also by Nan Shepherd

The Quarry Wood

The Living Mountain

A Pass in the Grampians

In The Cairngorms

THE WEATHERHOUSE

NAN SHEPHERD

INTRODUCED BY AMY LIPTROT

CANONGATE

This Canons edition published by Canongate Books in 2017

First published in 1988 by Canongate Books Ltd,
14 High Street, Edinburgh EH1 1TE

First published in Great Britain in 1930 by
Constable and Co. Ltd, London

www.canongate.co.uk

1

The publishers gratefully acknowledge general subsidy from the
Scottish Arts Council towards the publication of this title

British Library Cataloguing-in-Publication Data

A catalogue record for this book is available on request from the
British Library

ISBN 978 1 78211 886 2

Typeset by Falcon Graphic Art Ltd, Wallington, Surrey

Printed and bound in Great Britain by Clays Ltd, St Ives plc.

Contents

Introduction

'She threw the curtain about her, drew on a pair of galoshes, and ran into the night.'

When nineteen-year-old Lindsay Lorimer is drawn wildly out into the full moon, I knew that *The Weatherhouse* was not just a portrait of a community but a sensory thing that would speak to anyone who has known the Scottish land, or enjoyed Nan Shepherd's beloved work of non-fiction *The Living Mountain*. 'Running thus before the wind,' Lindsay 'had entered into peace that is beyond human understanding: she was at one with the motion of the universe.' This is one of the glittering moments that scatter this complex exploratory novel. These epiphanies, often coming when a character is alone and outdoors, are key to Shepherd's work and make it so exhilarating for me as a reader.

In the fictional Fetter-Rothnie, a small rural community in northeast Scotland, a cast of mainly female characters live their lives in the wake of World War One. The Weatherhouse of the title, with a 'quaint irregular hexagon' room, a glass door to the garden and a sundial, is home to ancient matriarch Lang Leeb and her three daughters. It is a microcosm of the country at that time, pursuing a traditional way of life in a changed world. Then there is the wider community, from old tramp Johnnie Rogie to Stella, a young adoptee, and the novel's other central character, Garry Forbes. When Garry returns to Fetter-Rothnie, scarred by a horrific trauma in the war, he is sceptical about the village: 'the reconstruction of the universe,' he thinks, 'would not begin in this dark hole, inhabited by old wives and ploughmen.' But in the path of the novel the place affects him deeply and his attitude changes.

The Weatherhouse was published in 1930 and was Shepherd's second book. She lived in the same house on the outskirts of Aberdeen for eighty-seven years and died in February 1981, three months before I was born. I grew up further north, in the islands, in an agricultural community almost one hundred years later, but many of the concerns remain the same. She explores what I recognise as both the pleasure and toughness of rural life. I have been that young woman escaping into the light of the full moon and also, returning after having lived away, I have felt like Garry, frustrated and conspicuous. It took a slowing down and an opening up to see the light and worth in what was around me.

Many of the characters are 'looking for the heart

of life.' We are repeatedly taken into the minds of women seeking some kind of self-realisation. Mrs Ellen Falconer longs for purpose, endeavour and imagination: 'It was life she wanted, strong current and fresh wind, no ignoble desire.' She encourages her daughter's connection to Garry to satisfy her own desires. Meanwhile, minister's daughter Louie Morgan wants to be admired: praying earnestly outdoors, hoping to be seen. Later she connects herself to the dead army engineer David Grey, saying: 'I wanted to be at the heart of life instead of on its margins.' Others dispute her version of their engagement, triggering a debate on the nature of truth and reality that is one of the themes of the book.

Compared to Garry's experiences in the trenches, Louie's fantasies seem inconsequential, but take up much more time and exploration. Shepherd shows how important minor scandal, reputation and gossip are in a small community. She uses the turning points and strivings that make a life, the friendships and misunderstandings, to prompt deeper meditations.

Nan Shepherd makes ingenious use of free indirect speech to create a novel of great empathy. Uneducated widowed Ellen, a 'nasty old woman,' is explored with depth and sensitivity, while crude Stella, born into poverty, comes to represent the future, finding employment and confidence by the end of the book. Characters can say things without really speaking: 'Garry is coming? I thought, I used to imagine – long ago – you were such friendly you two. I wondered sometimes – but then he went away.'

Shepherd's sympathy extends to embrace those is the grip of madness, as when Garry thinks, 'That's what they said about me: beside himself, cracked. I was in a fever, you see. But I'm convinced I saw clearer than in my right mind.' All the people in the novel are being exactly themselves and their motivations are presented with truth and kindness. With the Epilogue comes Ellen's work with the Working Girls' Guild, giving a sense of new possibilities and complications in the lives of women.

The novel's generous, calm attention to the inner lives of sidelined, unremembered women means it remains relevant for the twenty-first century. Shepherd herself lived happily without a man for many years and here we are shown women, often unmarried or widowed, as complex and passionate as they approach their later years. Perhaps my favourite moment in the book is when Garry returns from war and witnesses, before she has seen him, his aunt Barbara, 'a hard-knit woman of fifty-five,' alone in the kitchen, dancing.

Besides speaking generally for its time and country, *The Weatherhouse* is also of a very specific place – the outskirts of the Grampians – with a culture and language of its own. Characters go 'stravagin' and have 'collieshangie'. The words are specific to this area but have a control and understatement familiar to me from the isles.

Continually colliding with this controlled society is a wider desire for joy and understanding in Lindsay, Garry and others. There are several passages of quivering beauty and connection, where time and the individual cease to matter. 'He [Garry] saw everything he looked at not as substance, but as energy. All was life. Life pulsed in the clods of earth that the ploughshare were breaking, in the shares, the men. Substance, no matter what its form, was rare and fine.'

In these pantheistic sequences of unbridled energy, where the earthly and spiritual realms are linked through nature, *The Weatherhouse* seems pressingly modern, a response that will be familiar to readers of *The Living Mountain*. It is no surprise that there is currently such renewed interest in Shepherd's work. She has even become the latest woman to grace a Scottish bank note, appearing on the new Royal Bank of Scotland five-pound note, depicted in front of her beloved Cairngorm hills.

Although written in a period before conservation or industrial farming as we know it, *The Weatherhouse* pinpoints timeless philosophical debates about the naming of things and our relationship to the environment. Ellen says there is no need to learn the names of the birds: 'Her lips parted and her eyes shone; and Mrs Falconer longed to tell her of the strange secret of life – how all things were one and there was no estrangement except for those who did not understand.' The people of Fetter-Rothnie are linked into the bigger cycles of land and community, and what Garry comes to see as 'this astonishing earth.'

Amy Liptrot

The Main Characters

THE YOUNG PROTAGONISTS

Captain Garry Forbes (30), ('the Gargoyle'), son of the timid Benjamin Forbes who was half-brother to Barbara Paterson. Wounded in the trenches of the First World War.

Miss Lindsay Lorimer (19), daughter of Andrew Lorimer; sister of Frank, who served in the war with Garry Forbes.

Miss Louisa (Louie) Morgan (35), at Uplands, daughter of the previous minister at Fetter-Rothnie. Louie claims to be engaged to David Grey, Garry Forbes's engineer friend, who died of T.B.

THE LADIES AT THE WEATHERHOUSE

Aunt Craigmyle (Lang Leeb) (90+), cousin to Andrew Lorimer, the solicitor father of Lindsay and Frank. Widowed at 54, Leeb retired to the Weatherhouse and left things to her three daughters, namely:

Miss Annie Dyce (Paradise) Craigmyle, raised by her father to look after the farm, she took charge of it when he died until crippled by rheumatism.

Mrs Ellen (Nell) Falconer (60), married at 27 to Charlie Falconer who died in poverty, leaving Ellen to return to her old home along with her daughter, *Kate Falconer* (30), cook at a nearby convalescent hospital.

Miss Theresa (Tris) Craigmyle, Leeb's youngest daughter, housekeeper to her mother and sisters at the Weatherhouse.

FROM THE NEIGHBOURHOOD

Miss Barbara (Bawbie) Paterson (55), of Knapperley, maiden aunt to Garry Forbes.

Francie Ferguson, son to Jeames Ferguson who helped adapt the Weatherhouse; brother to 'Feel Weelum', finally husband (after 22 years engagement) to 'Peter Sandy's Bell', already father to her children, Stella Dagmar and Sidney Archibald Eric.

Mrs Barbara Hunter, of Craggie, ex servant girl and friend to Bawbie Paterson at Knapperley; wife of crofter Jake Hunter; mother of Dave, who returns wounded from the war to re-educate himself as a graduate and a school teacher.

Jonathan Bannochie, cobbler to trade, originator of the phrase 'Garry Forbes and his twa fools', referring to Garry, Bawbie and Francie.

The Prologue

The name of Garry Forbes has passed into proverb in Fetter-Rothnie.

One sees him gaunt, competent, a trifle anxious, the big fleshy ears standing out from his head, the two furrows cutting deeply round from nostril to chin, his hands powerful but squat, gift of a plebeian grandfather, and often grimed with oil and grease—hardly a figure of romance. Of those who know him, to some he is a keen, long-headed manager, with a stiff record behind him in the training of ex-service men and the juvenile unemployed, tenacious, taciturn, reliable, with uncanny reserves of knowledge; to others, a rampageous Socialist blustering out disaster, a frequenter of meetings: they add a hint of property (some say expectations) in Scotland; to some he is merely another of those confounded Scotch engineers; but to none is he a legend. They are not to know that in Fetter-Rothnie, where the tall, narrow, ugly house of Knapperley is situate, his name has already become a symbol.

You would need Garry Forbes to you. It is the local way of telling your man he is a liar. And when they deride you, scoffing at your lack of common sense, *Hine up on the head of the house like Garry Forbes and his twa fools*, is the accepted phrase. As the ladies at the Weatherhouse said, A byword and a laughing stock to the place. And married into the family, too!

ONE

To the Lorimers of a younger generation, children of the three Lorimer brothers who had played in the walled manse garden with the three Craigmyle girls, the Weatherhouse was a place of pleasant dalliance. It meant day-long summer visits, toilsome uphill July walks that ended in the cool peace of the Weatherhouse parlour, with home-brewed ginger beer for refreshment, girdle scones and strawberry jam and butter biscuits, and old Aunt Leeb seated in her corner with her spider-fine white lace cap, piercing eyes and curious staves of song; then the eager rush for the open, the bickering around the old sundial, the race for the moor; and a sense of endless daylight, of enormous space, of a world lifted up beyond the concerns of common time; and eggs for tea, in polished wooden egg-cups that were right end up either way; and queer fascinating things such as one saw in no other house—the kettle holder with the black cross-stitch kettle worked upon it, framed samplers on the walls, the goffering iron, the spinning wheel. And sometimes Paradise would show them how the goffering iron was worked.

Paradise, indeed, gave a flavouring to a Weatherhouse day that none of the other ladies could offer. Round her clung still the recollection of older, rarer visits, when they were smaller and she not yet a cripple; of the splendid abounding wonder that inhabits a farm. Not a Lorimer but associated the thought of Paradise with chickens newly broken from the shell, ducks worrying with their flat bills in the grass; with dark, half-known, sweet-smelling corners in the barn, and the yielding, sliding, scratching feel of hay; with the steep wooden stair to the stable-loft and the sound of the big, patient, clumsy horses moving and munching below, a rattle of harness, the sudden nosing of a dog; with the swish of milk in the pail and the sharp delightful terror as the great tufted tail swung and lashed; with the smell of oatcakes browning, the plod of the churn and its changing note of triumph, and the wide, shallow basins set with gleaming milk; with the whirr of the reaper, the half-comprehended excitement of harvest, the binding, the shining stooks; with the wild madness of the last uncut patch, the trapped and furtive things one watched in a delirium of joy and revulsion; and the comfort, afterwards, of gathering eggs, safe, smooth and warm against the palm.

Of that need for comfort Paradise herself had no comprehension. Rats, rabbits and weakly chicks were killed as a matter of course. There was no false sentiment about Miss Annie: nothing flimsy. She was hard-knit, like a home-made worsted stocking, substantial, honest and durable. 'A cauff bed tied in the middle,' her sister Theresa said rudely of her in her later years, when inactivity had turned her flabby; but at the farm one remembered her as being everywhere.

It was Andrew Lorimer, her cousin, who transformed her baptismal name of Annie Dyce to Paradise, and now his children and his brothers' children scarcely knew her by another. Not that Miss Annie cared! 'I'm as much of Paradise as you are like to see, my lad,' she used to tell him.

The four ladies at the Weatherhouse, old Aunt Craigmyle and her daughters, could epitomise the countryside among them in their stories. Paradise knew how things were done; she told of ancient customs, of fairs and cattle markets and all the processes of a life whose principle is in the fields. The tales of Aunt Craigmyle herself had a fiercer quality; all the old balladry, the romance of wild and unscrupulous deeds, fell from her thin and shapely lips. And if she did not tell a tale, she sang. She was always singing. Ballads were the natural food of her mind. John, the second of the three Lorimer brothers, said of her, when the old lady attained her ninetieth birthday, 'She'll live to be a hundred yet, and attribute it to singing nothing but ballads all her life.'

Cousin Theresa cared more for what the folk of her own day did—matter of little moment to the children. But she had, too, the grisly tales: of the body-snatchers at Drum and the rescue by the grimy blacksmith on his skelping mare; of Malcolm Gillespie, best-hated of excisemen, and the ill end he came by on the gallows, and of the whisky driven glumly past him in a hearse. To Cousin Ellen the children paid less heed; though they laughed (as she laughed herself) at her funny headlong habit of suggesting conclusions to every half-told tale she heard. Cousins Annie or Theresa would say, 'Oh, yes, of course Nell must know all about it!' and she would laugh with them and answer, 'Yes, there I am again.' But sometimes she would bite her lip and look annoyed. It was she too, who said, out on the moor, 'Look, you can see Ben A'an today—that faint blue line,' or talked queer talk about the Druid stones. But these were horizons too distant for childish minds. It was pleasanter to hear again the familiar story of how the Weatherhouse came to be built.

Mrs Craigmyle at fifty four, widowed but unperturbed, announced to her unmarried daughters that she was done with the farm: Annie could keep it if she liked—which Annie did. Theresa and her mother would live free. Theresa was not ill-pleased, when it became apparent that she was to be mistress of the new home. Theresa could never understand her mother's idle humour. The grace of irresponsibility was beyond her. But Mrs Craigmyle, whose straight high shoulders and legs of swinging length had earned her the family by-name of Lang Leeb, had been a wild limb, with her mind more on balladry than on butter; and her father, the Reverend Andrew, was thankful when he got her safely married into the douce Craigmyle clan. She had made James Craigmyle an excellent wife; but at fifty four was quite content to let the excellence follow the wifehood.

'We'll go to town, I suppose,' said Theresa, who liked company.

'Fient a town. We'll go to Andra Findlater's place.'

Annie and Theresa stared.

Andra Findlater was a distant cousin of their mother, dead long since. A stonemason to trade, he had lived in a two-roomed cottage on the edge of their own farmlands. When his daughters were seven and eight years old, Mrs Findlater decided that she wanted the ben-end kept clear of their muck; and Andra had knocked a hole in the back wall and built them a room for themselves: a delicious room, low-roofed and with a window set slanting.

'But if I could big a bit mair—' Andra kept thinking. Another but-and-ben stood back from theirs, its own length away and just out of line with the new room—now what could a man do with that were he to join them up? Be it understood that Andra Findlater had no prospect of being able to join them up; but the problem of how to make the houses one absorbed him to his dying day. It helped, indeed, to bring about his death; for Andra would lean against a spruce tree for hours of an evening, smoking his pipe and considering the lie of the buildings. He leaned one raw March night till he caught cold; and died of pneumonia.

Lang Leeb, as mistress of the big square farmhouse, had always time for a *newse* with her poor relations. She relished Andra. Many an evening she dandered across the fields, in her black silk apron and with her *shank* in her hands, to listen to his brooding projects. She loved the site of the red-tiled cottages, set high, almost on the crest of the long ridge; she loved the slanting window of the built-out room. A month after her husband's death she dandered down the field one day and asked the occupant of the cottage to let her see the little room again. 'It's a gey soster,' said she. 'The cat's just kittled in't.' Lang Leeb went home and told her daughters she was henceforth to live at Andra Findlater's place; and her daughters stared.

But Leeb knew what she was doing. She took the cottages and joined them. Andra's problem was, after all, easy enough to solve. She had money: a useful adjunct to brains. She knocked out the partition of Andra's original home and made of it a long living-room with a glass door to the garden; and between the two cottages, with the girls' old bedroom for corridor, she built a quaint irregular hexagon, with an upper storey that contained one plain bedroom and one that was all corners and windows—an elfin inconsequential room, using up odd scraps of space.

The whole was roofed with mellowed tiles. None of your crude new colourings for Leeb. She went up and down the country till she had collected all she required, from barns and byres and outhouses. Leeb knew how to obtain what she wanted. She came back possessed of three or four quern stones, a cruisie lamp and a tirl-the-pin; and from the farm she brought the spinning wheel and the old wooden dresser and plate racks.

The place grew quaint and rare both out of doors and in. One morning Leeb contemplated the low vestibule that had been a bedroom, humming the gay little verse it often brought to her mind:

The grey cat's kittled in Charley's wig,
There's ane o' them livin' an' twa o' them deid.

'Now this should be part of the living-room,' said she. 'It's dark and awkward as a passage. We'll have it so—and so.'

She knew exactly what she wanted done, and gave her orders; but the workman sent to her reported back some three hours later with instructions not to return.

'But what have you against the man?' his master asked.

'I've nothing against him, forbye that he's blind, and he canna see.'

She refused another man; but one day she called Jeames Ferguson in from the garden. Jeames was a wonder with his hands. He had set up the sundial, laid the crazy paving, and constructed stone stalks to the querns, some curved, some tapering, some squat, that made them look like monstrous mushrooms. 'Could you do *that*, Jeames?' 'Fine that.' Jeames did it, and was promptly dismissed to the garden, for his clumps of boots were ill-placed in the house. Mrs Craigmyle did the finishing herself and rearranged her curious possessions. Some weeks later Jeames, receiving orders beside the glass door, suddenly observed, 'I hinna seen't sin' it was finished,' and strode on to the Persian rug with his *dubbit* and tacketty boots. But no Persian rug did Jeames see. Folding his arms, he beamed all over his honest face and contemplated his own handiwork.

'That's a fine bit o' work, ay is it,' he said at last.

'You couldn't be angered at the body. He was that fine pleased with himself,' said Mrs Craigmyle.

But the house once to her mind, Mrs Craigmyle did no more work. Dismissing her husband in a phrase, 'He was a moral man—I can say no more,' she sat down with a careless ease in the Weatherhouse and gathered her chapbooks and broadsheets around her:

Songs, Bibles, Psalm-books and the like,
As mony as would big a dyke—

though, to be sure, daughter of the manse as she was, the Bible had scanty place in her heap of books. *Whistle Binkie* was her Shorter Catechism. She gave all her household dignity for an old song: sometimes her honour and kindliness as well; for Leeb treated the life around her as though it were already ballad. She relished it, but having ceased herself to feel, seemed to have forgotten that others felt. She grew hardly visibly older, retaining to old age her erect carriage and the colour and texture of her skin. Her face was without blemish, her hands were delicate; only the long legs, as Kate Falconer could have told, were brown with fern-tickles. Kate had watched so often, with a child's fascinated stare, her grandmother washing her feet in a tin basin on the kitchen floor. Kate grew up believing that her grandmother ran barefoot among tall bracken when she was young; and probably Kate was right.

So Lang Leeb detached herself from active living. Once a year she made an expedition to town, and visited in turn the homes of her three Lorimer nephews. She carried on these occasions a huge pot of jam, which she called 'the berries'; and having ladled out the Andrew Lorimers' portion with a wooden spoon, replaced the pot in her basket and bore it to the Roberts and the Johns. For the rest, she sat aside and chuckled. Life is an entertainment hard to beat when one's affections are not engaged. Theresa managed the house and throve on it, having found too little scope at the farm for her masterful temper. Her mother let her be, treating even her craze for acquisition with an ironic indulgence. Already with the things they had brought from the farm the house was full. But Theresa never missed a chance to add to her possessions. She had a passion for roups. 'A ga'in foot's aye gettin',' she said.

'She's like Robbie Welsh the hangman,' Lang Leeb would chuckle, 'must have a fish out of ilka creel.' And when Mrs Hunter told Jonathan Bannochie the souter, a noted hater of women, that Miss Theresa was at the Wastride roup, 'and up and awa wi' her oxter full o' stuff,' she was said to have added, 'They would need a displenish themsels in yon hoose, let alane bringin' mair in by.' 'Displenish,' snorted Jonathan. 'Displenish, said ye? It's a roup o' the fowk that's needed there.'

Miss Annie too, when she gave up the farm brought part of her plenishing. Ellen was the only one who brought nothing to the household gear. Ellen brought nothing but her child; and there was nowhere to put her but the daft room at the head of the stairs that Theresa had been using for lumber.

'It's a mad-like place,' Theresa said. 'Nothing but a trap for dust. But you won't take a Finnan haddie in a Hielan' burnie. She's no way to come but this, and she'll just need to be doing with it. She's swallowed the cow and needn't choke at the tail.'

Ellen did not choke. She loved the many-cornered room with its irregular windows. There she shut herself in as to a tower and was safe; or rather, she felt, shut herself out from the rest of the house. The room seemed not to end with itself, but through its protruding windows became part of the infinite world. There she lay and watched the stars; saw dawn touch the mountains; and fortified her soul in the darkness that had come on her.

TWO

Of the three Craigmyle sisters, Ellen was the likest to her mother. She too was long and lean, though she had not her mother's delicacy of fingers and of skin; and to Ellen alone among her daughters Mrs Craigmyle had bequeathed the wild Lorimer heart.

How wild it was not even the girl herself had discovered, when at twenty seven she married Charley Falconer. There was no opposition to the match, though Falconer was a stranger; well-doing apparently; quiet and assured: which the family took to mean reliable, and Ellen, profound. Her life had hitherto been hard and rigid; her father, James Craigmyle, kept his whole household to the plough; not from any love of tyranny, but because he had never conceived of a life other than strait and laborious. To work in sweat was man's natural heritage. His wife obeyed him and bided her time; Ellen obeyed, and escaped in thought to a fantastic world of her own imagining. The merest hint of a tale sufficed her, her fancy was off. Her choicest hours were spent in unreality—a land where others act in accordance with one's expectations. Sometimes her toppling palaces would crash at the touch of the actual, and then she suffered an agony of remorse because the real Ellen was so unlike the Ellen of her fancies. 'There I am again—I mustn't pretend these silly things,' she would say; and taking her Bible she would read the verse that she had marked for her own especial scourging: 'Casting down imaginations and every high thing that exalteth itself against the knowledge of God, and bringing into captivity every thought to the obedience of Christ.' For a day or two she would sternly dismiss each fleeting suggestion of fiction, striving to empty a mind that was naturally quick and receptive, and finding the plain sobriety of a Craigmyle regimen inadequate to fill it. Shortly she was 'telling herself stories' again. It might be wicked, but it made life radiant.

Concerning Charley Falconer she told herself an endless story. The tragedy of her brief married life lay in the clash between her story and the truth. Charley was very ordinary and a little cheap. He dragged her miserably from one lodging to another, unstable, but with a certain large indifference to his own interests that exposed his memory to Craigmyle and Lorimer contempt, when at his death Ellen could no longer deny how poor she was.

She came back to her mother's house, dependent, the more so that she had a child; at bitter variance with herself. She had been forced up against a grinding poverty, a shallow nature and a life without dignity. By the time she returned home her father was dead, the Weatherhouse built and Theresa comfortably settled as its genius. Ellen found herself tolerated. Power was too sweet to this youngest sister who had had none: the widowed and deprived was put in her place. Since that place was the odd-shaped upstairs room, Ellen did not grumble; but Theresa's management made it perhaps a trifle harder for her to come to terms with the world. Her own subordinate position in the house was subtly a temptation: it sent her back to refuge in her imaginings. After a time the rancour and indignity of her married years faded out. She thought she was experienced in life, but in truth she had assimilated nothing from her suffering, only dismissed it and returned to her dreams.

Two things above all restored her—her child and the country. It was a country that liberated. More than half the world was sky. The coastline vanished at one of the four corners of the earth, Ellen lost herself in its immensity. It wiled her from thought.

Kate also took her from herself. She was not a clever child, neither quaint nor original nor *ill-trickit*; but never out of humour. She asked nothing much from life—too easily satisfied, her mother thought, without what she could not have. Ellen, arguing from her own history, had schooled herself to meet the girl's inevitable revolt, her demand for her own way of living. But Kate at thirty had not yet revolted. She had wanted nothing that was not to her hand. She had no ambition after a career, higher education did not interest her, she questioned neither life nor her own right to relish it. Had she not been brought up among Craigmyles, their quiet domesticity was what she would have fancied. She liked making a bed and contriving a dinner; and since she must earn her living she took a Diploma in Domestic Science and had held several posts as housekeeper or school matron; but late in 1917 she entered (to the regret of some of her relations) upon voluntary work in a Hospital, becoming cook in a convalescent Hospital not far from her home.

Ellen had therefore carried for nearly thirty years the conviction that she had tested life; and mastered it.

At sixty she was curiously young. Her body was strong and supple, her face tanned, a warm glow beneath the tan. She walked much alone upon the moors, walking heel first to the ground with a firm and elastic tread. Her eyes were young; by cause both of their brightness and of their dreaming look. No experience was in their glance. She knew remote and unspeakable things—the passage of winds, the trembling of the morning star, the ecstasy of February nights when all the streams are murmuring. She did not know human pain and danger. She thought she did, but the pain she knew was only her own quivering hurt. Her world was all her own, she its centre and interpretation; and she had even a faint sweet contempt for those who could not enter it. The world and its modes passed by and she ignored them. She was a little proud of her indifference to fashion and chid her sister Theresa for liking a modish gown. She saw—as who could have helped seeing—the external changes that marked life during the thirty years she had lived in the Weatherhouse: motor cars, the shortening skirt, the vacuum cleaner; but of the profounder revolutions, the change in temper of a generation, the altered point of balance of the world's knowledge, the press of passions other than individual and domestic, she was completely unaware.

Insensibly as these thirty years passed she allowed her old fashion to grow on her. Fancy was her tower of refuge. Like any green girl she pictured her futures by the score. After a time she took the habit of her imaginary worlds so strongly that hints of their presence dropped out in her talk, and when she was laughed at she would laugh or be offended according to the vehemence with which she had created; but among the gentle scoffers none guessed the ravishment her creations brought her, and none the mortified despair of her occasional revulsions from her fairyland.

It did not occur to her that when Lindsay Lorimer came to Fetter-Rothnie her fairyland would vanish into smoke.

Lindsay came to stay at the Weatherhouse on this wise: her mother, Mrs Andrew Lorimer, arrived one day in perturbation.

'We don't know what to do with Lindsay,' she confessed. 'If you would let her come here for a little—? We thought perhaps the change—and away from the others. These boys do tease her so. They can't see that she's ill.'

'She's ill, is she?' said Theresa. 'And what ails her, then?'

Mrs Andrew took some time to make it clear that Lindsay's sickness was of the temper.

'Not that we have anything against him,' she said. 'He's an excellent young man—most gentlemanly. When he likes. But she's so young. Nineteen. Her father won't hear of it. "All nonsense too young," he says. But I suppose she keeps thinking, well, and if he doesn't come back. It's this war that does it.'

'It's time it were put a stop to,' said Miss Annie.

'Yes,' sighed Mrs Andrew. 'And let things be as they were.'

'But they won't be, said Ellen.

'No,' she answered. 'Frank'll never go to college now. He swears he won't go to the University and won't. And it's all this Captain Dalgarno. It's Dalgarno this and Dalgarno that. Frank's under him, you know. I wonder what the Captain means by it. He's contaminating Frank. Putting ideas into his head. He was only a schoolboy when it began, you must remember—hadn't had time to have his mind formed. And now he swears he won't go to the University and won't enter a profession. All my family have been in the professions.'

She sighed again.

'He wants to *do* things, he says. Things with his hands. Make things. "Good heavens, mother," he said to me, just his last leave—the Captain was home with him on his last leave, you know; it was then that Lindsay and he wanted to get married, and her father just wouldn't have it. "Good heavens mother, we've *un*-made enough, surely, in these three and a half years. I want to make something now. *You* haven't seen the ruined villages. The world will get on very well without the law and the Church for a considerable time to come," he said, "but it's going to be jolly much in need of engineers and carpenters." Make chairs and tables, that seems to be his idea. "Even if I could make one table to stand fast on its feet, I'd be happy. I won't belong to a privileged class," he said. "There aren't privileges. There's only the privilege of working." It *sounds* all right, of course, and I'm sure we all feel for the working man. But if Lindsay marries him I don't know what we shall all come to.'

Mrs Craigmyle, attentive in the corner, began to hum. No one of course heeded her. She sang a stave through any business that was afoot. She sang now, the hum developing to words:

Wash weel the fresh fish, wash weel the fresh fish,
Wash weel the fresh fish and skim weel the bree,
For there's mony a foul-fittit thing,
There's mony a foul-fittit thing in the saut sea.

And Ellen's anger suddenly flared. A natural song enough for one whose home looked down on the coast villages of Finnan and Portlendie; but it was Ellen the dreamer, not the sagacious Annie or Theresa, who had read in her mother that the old lady's was an intelligent indifference to life. She took no sides, an ironic commentator. Two and thirty years of Craigmyle wedlock had tamed her natural wildness of action to an impudence of thought that relished its own dainty morsels by itself. Her cruelties came from comprehension, not from lack of it. And had not Mrs Andrew said the word? 'Contaminating,' she had said. Ellen did well to be angry. She was angry on behalf of this young girl the secret of whose love was bandied thus among contemptuous women.

'But I know, I know, I understand,' she thought. 'I must help her, be her friend.' Already her fancy was off. She had climbed her tower and saw herself in radiant light, creating Lindsay's destiny.

She looked from under bent brows at her mother, who continued to sing, with a remote and airy grace, her long fine fingers folded in her lap. She sat very erect and looked at no one, lost apparently in her song. Ellen relaxed her frown, but remained gazing at the singer, falling unconsciously into the same attitude as her mother, and the singular resemblance between the two faces became apparent, both intent, both strangely innocent, the old lady's by reason of its much withdrawn, Ellen's from the enthusiasm of solitary dreaming that hedged her about from reality.

The Drama

ONE

Proposal for a Party

Miss Theresa Craigmyle opened the kitchen door in response to the knock, and saw Francie Ferguson holding a bag of potatoes in his arms.

'Ay, ay, Francie,' she said, 'you've brought the tatties. Who would have thought, now, there would be such a frost and us not to have a tattie out of the pit? It was a mercy you had some up.'

'O ay,' said Francie, 'and the frost's haudin'. There's the smell o' snaw in the air. It'll be dingin' on afore ye ken yersel.'

Miss Theresa took the potatoes, saying cheerily, 'And a fine big bag you've given us, Francie. But you were aye the one for a bittie by the bargain.'

Francie shuffled to the other foot and rubbed a hand upon his thigh.

'Well, ye like to be honest, but ye canna be ower honest or ye'd hae naething to yersel.' He added, spreading a dirty paw against the door-jamb, 'The missus is to her bed.'

'Oh,' said Miss Theresa. She said it tartly. The bag poised in her arms, she was judicially considering its weight. 'Not so heavy, after all,' she thought. Francie's way had formerly been, 'I just put in a puckle by guess like.' He hadn't been long at the school, he said, wasn't used with your weights and measures. But his lavishness, Miss Theresa could see, was receiving a check: beyond a doubt the work of the *missus*. Miss Theresa was not disposed to sympathy. 'She's a din-raising baggage,' she reflected, and heard Francie out with a face as set as the frost.

Francie was grumbling heartily at life. He knew fine that the potatoes were scanty measure. He did not confess it, of course, but since Miss Theresa was sure to discover, he detailed the mitigating circumstances: a sick wife, a cow gone dry, forty barren besoms of hens and a daughter soft-hearted to the point of letting all the rabbits off the snares—ay, and giving them a bit of her *piece*, no less, any one that looked pitiful at her. Francie had remonstrated, of course, but might as well speak to the wind blowing by. 'A gey-like swippert o' a queyne, she is that,' he said, not without a certain conscious pride. And meat-whole, he added, 'They're a' that—the wife as weel.'

'She would be,' said Miss Theresa. 'She's about stotting off the ground with fat. And what is't that ails her, like?'

Francie laboured to explain.

'Oh, a stoun' of love,' said Miss Theresa shortly. 'It'll have come out at the wrong place. Wait you.' And laying down the potatoes, she brought a good-sized pudding from the pantry and thrust it on Francie.

'You can't take that before the court and swear to it that you're hungered,' she said, and shut the door on him.

In the parlour she repeated the conversation.

'He does all the cooking himself, he tells me. I wouldn't be any curious about eating it. He stewed a rabbit. "It was gey tough," he says, "it gart your jaws wonder." '

'Fancy the little girl and the rabbits,' cried Lindsay. 'That's the child we saw yesterday, isn't it, Katie? With the coal-black eyes. She looked a mischief! She's not like her father, anyway. You'd never suppose she was his daughter.'

'You never would, for the easy reason that she's not.'

'I'm glad to see he calls her his daughter, it's kindly of the body.'

'What other could he do? You can't give a gift a clyte in the mouth, and the bairns were her marriage gift to the craitur, as you might say.'

'They looked so neglected, these children,' cried Lindsay. 'And with their mother ill. Couldn't we give them a party? They can't have had much of a Christmas.'

'Oh, party away at them,' conceded Theresa. 'Would you really like it, Lindsay?'

Lindsay was aglow with eagerness. 'And a Christmas tree?' she said. 'Oh, I know it's January now, but I don't believe they've ever seen a tree. One of those big spruce branches would do.' She was given over entirely to her excitement. A mere child, thought Theresa. Well, and here was a change of countenance from the earlier days. The affair could not mean much when she threw it off so easily. The pale and moody Lindsay who had gone wanly about the house on her arrival, displeased Miss Theresa, who disliked a piner. Like many robust people, she resented the presence of suffering; pain, physical or mental, was an inconvenience that she preferred not to see. A Lindsay absorbed in trifling with a Christmas tree was a relief Miss Theresa might well afford herself; and she afforded it with grace.

'Have you time, Kate,' she asked of her niece Kate Falconer, who was spending her hour of leave at home, 'to go round on your way back to the Hospital and bid them come?'

'Why, yes,' said Kate, 'if we start at once. You come too, Linny.'

'Go in by to Craggie,' pursued Miss Theresa, 'and bid Mrs Hunter too. We've been meaning to have her to tea this while back. She'll be grand pleased at the tree. She's like a bairn when you give her a thing.'

Kate went to make ready, and Lindsay would have followed; but as she passed, her grand-aunt detained her with a look. Mrs Craigmyle had few gestures; she held herself still; only her eyes glittered and her lips moved, and often her fingers went to and fro as she knitted—a spider stillness. The film of delicate lace upon hair as fine as itself was not the only thing about her that betokened the spider. One had the sense of being caught upon a look, lured in and held.

Lindsay drew up to her, and stood.

'So, so, you are to turn my house into a market, Leezie Lindsay?'

'Why do you call me that, Aunt Leeb?'

Lang Leeb sang from the old ballad.

'Surely you know,' she said, 'that Leezie Lindsay came to Kingcausie with that braw lad she ran away with, and it's not far from Kingcausie that you've come, Mistress Lindsay.'

The scarlet rushed on Lindsay's brow and stood in splatches over neck and chin.

She pushed back her mop of curls and stared at the old woman; and her words seemed to be drawn from her without her will.

'Kingcausie? That's—isn't that the place among trees, a line of beeches and then some scraggy firs? Beyond the Tower there.'

'Hoots! Never a bit. That's Knapperley. Daft Bawbie Paterson's place. Kingcausie lies to the river.'

The scarlet had deepened on Lindsay's throat. 'Have I given myself away?' she was thinking.

She had discovered what she had wanted to know since ever she came to Fetter-Rothnie. Often as she had visited the Weatherhouse, she had not stayed there, and its surroundings were unfamiliar. It had seemed so easy, in imagination, when she walked with Kate, to ask it in a careless way, 'Isn't that Knapperley over there, Katie?' or 'What place is that among the trees?' But when the moment came her heart had thumped too wildly; she was not strong enough to ask. Now that she knew she sheered off nervously from the subject, as though to linger were deadly. And she plunged, 'But why a market, Aunt Leeb? I'm sure we shan't be very rowdy.'

'A lot you know about the fisher folk, if that's your way of thinking. It was them that cracked the Marykirk bell, jingle-janglin' for a burying.'

'But they're not fisher folk here—Francie?'

'She is.'

And Lindsay, because she was afraid to hear further of the lady who had brought the black-eyed bairns as a wedding gift to her husband, glanced rapidly around, and saw Mrs Falconer put her head in at the door and look at them. There was something pathetic about Cousin Ellen, Lindsay thought—her straying gaze, her muttering to herself. A poor old thing. And what was she wanting now, watching them both like that?

A poor young thing, Ellen was thinking. She must protect her from her mother's sly and studied jests. So she said, 'Kate must be off, Linny,' and the girl fled gladly.

Francie was shouting a lusty song as he worked:

I'll never forget till the day that I dee
The lumps o' fat my granny gied me,
The heids o' herrin' an' tails o'cats—

He broke off abruptly and cried, 'Are ye cleanin' yersels, littlins? Here's ladies to see you.'

The children hove in sight, drying their half-washed hands on opposite ends of a towel. Bold-eyed youngsters, with an address unusual in country bairns. Each hurried to complete the drying first and so be saved from putting away the towel; and both dropping it at one moment, it fell in a heap. The children began to quarrel noisily.

'Put you it by, Stellicky,' said the man, who stood watching the bickering bairns for awhile with every appearance of content. Francie had a soft foolish kindly face, and while the girl, with black looks, did as she was bidden, he swung the loonie to his shoulder and said, 'He's a gey bit birkie, isna he, to be but five year auld?'

'And how's the wife?' said Kate.

Francie confided in her that whiles she took a tig, and he thought it was maybe no more than that.

'They were only married in August,' said Kate, laughing, as the girls followed a field path away from the croft.

'Oh, look,' cried Lindsay. 'A bramble leaf still. Blood-red.'

'So it is,' Kate replied. 'And engaged for over twenty years.'

'I don't particularly want to hear about it, Katie.'

'But why,' said Kate, 'it's an entertaining tale.'

And she began to relate it.

Francie was son to old Jeames Ferguson, who had helped to make the Weatherhouse; and Francie's taking of a wife had been a seven days' speak in Fetter-Rothnie. He had been betrothed for two and twenty years. All the countryside knew of the betrothal, but that it should end in marriage was a surprise for which the gossips were not prepared. A joke, too. A better joke, as it turned out, than they had anticipated.

The two and twenty years of waiting were due to Francie's brother Weelum. Weelum in boyhood had discovered an astounding aptitude for craftsmanship. He had been apprenticed to a painter in Peterkirk, and in course became a journeyman. From that day on Francie referred invariably to his brother as 'The Journeyman.' Weelum's name was never heard to cross his lips; he remained 'The Journeyman,' though he did not remain a painter.

Weelum's career as a journeyman was mute and inglorious. He was a taciturn man: he wasted no words; and when his master's clients gave orders about the detail of the work he undertook he would listen with an intent, intelligent expression, and reply with a grave and considering nod. Afterwards he did exactly what he pleased. Folk complained. Weelum continued to do what he pleased. In the end his master dismissed him; reluctantly, for he had clever hands.

He established himself with Francie. There was not work on the croft for two men; but as there was no woman on it, Weelum took possession of the domestic affairs. He did what he pleased there too, and made much to-do about his industry. Francie could not see that there was much result from it all. 'He's eident, but he doesna win through,' he would sometimes say sorrowfully. 'Feel Weelum,' the folk called him. 'Oh, nae sae feel,' said Jonathan Bannochie the souter. 'He kens gey weel whaur his pottage bickers best.' To Francie he was still 'The Journeyman.'

When Weelum came home to bide, Francie was already contracted to a lassie in the fishing village of Bargie, some twenty miles away, down the coast. A bonny bit lass, but her folk were terrible tinks; they had the name of being the worst tinks in Bargie. Weelum had some family pride, if Francie had none, and there were bitter words between the brothers. The Journeyman set his face implacably against the marriage, and stood aggrieved and silent when Francie tried to thresh the matter out. 'He has ower good a downsit, and he kens it,' said the folk. Francie's respect for his brother was profound. On the Sunday afternoons when he cycled across to Bargie, he would slink out in silence by the back way from his own house. One Sunday the brothers came to high words. Francie mounted his cycle, and trusted—as he always did trust—that all would be well on his return. That Weelum did not speak on his return gave him no anxiety: Weelum often *stunkit* at him and kept silence for days. But this time Weelum kept silence for ever. He never again addressed a word to his brother, though he remained under his roof, eating of his bread, for over twenty years. Through all that time the brothers slept in the same bed, rising each in the morning to his separate tasks.

One afternoon the Journeyman fell over with a stroke. That was an end to the hope of his speaking. 'I some think he would have liked to say something,' Francie declared. He climbed in beside his brother to the one bed the room contained, and wakened in the hour before dawn *geal cauld* to find the Journeyman dead beside him.

Some months later Francie was cried in the kirk. A burr of excitement ran through the congregation. So the Bargie woman had waited for him! When the day of the wedding came, Francie set out in the early morning, with the old mare harnessed to the farm cart.

'Take her on the hin step o' yer bike, Francie, man,' cried one of the bystanders. 'That would be mair gallivantin' like than the cairt.'

'There's her bits o' things to fesh,' Francie answered.

'She'll hae some chairs an' thingies,' said the neighbours. 'The hoosie'll nae be oot o' the need o' them. It's terrible bare.'

Francie had not dreamed of a reception; but when, late in the evening, the bridal journey ended and the cart turned soberly up the cart-road to the croft, he found a crowd about his doors.

Francie bartered words with no man. He handed out his bride, and after her one bairn, and then another; and then a bundle tied up in a Turkey counterpane. The bride and the bairns went in, and Francie shut the door on them; and turned back to tend his mare.

'She'll hae been a weeda, Francie?' said Jonathan Bannochie. A titter ran round the company.

Francie unharnessed the mare.

'Weel, nae exactly a weeda,' he said in his slow way;

and led the mare to stable.

Next morning he harnessed her again and jogged in the old cart to town. All Fetter-Rothnie watched him come home with a brand-new iron bedstead in the cart. 'For the bairns,' they said. 'He might have made less do with them.' But the bed was not for the bairns.

'Aunt Tris was the first of us to see her,' Kate told Lindsay. 'She invented an errand over. Aunt Tris would invent an errand to the deil himself, Granny says, if she wanted something from him. She came home and sat down and took off all her outdoor things before she would say a word. And then she said, "He was fond of fish before he fried the scrubber." She told us about the bed. "She won't even sleep with him," she told us. "Him and the laddie sleeps in the kitchen, and her and the lassie's got the room. It's six and sax, I'm thinking, for Francie, between the Journeyman and the wife." And she told us the bairns' names.'

The bairns' names were a diversion to Fetter-Rothnie. In a community that had hardly a dozen names amongst its folk, Francie's betrothed had been known as Peter's Sandy's Bell; but she was determined that her children should have individual names, and called the girl Stella Dagmar and the boy Sidney Archibald Eric. Bargie treated the names after its fashion. The children became Stellicky Dagmaricky and Peter's Sandy's Bellie's Sid.

'Granny sat and listened to Aunt Tris,' Kate continued. 'Licked her lips over it. Granny loves a tale. Particularly with a wicked streak. "A spectacle," she said, "a second Katherine Bran." Katherine Bran was somebody in a tale, I believe. And then she said, "You have your theatres and your picture palaces, you folk. You make a grand mistake." And she told us there was no spectacle like what's at our own doors. "Set her in the jougs and up on the faulters' stool with her, for fourteen Sabbaths, as they did with Katherine, and where's your picture palace then?" A *merry prank*, she called it. Well!— "The faulter's stool and a penny bridal," she said, "and you've spectacle to last you, I'se warren." Granny's very amusing when she begins with old tales.'

Lindsay's attention was flagging. 'Besides,' she thought,

'I don't like old tales. Nor this new one either.' They had come out of the wood on to a crossroad and the country was open for miles ahead.

'And that's Knapperley, is it, Katie?' she asked.

'Yes,' said Kate. 'But we don't go near it to get to Mrs Hunter's.'

TWO

The January Christmas Tree

Snow fell that night, and the night following, and the frost set harder than before. The guests were stamping at the doorstep, knocking off the snow that had frozen in translucent domes upon their heels, shaking their garments free from the glittering particles of ice that hung in them. The children eyed the house with awe, mingled in Stella Dagmar with disdain. 'It's a terrible slippery floor, I canna get traivelled,' she objected in the long, polished lobby. But the glories of the Christmas tree silenced criticism for awhile. Lindsay had made a very pretty thing of it; and when by and by she slipped from the room and Miss Theresa said ostentatiously, 'She's away to take a rest—she's been ill, you see,' the girl herself was as deliciously excited as any bairn. She giggled with pleasure as she draped an old crimson curtain round her and adjusted her Father Christmas beard. 'Now what all nonsense shall I say?' And she said it very well, disguising her voice and playing silly antics.

'My very toes is laughin',' Mrs Hunter declared.

The room grew hot, and Lindsay in her wrappings choked for air. She slid her hand behind the curtain that covered the glass door to the garden. But the door blew open at her touch. The wind and a woman entered together: a woman in the fifties, weathered and sinewy, clad in a rough, patched Lovat tweed and leggings caked with mud and battered snow. On her head sat a piece of curious finery that had been once a hat and from it dangled a trallop of dingy veiling.

'Bawbie Paterson,' cried Miss Theresa. 'Who would have expected that?'

Miss Paterson marched across the room.

'It's you I'm seekin', Barbara Hunter,' she announced. 'Will you send for Maggie? There's my lassie up and left me. The third one running. Will you send for Maggie? Maggie's the lass for me.'

'Barbara Paterson,' said Mrs Hunter, 'that I will not. Maggie's in a good place. I'd be black affronted to bid her up and awa'. And mair than that, Miss Barbara, nae lass o' mine'll ever be at your beck and ca'. Ye dinna feed your folk, Miss Barbara. I've seen my chickens hanging in to the bare wa's o' a cabbage as though they hadna seen meat this month an' mair, and your kitchen deemie, Barbara Paterson, had the same hungry e'e. Ye'll nae get Maggie.'

'And what am I to do wanting a kitchen lass?'

'Ye can tak the road an' run bits, Miss Barbara.'

'Since you are in my house, Bawbie Paterson,' said Miss Theresa, 'you'd better take a seat.'

'I'll not do that, Tris Craigmyle. You'd have me plotted with heat, would you? But I'll wait a whilie or I go in a lowe. And who might this be?' And she wheeled round to stare at Lindsay, who had dropped the curtain and was staring hard at her.

'A likely lass,' said Miss Barbara; and she clutched at Lindsay, who did not resist, but allowed herself to be drawn closer. 'And are you seeking a place? Can you cook a tattie? A' to dross?'

'Hoots, Miss Barbara,' cried Mrs Hunter, scandalised. 'That's nae a servant lass. That's Miss Lorimer—Andrew Lorimer the solicitor's daughter. Ye're nae at yersel.'

Lindsay's heart was beating fast. She said nothing, but stared at the great rough face above her. She had a feeling as though some huge elemental mass were towering over her, rock and earth, earthen smelling. Miss Barbara's tweeds had been sodden so long with the rains and matted with the dusts of her land, that they too seemed elemental. Her face was tufted with coarse black hairs, her naked hands that clutched the fabric of Lindsay's dress were hard, ingrained with black from wet wood and earth. 'She's not like a person, she's a thing,' Lindsay thought. The girl felt puny in her grasp, yet quite without fear, possessed instead by a strange exhilaration.

Held thus against Miss Barbara's person and clothes, the outdoor smell of which came strongly to the heat of the parlour, Lindsay, her senses sharpened by excitement, was keenly aware of an antagonism in the room: as though the fine self-respecting solidity of generations of Lorimers and Craigmyles, the measured and orderly dignity of their lives, won at some cost through centuries from their rude surroundings, resented this intrusion into their midst of an undisciplined and primitive force. The girl waited to hear what Miss Theresa would say, sure that it was Miss Theresa who would act spokesman against this earthy relic of an older age.

But before Miss Theresa could speak, Stella Dagmar, angry at her interrupted play and offended that no one noticed her, began a counting rhyme, running about among the women and slapping each in turn:

I count you out
For a dirty dish-clout.

Miss Theresa's wiry hands were on the culprit. 'A clout on the lug, that's what you would need. Francie hasn't his sorrow to seek.'

Stella dodged and screamed. The whole room was in an uproar. And suddenly Miss Barbara, loosening her grasp on Lindsay, broke into a bellow of laughter; and in a moment was gone.

Miss Theresa was scarlet in the face from fury.

'Saw you ever such an affront to put on a body?' she cried, cudgelling Stella to the rhythms of her anger. 'Coming into a body's house at a New Year time a sight like yon. Coming in at all, and her not bidden. And I'm sure you needn't all be making such a commotion now. You couldn't tell what's what nor wha's Jock's father.'

They were all talking together. Lindsay stood amazed. The voices became appallingly distinct, resounding in her very head; and the hot, lit room, the excited ladies in their rich apparel, burdened her. She wanted to run after Miss Barbara, to escape; and, picking up her crimson curtain, she said, 'I'll put this past.'

'I kent it was you all the time,' Stella flung at her. But Lindsay was already gone. She closed the door from the parlour and stood in the cold, still hall. Through the windows poured the light of full moon. And Lindsay had a vision of the white light flooding the world and gleaming on the snow, and of Miss Barbara convulsed with laughter in the middle of the gleam.

She threw the curtain about her, drew on a pair of galoshes, and ran into the night.

The night astonished her, so huge it was. She had the sense of escaping from the lit room into light itself. Light was everywhere: it gleamed from the whole surface of the earth, the moon poured it to the farthest quarters of heaven, round a third of the horizon the sea shimmered. The cold was intense. Lindsay's breath came quick and gasping. She ran through the spruce plantation and toiled up the field over snow that was matted in grass; and, reaching the crest, saw without interruption to the rims of the world. The matted snow and grass were solid enough beneath her feet, but when she looked beyond she felt that she must topple over into that reverberation of light. Her identity vanished. She was lost in light and space. When she moved on it surprised her that she stumbled with the rough going. She ought to have glided like light over an earth so insubstantial.

Then she saw Miss Barbara.

Miss Barbara Paterson came swinging up the field, treading surely and singing to herself. Her heavy bulk seemed to sail along the frozen surfaces, and when she reached the dyke she vaulted across it with an impatient snort.

'O wait for me!' Lindsay cried. She too was by the dyke, and would have leaped it, but was trammelled with her curtain.

'Wait for me,' she cried. 'I want to speak to you.'

But when Miss Barbara turned back, there was nothing she could find to say.

'Were you wanting over?' asked Miss Barbara. She leaned across the dyke, lifted the girl in her arms and swung her in the air. 'You're like the deil, you'll never hang, for you're as light 's a feather.'

'Oh, put me down. But I want to go with you. Will you show me Knapperley?'

'Ca' awa' then.' Miss Barbara, without further ado, made off up the top of a furrow, pushing the girl firmly along by the elbow. Lindsay kept her footing with difficulty, sinking ever and again in the deep snow that levelled the furrows. She wondered what her mother would think. It was like an escapade into space. Her safe and habitual life was leagues away.

Miss Barbara made no attempt to speak. They passed through a woodland and came out by a gap.

'There's Knapperley for you,' its owner said.

Lindsay stared. From every window of the tall narrow house there blazed a lamp. They blazed into the splendour of the night like a spurt of defiance.

'But the Zepps,' she gasped.

'They don't come this length.'

'But they do. One did. And anyway, the law.'

'That's to learn them to leave honest folks alone.'

A spasm of terror contracted Lindsay's heart. Miss Barbara had clambered on to the next dyke. She made little use of stile or gate, preferring always to go straight in the direction she desired. She stood there poised, keeping her footing with ease upon the icy stones, and pointed with an outstretched arm at the lights, a menacing figure. Then she bent as though to help Lindsay over.

'Will she lift me again?' thought the girl. The insecurity of her adventure rushed upon her.

'Will she kidnap me and make me her servant girl? But I couldn't live in a house with lights like that. There would be policemen if there weren't Zepps.'

She twisted herself out of reach of the descending hand and fled, trailing the scarlet curtain after her across the snow.

THREE

Knapperley

Meanwhile in the Weatherhouse parlour Mrs Hunter was discussing Miss Barbara.

'If she wasna Miss Barbara Paterson of Knapperley she would mak you roar. You would be handin' her a copper and speirin' if she wanted a piece.'

'O ay, she's fairly a Tinkler Tam,' said Miss Theresa. 'Coming into a body's house with that old tweed. But she hasn't any other, that's what it is.'

'That's where you're mistaken, Miss Craigmyle. She's gowns galore: silk gowns and satin gowns and ane with a velvet lappet. Kists stappit fu'. But whan does she wear them? That's the tickler. It's aye the auld Lovat tweed. And aye the black trallop hangin' down her back.'

'It's her only hat, that I can wager.'

'It or its marra. Wha would say? She bought it for a saxpence from a wifie at the door and trimmed it hersel' with yon wallopin' trash. "If you would do that to your hat, Barbara Hunter, it would be grander." "God forbid, Barbara Paterson, that I should ever wear a hat like that." But she's aye worn it sin' syne. Some says it's the same hat, and some says it's its marra and the auld ane gaes up the lum on a Sabbath night whan there's none to see.'

Mrs Hunter talked with enjoyment. She was entirely devoted to the spanking mare on whose land she and her husband held their croft, and entirely without compunction in her ridicule of Miss Barbara's departures from the normal. She liked to talk too—gamesome cordial talk when her hard day's work was over; and the Craigmyle ladies, with their natural good-heartedness, allowed her to talk on.

'Auld Knapperley gave her an umbrella and her just the littlin, and she must bring it to the Sabbath school as prood's pussy. "What'll I do with my umbrella?"—hidin' it in ahin her gown—"it's rainin'." "Put up your umbrella, Barbara." "I won't put it up, Barbara. I won't have it blaudit, and it new." And aye she happit it in the pink gown. Me and her was ages and both Barbara Paterson then, and she took a terrible notion o' me. If I had a blue peenie she must have a blue peenie as well. And syne I was servant lassie at Knapperley for a lot of years. I couldna but bide, her that fond of me and all.'

'But you won't let Maggie go, Mrs Hunter?'

'I will not that. She was queer enough whan the auld man was livin', and she's a sight queerer now. I was there whan he dee'd and whan Mrs Paterson dee'd an' a'. Ay, I mind fine, poor body, her thinkin' she would get him to mak her laddie laird o' the placie and nae Miss Barbara. She liked her laddie a sight mair than ever she liked her lassie. But she married Donnie Forbes for love and Knapperley for a down-sit. And she thought, poor soul, that she had nae mair a-do than bid him say the word and Knapperley would be her laddie's. But she aye put off the speirin'. And syne whan she kent she wouldna rise again, she bids Knapperie in to her bedside. "What's that you're sayin'?" says he. "Say't again, for I'm surely nae hearin'." So she says it again. "And him a Forbes," she says, "a family of great antiquity." "O ay, like the shore porters o' Aberdeen, that discharged the cargo from Noah's Ark." "You're mockin' me," she says. "I'll grant you this," he says, "there was never a murder in this parish or the next but there was a Forbes in it. There was Forbes of Portlendie and Forbes of Bannochie, and a Forbes over at Cairns that flung his lassie's corp ahin a dyke. But there's been nae murder done at Knapperley and nae Forbes at Knapperley—" "But there wasna aye a Paterson at Knapperley, and some that kens," she says, meanin'-like, "says the first that ocht the place didna rightly owe the name." "It's a scant kin," he says, "that has neither thief nor bastard in it, and for my part I'd rather have the bastard than the thief. The lassie'll mak as good a laird as the laddie. The place is hers, and you needna set any landless lads on thievin' here. I'll keep my ain fish-guts for my ain sea-maws." She didna daur say mair, but aye whan he gaed by her door there cam the t'ither great sigh. "You can just sigh awa' there," he would say. And whiles he said, "Jamie Fleeman *kent* he was the Laird o' Udny's feel." Well, well, he was a Tartar, auld Knapperie. But he's awa' whaur he'll have to tak a back seat. He dee'd in an awfu' hurry.'

'And Mr Benjamin has never come back since.'

'O ay. O fie ay. He cam' back. But just the once. "This is a great disappointment to me, Barbara. Bawbie's getting near. You see the weather it is, and you could hold all the fire in the lee of your hand. There's the two of us, one on either side, and greatcoats on to keep us warm. And nothing but a scrap end of candle to light you to your bed." "You may thank your stars, Mr Benjamin, she didna stand and crack spunks or you were in ower." So he never cam again. But he let his laddie come.'

'She'll be making him her heir,' said Miss Annie.

'I wouldna wonder. They're chief, Miss Barbara and Mr Garry.'

'A halarackit lump,' Theresa said.

'O, a gey rough loon. Mair like auld Knapperie's son than Mr Benjamin's. But a terrible fine laddie. Me and Mr Garry's great billies. "Will you dance at my wedding, Mrs Hunter? I'll give you a new pair of shoes." "I will do that, laddie. But wha is the bonny birdie?" '

'Yes, who?' thought Mrs Falconer. She made a running excursion into the past. Once she had fancied that Kate was not indifferent to Garry Forbes. At one time they had been much together, when he came on holiday to Fetter-Rothnie. But Theresa's tongue had been so hard on the boy—the intimacy ceased. Mrs Falconer remembered her own impotent fury against her sister. And, after all, Kate had given no sign. 'Another dream of mine, I suppose,' thought Mrs Falconer. And she sighed. It was not easy to include Kate in any dream. 'And she's all I have to love,' thought her mother wistfully.

Mrs Hunter ran on. ' "O, that's to see," he says. "I've never found a lassie yet that I love like your ain bonny self." "You flatterer," I says. "Unless it would be my aunt." And we both to the laughin'. But he's fair fond of her, mind you. There's nae put-on yonder.'

'He would be,' said Theresa. 'Sic mannie sic horsie. She's a Hielan' yowe yon.'

Mrs Hunter bridled. 'She's a good woman, Miss Craigmyle. There's worse things than being queer. There's being bad. There's lots that's nae quite at themsels and nae ill in them, and some that's all there and all the worse for that. There's Louie Morgan, now—queer you must allow she is, but bad she couldna be.'

Whether because the affront put on her by Miss Barbara's rash incursion was still rankling, or whether by reason of the naturally combative quality of her mind, Miss Theresa stormed on the suggestion.

'Louie!' she said. 'Hantle o' whistlin' and little red land yonder. And you don't call it bad to bedizen herself with honours and her never got them?'

'Meaning' what, Miss Craigmyle?'

'This tale of her engagement,' said Theresa with scorn.

'Poor craitur! That was a sore heart to her. Losin' young Mr Grey that road, and them new promised. It'll be a while or she ca' ower't.'

'She never had him.'

'Havers, Miss Theresa, she has the ring.'

'Think of that, now.'

'She let me see the ring.'

'She bought it.'

'She didna that, Miss Theresa. It's his mother's ain ring, that she showed me lang syne, and said her laddie's bride would wear whan she was i' the mools.'

Miss Theresa took the check badly. To be found in the wrong was a tax she could not meet. She had grown up with a hidden angry conviction that she was in the wrong by being born. As third daughter, she had defrauded her father of a son. It was after Theresa's birth that James Craigmyle set himself to turn Annie into as good a farmer as himself. He never reproached Tris to her face, but the sharp child guessed her offence. When he was dead, and she in the Weatherhouse had power and authority for the first time in her life, she developed an astounding genius for being in the right. To prove Theresa wrong was to jeopardise the household peace.

She was therefore dead set in her own opinion by Mrs Hunter's apparent proof of her mistake. The matter, to be sure, was hardly worth an argument. Louie Morgan was a weak, palavering thing, always playing for effect. The Craigmyle ladies knew better than to be taken in with her airs and her graces, that deceived the lesser intellects; but they had, like everyone else, accepted the story of her betrothal to David Grey, a young engineer brought up in the district, although David Grey was already dead before the betrothal was announced. Even Theresa had not openly questioned the story before. Irritation made her do it now, and the crossing of her theory drove her to conviction.

'It's as plain as a hole in a laddie's breeks,' she said. 'There was no word of an engagement when the young man was alive, was there?'

The whole company, however, was against her. The supposition was monstrous, and in view of Mrs Hunter's evidence upon the ring, untenable.

'And look at the times she's with auld Mr Grey,' said Mrs Hunter, 'that bides across the dyke from us, and him setting a seat for her that kindly like and cutting his braw chrysanthemums to give her.'

'She had sought them,' said Theresa.

'Oh, I wouldna say. She's fit for it, poor craiturie. But she wouldna tell a lee.' Mrs Hunter frankly admitted the failings of all her friends, but thought none the worse of them for that. 'She's her father's daughter there. A good man, the old Doctor, and a grand discourse he gave. It was worth a long traivel to see him in the pulpit, a fine upstandin' man as ever you saw. "Easy to him," Jake says. Jake's sair bent, Miss Craigmyle. "Easy to him, he's never done a stroke of work in his life." His wife did a' thing—yoked the shalt for him whan he went on his visitations, and had aye to have his pipe filled with tobacco to his hand when he got hame.'

'Where's Lindsay gone to?' Theresa cut abruptly across the conversation. 'She's taking a monstrous while to put away her cloak. And it's time these bairns were home.'

She pulled the coloured streamers from the tree out of Stella's hands.

They called for Lindsay, but had no answer. When it became plain she was not in the house, there was a flutter of consternation.

'Out?' said Miss Annie. 'But she'll get her death. And what could she be seeking out at this time of night?'

Only Mrs Falconer held her peace. A light smile played over her features, and her thoughts were running away by the upland paths of romance. She had a whole history woven for herself in a moment—a girl in love and escaping into moonshine on such a pure and radiant night as this: did one require pedestrian excuse?

She said, 'I'll put on my coat and take these children home. I'm sure to meet her on the way.'

Like Lindsay, she had the sense of escaping into light. She went along with a skipping step, her heart rejoicing; and almost forgot that she had come to look for a runaway whose absence caused concern.

She delivered over the children to Francie, who shut the door on them and said, 'I'll show you a sight, if you come up the park a bit.' Mrs Falconer followed, caring little where she went in that universal faerie shimmer. It seemed to her that she was among the days of creation, and light had been called into being, but neither divisions of time nor substance, nor any endeavours nor disturbances of man.

'What think you o' that in a Christian country?' Francie was asking; and Mrs Falconer saw, as Lindsay had seen, the blazing lights of Knapperley.

'What a strange pale beauty they have,' she said, 'in the moonlight.'

'Beauty, said ye?' echoed Francie, with supreme scorn. 'It's a beauty I can do fine wantin' in a war-time, and all them Zepps about.'

'Hoots, Francie,' said Mrs Falconer, recovering herself, 'it's as light as day. The house lights 'll make little difference in the sky tonight.'

'I've seen that lights, Mrs Falconer, in the darkest night o' winter. It's nae canny. She'll come by some mishaunter, ay will she, ay will she that.'

'A fine, maybe. Don't you worry, Francie. If she carries on like that the police 'll soon put a stop to her cantrips.'

Francie went away muttering. Mrs Falconer returned home, having forgotten to look very hard for the runaway. Lindsay was still absent.

'You can't have looked sore all the time you've been,' said Theresa.

Ellen did not, of course, confess that she had forgotten the girl. She said, 'What harm can she come to? She's gone out to see the moon.'

'Fiddlesticks and rosit! Everybody's not so daft about a view as you.'

'I'll go again,' said Ellen, nothing loth; but as she opened the door Lindsay arrived, running.

She was plainly in terror, and throwing herself on the sofa broke into sobbing.

'Whatever made you want to go there?' they asked when she told where she had been.

'I don't know,' sobbed Lindsay. She was like a little frightened child, and very lovely in her woe. They made much of her, and miscalled Bawbie Paterson to their hearts' content.

Lindsay told her story over again to Kate, when Kate had arrived home for the night and the girls were in the windowed room that Kate shared habitually with her mother. Ellen had yielded her tower to the guest.

'They wanted to know why I went, Katie, but they mustn't. Oh, I wish she weren't like that—she's dreadful.'

'But you needn't go near her, need you?'

Lindsay began to laugh and to sob. 'Katie,' she whispered, 'she's his aunt, you know.'

Kate was silent from astonishment.

She had heard her aunt's account of Mrs Andrew Lorimer's story—'Captain Dalgarno,' Mrs Andrew had said.

'I see,' she said at last. Captain Dalgarno was therefore Garry Forbes.

'Mother told you about me, didn't she? Didn't she, Katie? She had no right—they treat me like a child. She did say, didn't she?'

'I wasn't here, Linny. Yes, she said.'

'Said what? How much, Katie? Oh, I couldn't bear them to know that was why I ran after her. I wanted to see—Do you suppose they know, Katie?'

'I am sure they don't. But is it secret, Linny?'

'No. But running after her like that—' She began to writhe on the bed. 'I'm so unhappy, Katie.'

'Yes,' said Kate.

Kate was dumb before emotion. Her own was mastered and undivulged. She remained silent while Lindsay sobbed, and in a while the girl grew quiet, and fell asleep.

But Kate, after her young cousin slept, stole out of bed and crossed the room. Bending, she pulled the cover over Lindsay's naked arm. 'In this frost—she'd starve.' And for a moment Kate stood looking down on the flushed young face. So this was the woman whom Garry Forbes had chosen. Kate returned to bed and went to sleep. She had a long day's work ahead of her and a long day's work behind; and lying awake brought scanty profit.

FOUR

Coming of Spring

Lindsay's escapade on the night of the Christmas tree provided much matter for talk and for allusion. The ladies had their ways. Paradise, genial and warm, would cry, 'Out again, Lindsay. Stay you by the fire, my lass. But you don't seem to feel the cold, stravaigin' in the snow. You'll be stiffer about the hunkers before you come to my time of life. Put some clothes on, lassie, you'll starve.'

Theresa, hearing, would retort, 'She's not like you, rowed up like a sair thoomb. She's youth to keep her warm.'

'Ay, ay, here's me that needs the fire. And me to have been so active all my days.'

'Like Vesuvius.'

'Don't you heed her,' said Paradise, laughing. 'I could dander at night with the best when I was younger. O ay, frosty nights and all. Many's the lad that's chased me up the park and in by the woodie side.'

'But she aye took care of herself. Catch a weasel sleeping. You'd better have a care, Lindsay, going out alone by night, in a place you don't know.'

'There's somebody you would have liked fine to be meeting out there, my lady,' Paradise would add.

And Lindsay's face burned, as she watched them under narrowed lids. They had no mind to disconcert her, but had lived too long and heartily to remember the reticence of youth; and old Mrs Craigmyle, with her fine regard, Lindsay felt, enjoyed her young discomfort—not in a thoughtless frankness, like the others, but pondering its quality.

'Leezie Lindsay,' her grand-aunt would say—the very name made Lindsay's cheek grow hot—'you never ask the old dame for a song. When you were a littlin, it was, "And now a song, my grand-aunt," and when she sang you danced and you trebled. You have other ploys to please you now.'

Lindsay, knowing that she avoided the old lady's presence, blushed the more. And there was nothing in the words, yet everything. Her rare low words had a choice insolence that astounded the girl; but she dared not take offence, so delicate was the insinuation, lest she had mistaken her grand-aunt's meaning and herself supplied the subtle sting she felt. She would leave Lang Leeb's presence bewildered, in a sorry heat of shame that she had a mind so tainted.

Mrs Falconer had other modes of leading to attack. She would make up on the girl as she tramped the long moor roads and walk musing by her side. An ungainly figure, Lindsay thought. And rather a nuisance. She could never get accustomed to Cousin Ellen's habit of muttering to herself as she walked, and when Mrs Falconer began to address her, in her low hesitating voice, it was hard to be sure that she was not still talking to herself. Hard, indeed; because Ellen had no plain path out from her dreams, and her queer ends of talk were part of the story she had woven around herself and Lindsay.

'There's hard knowing what to do,' she would say. 'I've had to suffer, too. I fought for my own way of seeing things.' That battle of thirty years before came fresh and horrible to her memory. 'One generation forgets another's war. But, you see, I came out the conqueror.'

She let her thought hover upon her own past. It was a glancing embroidery now, pleasant to sight. But Lindsay saw only a tarnished and tangled thread or two that had no connection with herself, and thus a scanty interest.

'So I didn't hurry you,' Cousin Ellen went on. ' "Seek her out," they said, "seek her out. There's danger." But I knew, you see. Oh yes, I knew. Not the danger *they* meant. So I didn't look sore. I let you bide your time. There's some sorts of danger you have to meet, and where better to meet them than under a moon like yon? Oh yes, I knew.'

'Knew what?' Lindsay pondered. 'Why I went out at night? But I am sure she doesn't. What danger was there?'

Only Kate, who knew, said nothing. Kate had no words. Lindsay thought her callous, and writhed angrily to remember how she had given her secret self away. But she could have given it to no better heart than Kate's. Kate took it in and loved it.

Lindsay, unaware of her devotion, had hours of embarrassment among these elderly women who barbed their chance words with a story half heard from her mother and an escapade whose reason they did not understand. The allusions were sufficiently rare, except on the part of Mrs Falconer, who continued to puzzle Lindsay with her air of secret communion; but their mere possibility was enough to alarm the girl and soil the pleasantness she had always expected of a Weatherhouse sojourn. When, therefore, the frost gave and the roads were filled with slush and the whole countryside was dirty, Lindsay went home without regret.

It was a black February, wet, with an east wind 'hostin' through atween the houses.' At the end of the month trains were blocked by snow and fallen trees, and March came in bleak and bitter. Lindsay found the time long. She had wanted to be a nurse and they would not let her—she was not strong enough, they said—and there was nothing else that she particularly desired to do. So she made swabs and waited at the Station Rest Room Canteen, and thought herself a little hardly used by fate, but would not confess it, since she saw others around her used more hardly. She was to think it shortly with more justice, for Garry ceased to write to her. She would not confess at home to the lapse, but searched casualty lists and grew pale and restless. Before March ended spring suddenly filled the world. Buds were swollen in a night. Crocuses and scilla broke from the black earth; and Mrs Andrew Lorimer, watching her daughter's thin, strained face, sent her back to the Weatherhouse. She knew well enough that no letter had come for Lindsay, but would show no sympathy in an affair of which she disapproved.

The Weatherhouse ladies had had time to forget Lindsay's escapade. It was no longer matter for stupid allusion. They seemed also to have forgotten the love affair. There were no covert allusions to that either. Perhaps the girl's bearing, a little proud, steeled to show no hurt even when hurt was taken, made a hearty farm allusiveness fall flat. Kate remembered in silence. Mrs Falconer again waylaid the girl with queer talk that she could not understand. Lindsay could have no idea of the rush of life that came to Cousin Ellen by touching even so distantly the vital experience of a young girl's love and growth. Ellen had touched no vital experience other than her own. Kate had apparently had none to show her. No one had opened a heart to her or shared with her the strange secrecy of living, and in the hours of remorse when she chid herself for the false fictions of her brain she recognised sadly that she created these because she had had so little of the real stuff of living to fill her mind. So Lindsay, coming to Fetter-Rothnie charged with the splendours of a real romance, intoxicated Mrs Falconer. The elderly woman watched her with a sort of adoration, and would have purchased her confidence at a price; but she did not know how to reach the girl's confidence. Lindsay thought her queer and avoided her.

The others she did not avoid. Suspense, she found, was easier to bear up here in the sun and wind, where no one knew that she was waiting. It surprised her to find how she slipped into the life of the countryside, learned its stories, its secret griefs and endeavours. She had not dreamed how much alive a few square miles of field and moor could become. Miss Annie taught her to understand the earth and its labourers—the long, slow toil of cultivating a land denuded of its men. She learned to despise Peter Cairnie, a shrewd shirker in a rich farm by the river, who ploughed Maggie Barnett's land to her at an exorbitant figure; and to honour Maggie, wife of a young crofter at the Front, who managed the croft and reared her three bairns alone.

'Do you hear from him often?' Lindsay said to Maggie.

'Whiles, whiles,' the wiry woman answered. 'But he's nae great sticks at the pen. I heard five weeks syne.'

Five weeks, Lindsay thought, and she takes it as of course. She watched Maggie whack the cow round in her stall and set to milking, and followed Miss Theresa a little thoughtfully to Mrs Hunter at Craggie.

Another croft; its man not gone this time, but slow and frail; Dave, the eldest boy, in the Gordons.

'And does he write?' asked Lindsay. It was something to say.

'Write!' cried Mrs Hunter in her glowing fashion. 'There was never a lad to write like our Dave. And money coming home to keep the loonies at the school. "Keep you Bill and Dod to their books, Mother," he says. "This war's bound to go over some time, and the boys'll need all the education they can get. I'll put them through college," he says. It's himsel should have been at the college, if I had my way of it. His heart was never in the joinering, but there, it couldna be. But the young ones, they're to town to the school, a gey lang way, and a gey lang day; their father could do fine with a hand from them with the beasts and about the place, but there you are, you see. "Keep them to their books, mother," says Dave. "They'll get what I couldn't get." And I can aye lend a hand with the beasts mysel.'

Lindsay went often to Mrs Hunter's. Mrs Hunter had been servant lass for so long at Knapperley, and she talked freely of Miss Barbara and Mr Garry, not suspecting the avid interest of her listener. Talk lightened the heart to Mrs Hunter. Good reminiscent unprejudiced talk was the salt of earth to her; and she had earth enough in her laborious life to require salting.

Lindsay would come in, swing herself to the table or squat upon a creepie, and manoeuvre Mrs Hunter to the subjects she desired. It was thus that she heard the story of David Grey. David had been Garry's friend. And he was dead. His father, John Grey, lived across the dyke from Mrs Hunter. This indomitable old man, approaching the seventies, spare, small and alert, lived alone except for the woman who kept his house. Son of a petty crofter in a Deeside glen, he had laboured on the croft, taken his schooling as he could, and fought his way to apprenticeship in an engineering shop. The master of the country school where he had spent his winters did well by him; in night school he rose steadily, until by the end of his apprenticeship he was teaching draughtsmanship and mechanics. He went out early on Sunday mornings and took long walks in the coun try, in the course of which he studied botany and learned by heart the works of the English poets. He even wrote verses, in Tennyson's early manner; and studied Carlyle and Ruskin, John Locke and Adam Smith. His books were bought from second-hand bookstalls; it was thus that he became possessor of an eighteenth-century *Paradise Lost*, leather-bound, with steel engravings of our First Parents in a state of innocence. To these engravings he had added, for Eve a skirt, for Adam short pants, of Indian ink. He married, became Works manager of the Foundry where he had served his apprenticeship, settled within reach of town and cultivated his garden. He rose with daylight, laboured in the earth till the breakfast hour, made a rapid but thorough toilet, went to town. At the end of his garden, the beauty of which was celebrated through all the district, was a workshop: there was nothing connected with a homestead that he could not make or mend. His fingers, clumsy, broad and seamed, were incredibly delicate in action. His figure was squat and plebeian, but redeemed by its alert activity and by the large and noble head. The brow was wide and lofty, the nose aquiline, shaggy eyebrows emphasised the depths of the eye-sockets, in which there shone a pair of dark, piercing and kindly eyes. Children loved him. His voice was soft and persuasive. His men revered him and trusted his judgment. He spoke evil of no man.

In youth his hair, brows and beard (which he never removed) were intensely black, but by the time of this story, white; and so much of his forehead and temples was now bare as gave a singularly lofty and serene appearance to his head. One felt him as a man of peace. In the spring of 1914 he had retired from work and given himself with a child's delight to his garden; but early in the war, feeling that his specialised knowledge and training should be put at the service of his country, he offered himself to the Munitions Department of his city, and was engaged as a voluntary and unpaid Inspector of Shells; he stipulated only that his travelling expenses should be paid—his salary had always been small, and he had saved no more than would suffice for his old age. The lifting and handling of shells was too much for his failing strength. He toiled home at night exhausted; but was up on the following morning to work in his garden. He had even taken in another piece of ground and was growing huge crops of potatoes and green vegetables, which he distributed among the local hospitals.

His wife was dead. His only son, a brilliant boy, unlike his father in appearance and temperament, had inherited and intensifed his genius. David was tall, red-headed, fiery-tempered, wild and splendid, but with his father's capacity for engineering and his power over those who worked for him. John Grey saw his own dreams fulfilled in his son. The boy marched triumphantly through school and college, and, entering Woolwich Arsenal in the war, became night manager of a new fuse factory. His work was his passion. Brilliant, inventive, steady in work as his father, he lacked the older man's composed serenity. The artist's sensibility, the lover's exaltation, went to his work; and broke him. He developed tuberculosis, and in three months' time was dead.

John Grey took the blow in silence. He spoke to no one of his son, but went on his steady, quiet way. Only the professional books that he and the boy together had amassed ceased to interest him. He never read them again, and his tired mind had no further concern with the modern developments of which, for the boy's sake, he had kept himself informed.

When Lindsay learned, through Mrs Hunter, that David Grey had been Garry's friend, she placed both the old and the dead man in her shrine of heroes. This shy and undeveloped girl at nineteen had the Lorimer passion, exemplified in Mrs Falconer's day-dreams and the balladry of Lang Leeb her mother, for a romantic enlargement of life. Lindsay was given to hero-worship. On these spring evenings and on Saturday afternoons she would watch the old man at work in his garden. Sometimes, as he crawled weeding among the beds, in his old garments that had turned the colour of earth itself, with his hands earth-encrusted, he seemed older than human—some antique embodiment of earth. One could fancy a god creating an Eden. Steady and happy. Absorbed. Like a part of what he worked in, and yet beyond it. The immanent presence.

The stooping figure, moving back and forth like a great silent animal, would raise itself, the noble forehead come into view; and rising on stiff knees, the old man would greet the girl with a perfect courtesy, sit by her pulling at his pipe. Once, in the sun, he fell asleep as he sat beside her, nodding in an old man's light and easy slumbers.

Once or twice Louie Morgan came to the garden. Lindsay had heard her story too; how she was betrothed to young David Grey—an unannounced betrothal, to which she had confessed only after his death. One evening, walking away with her from the garden, Louie showed Lindsay a ring, which she wore about her neck.

'Why should I flaunt it for everyone to see?' she had said; and with her head on one side she gazed at the ring. Her face was all curious little puckers—a study for a Lady in Anguish. She made funny twists with her mouth. But Lindsay was excited. It was her first intimate personal contact with the bereavement of war, and she exalted Louie also to a place in her shrine.

So the spring wore on. There on the upland one saw leagues of the world and leagues of sea, all milky-blue, hazed like the bloom upon a peach. And how good it was to watch the country changing with the spring!

'Come,' Paradise would say. 'Tomorrow the chickens should be out. We'll sprinkle water on the eggs today.' Tomorrow came, and the shells broke—small, soft, delectable living things were there.

'Oh, how I love them! I have never seen them so young. Oh, it's running, it's running on my hand! But why can't I feed them?'

Paradise, taking the broken shells from the coop, told her they were too young for food; but Lindsay was not listening. She had heard somewhere a loud harsh cry.

'Look, look! Oh, there! See them! What can they be?' And she pointed far overhead, into the height of the blue sky. Birds were flying there, one bird, and others following in two lines that made an open angle upon the blue; but while one arm of the angle was short, the other stretched far out across the sky, undulating, fine and black.

'One, two three—twenty, twenty one—Oh, I have counted ninety birds! My neck is aching.' She held her hands to her neck, moving her head about to ease its pain. 'Paradise, tell me what they are.'

'Why, that is the wild geese. Have you never seen them fly before?'

'Never. Wild geese, wild geese! How wonderful the country is!'

When Cousin Ellen walked with her she assailed her with questions.

'And see, Cousin Ellen, this one. Look at him. Has he a nest there, do you think? Where do you look for nests? What kind is he? What is his name?'

Ellen shook her head.

'I hardly know their names, Linny.'

'But don't you love birds?'

'Oh, yes.' Ellen paused, gazing at the eager girl. 'They are a part of myself,' she wanted to say; but how could one explain that? Where it had to be explained it could not be understood. 'You are a part of me, too,' she thought, with her eyes fixed on Lindsay's where she waited for her answer. Her lips were parted and her eyes shone; and Mrs Falconer longed to tell her of the strange secret of life—how all things were one and there was no estrangement except for those who did not understand. But all that she could find to say was, 'I know hardly any of their names.'

The girl's clear regard confused her, and she dropped her eyes. She felt ashamed. 'Names don't matter very much, do they?' she asked hurriedly.

'Oh, yes. Names—they're like songs.' And she chanted in a singing voice, 'Wild duck, wild duck, kingfisher, curlew. Their names are a part of themselves. Can you tell me where to see a kingfisher, Cousin Ellen?'

'No . . . I'm afraid not.'

Ellen had been found wanting, Lindsay felt. To walk with her held no allurement.

Only once a spontaneous feeling of love for Cousin Ellen welled up in her heart.

Lindsay had come to the Weatherhouse bringing gifts.

'I've brought presents for you all. See, a poor woman made them. She can do nothing for the war, so she makes these lovely things and gives the money.'

Theresa and Paradise took their boxes, which were of embroidered silk exquisitely fashioned, and put them instantly to use. But Cousin Ellen's gift lay on the table.

'Don't you like your gift? I'm sorry you don't like it.'

'Oh yes, I like it. It is very beautiful. Please don't think because I don't use it that I am not grateful for it. I have never cared for many possessions. I have never had many possessions to care for,' she added, smiling brightly. 'A man's life consisteth not in the abundance of things that he hath.'

A week later Miss Theresa stamped into the parlour.

'Well, really, Nell! To give Lindsay's beautiful box away. Something commoner would have done, surely to peace, if you must be throwing things at that Stella Ferguson's head. A nice appreciation you show, I will say.'

'Yes, I gave it to Stella. Possessions mean a lot to her.'

Theresa continued to bluster; but Lindsay jumped from the stool where she had been seated with her book, and cried, 'Oh, I love you for giving it to Stella, Cousin Ellen.'

'Lindsay'—Miss Theresa changed the subject sharply—'you'll spoil your eyes, poring over these great books. You are quite wrinkled.'

Lindsay turned a flushed and troubled face, pushing the hair from off her brow.

'But I must be ready. The world will need us all. I'm doing nothing now, but I can prepare myself for afterwards. There will be ten years of trouble to live through.'

She quoted the phrases she had heard from Garry's lips, and set herself to study the books that he had read. 'We shall all have our part to play in the reconstruction.'

Into this life Garry Forbes came in the second week of April. All spring was in that week—its tempestuous disinclinations, its cold withdrawals, its blaze of sun, its flowers, its earthy smell. On all hands was a breaking: earth broken by the ploughshare, buds broken by the leaf. The smooth security of seed and egg was gone. Season most terrible in all the cycle of the year, time of the dread spring deities, Dionysus and Osiris and the risen Christ, gods of growth and of resurrection, whose worship has flowered in tragedy, superb and dark, in Prometheus and Oedipus, massacre and the stake. Life that comes again is hard: a jubilation and an agony.

Garry was at this time some thirty years of age. Tall, dark-skinned, black stubbs on his chin and cheek that no shaving would remove, with prominent nose and cheek bones and outstanding ears, the two deep furrows that were later so marked a feature of his appearance already ploughing their way from above the nostrils to encircle the mouth, and just now lank and haggard from war and influenza; he came to spend a brief sick leave with his aunt, Miss Barbara Paterson, at Knapperley.

'What do you want with a kitchen lass?' he said to her. 'I'll be your kitchen lass.'

Miss Barbara sat back in her deep chair and flung yowies from her pockets on to the blazing fire. She, who could spread dung and hold a plough with any man, disliked the petty drubs of housework.

'You're Donnie Forbes's grandson,' she said, watching her nephew as he washed the supper dishes. 'I'm a Paterson of Knapperley. A Paterson of Knapperley doesna fyle their fingers with dishwater.'

Benjamin Forbes, Miss Barbara's half-brother, son of the despised Donnie Forbes whom Mrs Paterson had wedded merely for love, had, like his mother, been timid and incapable in his relations with other people. He lived with his boy in the mean suburb of an inland town. When charwomen cheated and neglected them, it was the boy who found fault, dismissed and interviewed. The fiction was faithfully preserved between father and son that the father habitually did these things, but delegated them upon occasion to the son. Garry put a bold front upon the business, and won the praises of the women in the block for his assured and masterful bearing. They could not know that the child sometimes cried himself to sleep, and he would have perished rather than confess to it. When service was not to be had, Garry waited on his father;

and broke the nose of the boy who taunted him with it at school.

'I'll sweel out the slop-pail if I like,' he shouted.

He was a powerful fellow, able easily to wipe out insults, and far too proud to acknowledge his own secret abasement at doing a woman's jobs.

Benjamin talked often to the boy of Knapperley. 'Yon's the place, laddie,' he would say. Garry choked as he listened; he felt he must perish of desire for the burns and the rocky coast. But when he begged his father to let him go to Knapperley, Benjamin demurred. He shrank from a second encounter with his half-sister. One day, when Garry was twelve years old, Benjamin came home to find the boy on the next-door roof, mending a broken gutter-pipe, and learned that his son mended for all the women in the row—and took his wages. Shamefaced but voluble, Garry produced his money-box; he had not spent a penny of his earnings; all was saved—to pay his fare to Knapperley. Benjamin swore softly, but wrote to Miss Barbara; and though no answer was received, the boy set off alone as soon as his holidays began. He tramped the eight miles out from Aberdeen with his belongings on his back, and was dismayed at the ease of the journey. It was unbearably tame to walk in to Knapperley and sleep in a bed; and his secret hope (that his aunt would not receive him: a contingency for which he had made elaborate preparations) vanished like smoke when he saw the actual place. He was sure she would take him in and bid him wash his hands.

'That Knapperley?' he asked a man who was lounging against a gate.

'Who was ye seekin'?'

'Oh, nobody much. I just wanted to know.'

He walked away.

'Ay is't,' the man shouted after him

Garry did not turn.

He came in a little to the moor and saw the sea. That night was full moon. The boy wandered all night like a daft thing. He had drunk magic. At dawn he fell asleep, and the sun was well up when he awoke, furiously hungry, and made for Knapperley. He had no intention of telling where he had spent the night.

But the first person he saw was the fellow who had spoken to him by the gate. Miss Barbara was standing on a cart, forking straw from the cart into a great bundle beside the stable door.

'Ay, ay,' said the man. 'Ye've gotten your way. I tell't her ye was in-by the streen.'

'Let's see you with the graip,' said Miss Barbara, descending from the cart and handing the fork to her nephew.

Garry threw his knapsack from his shoulders and clambered on to the cart. He would not be outdone by anybody; but the horse moved and set the cart in motion; he lost his balance, plunged violently and swung his graip high in the air.

Miss Barbara and the man roared with laughter. A dozen dogs, as it seemed, arrived from nowhere and barked.

'I'll show you how to laugh at me!' cried Garry, recovering his footing. He was mortified to the soul, and began to handle the straw with all the skill and vigour he could command. Miss Barbara folded her arms and watched. Rabbie Mutch could be heard recounting the affair to the kitchen lass, and there followed a guffaw of laughter from them both.

'You'll be ready for your porridge, I'se warren,' said Miss Barbara in a little; and she led the way to the kitchen, where breakfast was ready for herself, her man and her kitchen girl. 'Where spent you the night?'

'Up beside a tower kind of place.'

'You never got in?'

'Oh no, just outside.'

'Gweed sakes!' roared Rabbie. 'Like the—nowt.'

'Dinna you do that,' said the kitchen lass earnestly. 'The moon'll get you. You'll dwine an' dee.'

Far from bidding him wash his hands, Miss Barbara let her nephew come to table with his clothes sullied from the moor. The rough free life she led suited the spirited lad. His manners grew ruder. Rabbie Mutch kept up on him the joke about his sprawling from the cart. He would say at dinner-time, 'O ay, ye can haud the forkie better'n the graip. Yon was a gey like way to haud a graip. Forkin' the lift, was ye?'

The sensitive boy was too proud to show his resentment. He retaliated in kind. Rabbie and he made rude jokes at each other's expense and became fast friends.

For his aunt, the boy admired her wholeheartedly. She knew so much that he had never heard. The country became a new possession. He was free, too, from the indignity that harassed him at home; the endless squabbling with washerwomen. Miss Barbara found fault often enough, but in a coarse and hearty manner, that was followed by guffaws of laughter from all concerned. Garry developed a poor opinion of his own and his father's assertion of authority, and determined to try Miss Barbara's methods on the next woman who offended.

He would secretly have preferred to leave these offenders unchallenged, but, being plagued with a passion for the ideal, could not let ill alone.

When, at the age of twenty nine, on leave at the Lorimer's house with the young Frank, he met and loved Lindsay, this passion had not abated. 'Well, I've done it now,' he thought. He rushed about the house, forgot his manners, played absurd practical jokes, swore himself to secrecy over his love, and blurted it out immediately to Lindsay. To his consternation she flung her arms around his neck.

'I've loved you for ever and ever so long,' she cried. 'You should hear how Frank talks of you.'

Her girl friends called him the Gargoyle.

'One could forgive the ears,' her mother declared, 'if he knew how to conduct himself.'

Garry's lapses from a Mrs Andrew Lorimer standard were not always due to ignorance. He resented those refinements that suggested privilege. This shy lover of the ideal, this poet who clowned away the suspicion of poetry from himself, burned in his heart with no less a fire than love for all mankind. A simple fool, not very fit for Mrs Andrew Lorimer's drawing-room, where such an enormous appetite was found ill-bred. The well-bred love with discrimination.

'Such waste of furrow,' said Mrs Robert Lorimer. 'Those architectural effects of feature. In a gentleman, how distinguished! A man of race and breeding could arrive where he liked with a face of that quality.'

Garry's race being that of the despised Donnie Forbes and his breeding of the back street, his ugliness was pronounced not distinguished, but common.

'You've got a rarity there, Miss Lindsay,' mocked her aunt Mrs Robert.

'I know he is rare,' the girl answered steadily. She and Frank alone appreciated the rareness. Both listened vehemently to his interminable plans for reconstructing the universe. They talked far into the night, until Mrs Andrew despatched her husband from his bed to round them up.

'Leave them alone,' he grumbled. 'There's a war on. Those boys'll be in the trenches again soon enough, God knows.' But he obeyed the mandate.

'Your mother thinks it's time you were in bed, Linny.'

He blinked in the glare of light. Standing there in his pyjamas and dressing-gown, an unimaginative man, he felt nevertheless the tense elation in the room.

'So courting's done in threes nowadays—eh?'

Lindsay flung back her head. 'O daddy, nights like this don't come again.'

She met her mother's morning eye with a clear regard.

'Europe is in the melting-pot, mother—is a slight alteration in one's bedtime of importance?'

'Ler her keep her phrase,' said Mr Lorimer. 'She'll outgrow that.'

Inflamed by Garry's letters, she continued to keep her phrase.

The letters ceased when Garry took influenza, after a day and a night's exposure in a shell hole, where, up to the thighs in filthy water, he had tried to suck the poison from another man's festering arm. The other fellow died where he stood, slithered through his fingers and doubled over into the filth, and Garry was violently sick. He stared at the horror beside him, and now he saw that blood had coagulated in the pit between the man's knees and his abdomen. Poor beggar, he must have had another wound . . . He must get out of sight of that, but his feet were stuck, they would never pull free again. He stooped, plunging his arm in the slimy water. Branches came up, dripping long strings of ooze. Now he had detached the other man's feet; the body canted over, a shapeless rigid mass, and he saw the glaring eyes, the open mouth out of which slime was oozing. He pushed with all his might, thrust the thing under; barricaded himself with branches against its presence. Rain fell, sullen single drops, that burrowed into the surface of the slime and sent oily purplish bubbles floating among the ends of branch that were not submerged. Clots of blood appeared, washed out from the body.

'A wound I didn't know of,' he thought. 'A wound you couldn't see.' Perhaps his own abdomen was like that—black with blood. Squandered blood. Perhaps he too was wounded and did not know it. 'I put him there—I thrust him in.'

Delirium came on him. A wind roared hideously. He knew it was an advancing shell, but shouted aloud as he used to do when a boy in the hurricanes that swept the woods at Knapperley. Again the rushing mighty wind. Night came at last. He knew he must escape. 'Can't leave you here, old man.' In some queer way he was identified with this other fellow, whom he had never seen before, whose body he had thrust with so little ceremony under the slime. 'Tra la la la,' he sang, tugging at the corpse. 'Come out, you there. Myself. That's me. That's me. I thrust him in—I am rescuing myself.'

He was found towards morning in a raging fever, dragging a grotesque bundle at his heels—a corpse doubled over, with bits of branch that protruded from the clothing, plastered with slime. They had to bring him in by force.

'Don't take him from me, you chaps. It's myself. I have been wounded—here, in the abdomen. Here,' he shouted. And he put his arms round the shapeless horror he had dragged bumping from its hole.

He never knew what came of the body, nor whose it was. When he regained his senses he was in hospital, too weak to think or speak, but sure he had been wounded. 'Queer business that,' he said later, 'about my wound. I was convinced I had a wound. I saw myself. Oh, not a pretty sight. Obstinate old bag of guts. I had to haul myself out. I hauled for hours. And I knew it was myself and the other man too. I thrust him in, you see, and I had to haul myself out. Queer, isn't it, about oneself? Losing oneself like that, I mean, and being someone else.'

He lay pondering the hugeness of life. Sometimes he was so weak that he cried. Nurses said to one another, 'Poor fellow—that huge one in the corner. Crying like a baby. He has delusions.'

He fumed at their pity as he had fumed at ridicule in his boyhood; but in a gush of charity allowed himself even to be pitied. One could not refuse to meet other people halfway.

'It's because it's so big,' he tried to explain to one of the nurses.

'Yes, I know,' she answered, pressing his hand.

Of course she didn't know. It wasn't the war that was big, it was being alive in a world where wars happened—that was to say, in a world where there were other people, divinely different from oneself; whole Kingdoms of Heaven, clamouring to be taken by violence and loved in spite of themselves. No nurse could know that; but he permitted her to put her hand on his, and even when she pressed it he did not fling it off. But then he was so tired.

Some weeks later Garry left his valise at the station and set out to walk the four cross-country miles to Knapperley. Night had fallen—a night of war-time, unrelieved. Behind him, along the line of railway where the houses were clustered, dull blurs of light were visible; in front all was dark. Slowly the vast heaven detached itself from the earth. Trees took shape—bare, slender branches striking upward into the sky. It seemed as though out of the primal darkness the earth once more were taking form: an empty world, older than man, silent. In a while Garry became acutely aware of the silence. It burdened him. He stood to listen. A bird was stirring, dead dry leaves rustled in the beech hedge; far off, a dog barked. The lonely echo died, there was no wind, the world was still as dream. Life had not yet begun to be, man had not troubled the primordial peace. Strange stagnant world—he hated its complacency. Standing there on the ridge, dimly aware of miles of dark and silent land, Garry felt a sort of scorn for its quietude: earth, and men made from earth, dumb, graceless, burdened as itself.

'This place is dead,' he thought. The world he had come from was alive. Its incessant din, the movement, the vibration that never ceased from end to end of the war-swept territory, were earnest of a human activity so enormous that the mind spun with thinking of it. Over there one felt oneself part of something big. One was making the earth. Here there were men, no doubt, leading their hapless, misdirected, individual lives; but they were a people unaware, out of it. He felt almost angry that Lindsay should be dwelling among them. He knew from her letters that she was in Fetter-Rothnie, and, convalescent, had written her that he would come to Knapperley; but that her young fervour should be shut in this dead world annoyed him. She was too far from life. The reconstruction of the universe would not begin in this dark hole, inhabited by old wives and ploughmen.

But as he mounted farther into the night, the night, growing upon his consciousness, was a dark hole no longer. The sky, still dark, brooded upon a darker earth, but with no sense of oppression. Rather both sky and earth rolled away, were lost in a primordial darkness whence they had but half emerged. Garry felt himself fall, ages of time gave way, and he too, was a creature only half set free from the primordial dark. He was astonished at this effect upon himself, at the vastness which this familiar country had assumed. Width and spaciousness it always had, long clear lines, a far horizon, height of sky; yet the whole valley and its surrounding hills could have been set down and forgotten in the slum of the war territory from which he had crossed. All the generations of its history would not make up the tale of the fighting men.

He paused a little, contemplating that history. Fierce and turbulent men had made it: Picts and Celtic clansmen, raiders and Jacobites. Circles and sculptured stones, cairns and hill-forts, tall grim castellated strongholds, remained as witness to its past. In its mountain glens there were recesses, ledges at the waterside under overhanging crag a hundred feet in height, where fugitives had hidden from their foes; on its coasts dangerous caves, where smugglers had operated, caught the resounding seas. Craft put out and were tossed on the waters in adventures of piracy and merchandise and statesmanship. Fishermen knew its landmarks. Wrecks were strewn about its shores. Monarchs and chieftains had ridden its passes; a king had fled that way to his destruction, a queen watched the battle on which her fortune hung; and its men had gone to every land on earth following every career. Yet, a small land; poor; ill to harvest, its fields ringed about with dykes of stone laboriously gathered from the soil. Never before had Garry felt its vastness; and he paused now, watching and hearkening. A sound broke the stillness, faint bubble of a stream, the eternal mystery of moving water; and now the darkness, to his accustomed eyes, was no longer a covering, but a quality of what he looked upon. Waste land and the fields, in common with the arch of sky, and now a grandeur unsuspected in the day. Light showed them as they were at a moment of time, but the dark revealed their timeless attributes, reducing the particular to accident and hinting at a sublimer truth than the eye could distinguish. Garry felt for a moment as though he had ceased to live at the point in time where all his experience had hitherto been amassed.

He was recalled to his accidental point in time by a woman's voice, shrill and clamorous, carrying across the night. A man's voice answered, like a reverberating boom. Garry walked on. Knapperley was just ahead.

The dogs were on him as soon as he entered, but not before he had seen Miss Barbara, alone on the kitchen floor, in her swinging Lovat tweed, dancing a Highland fling. How she lifted her supple sinewy legs, and tossed her arms, and cracked her fingers! 'That's you, is it?' her nod seemed to say as she glanced towards her nephew and went on with the step. Garry laughed, weary as he was, and swung into the dance. How much of the character of the land had not gone into this vigorous measure, which a hard-knit woman of fifty five was dancing alone on her kitchen floor in the middle of a world war, for no other reason than that she wanted to!

But in a moment he caught his breath and sat down. Miss Barbara sat also, pulled a handful of raisins from her pocket and began to munch. She asked no questions of her nephew, accepting him as she accepted rain or a litter of pups.

'That's better than jazz, aunt.'

'And what might jazz be?'

'It's a thing some people do.'

'Don't you come here, my lad, with your things some people do. This is a decent house.'

The man lay back, face seamed and drawn, eyes sunken, and looked at the house. Since the war began he had not come to Knapperley till then.

'Not a mortal thing is changed. The war just hasn't touched you, has it, aunt?'

To which she answered with an indignant flash, 'Change and change enough. There's nae near so many bodies about the roads. Tinkler bodies. There's just nane ava, and they're a terrible miss. I aye liked them coming in about for a sup and a crack. Many's the collieshangie we've had in this very ingle—Jeemsie Parten that has nae teeth but on the Sabbath, and Tammas Hirn, he had aye a basket with trappin' and aye time for a newse, and an auld orra body that hadna a name—pigware he brought, bowls and bonny jugs. I hinna had a new bowl since I kenna the time. And Johnnie Rogie, a little shauchlin' craitur, but the king o' them a'.'

Garry went to his room and fell asleep; but awoke in a little shivering violently. The bed—he might have known it—was damp. He dressed and crawled shaking down to the embers. The dogs stirred, but soon were quiet. An owl called. Miss Barbara made no sign; and for the rest of the night Garry sat by the blaze that he rekindled, staring into its heart and attempting to reconcile his aunt's vivid enjoyment of the moment with the dark truth he had been thrust upon in his walk that evening, where time and the individual had ceased to matter.

FIVE

Problem set for Garry

Lindsay was on the moor next morning to meet her lover. She was glad that she had taken his letter herself from the postman, that the old women need not know. The five last empty weeks had collapsed, the moment was enough.

'There are tassels on the larch, Garry. Look, and purple osiers. And oh, do you smell the poplar? I forgot—you are laughing, you know all these places so much better than I. I have never been in the country in spring before.'

'But now that I think of it, neither have I.'

'Not here?'

'Why, no. They were schoolboy holiday visits. Once or twice since, in midsummer.'

'You've never bird's-nested here?—I am so glad. Then I can show you things . . . These are the osiers.'

'No matter what they are. They are too lovely to require a name.'

On the willows by the pool the catkins were fluffed, insubstantial, their stamens held so lightly to the tree that they seemed like the golden essence of its life escaping to the liberty of air. Once, as the two wandered in the wood, they saw a rowan, alone in the darkness of the firs, with smooth grey branches that gleamed in the sun. The tree had no seeming substance. It was like a lofty jet of essential light.

But farther into the wood, in a sheltered clearing, the sun blazed upon a woman, picking gleams from her feathery yellow hair. She was kneeling on the ground, her hands clasped together and her head thrown back. They could see that her eyes were squeezed close and her lips were moving.

'Saying her prayers,' cried Lindsay. 'It's Louie Morgan. She's pi, you know.'

Louie continued to pray. They could hear now the words that issued from her lips. Bowing and smirking to an audience that was not there, Louie was petitioning: 'I'm on the Fetter-Rothnie Committee—may I introduce myself? I'm on the Fetter-Rothnie Committee—may I introduce myself?'

Lindsay checked her gurgle of laughter. 'But it's a shame to laugh at her. Poor soul, she's had so hard a time.'

'How?' Garry asked, carelessly; amused at the creature's antics.

'But don't you know? Your friend David Grey.'

She told him the story of Louie's betrothal.

There began for Garry at that moment the tussle that made his name a byword in Fetter-Rothnie.

'Dave,' he repeated stupidly. 'Dave.'

He had shared rooms with David Grey when they were students at Glasgow Technical College. David's death had touched him closely. Lindsay knew little of the depth and strength of that affection, of which indeed he had never spoken.

'David Grey,' he repeated. 'That creature there.'

Louie was still becking and bowing, swaying upon her knees, with clasped hands and eyes squeezed close. The exhibition, which had been ludicrous, became offensive. But the eyes opened suddenly, and the antic creature scrambled, not ungracefully, to her feet.

Louie Morgan was a slight, manoeuvring figure, in the middle thirties. Her large eyes were melting and beautiful. She studied her movements of arm and throat. When a stranger asked the way of her, she heard him think, 'What a beautiful girl! What poise! I am glad I missed my way. That is a face one must remember.' She studied to have a face one must remember. She had solid respect in Fetter-Rothnie as the daughter of her father, who had been its minister; and of her mother, who made the tea at every Sale of Work and Social Meeting. As Jonathan Bannochie had said, in proposing her a vote of thanks at the last Congregational Meeting, 'It would be a gey dry tyauve wantin' the tea, and Mistress Morgan's genius lies in tea.' She had a further genius in her admiration for her only child. She thought Louie only a trifle less wonderful than Louie thought herself. Mrs Morgan was small, plain and collected. Louie, she said without a tinge of envy, took her charm and temperament from the father's side.

As became the daughter of her father, Louie was devout. She carried a pocket Testament and read it on ostentatious occasions. She wanted to hear strangers think, 'What beautiful piety! How fine the expression it gives the countenance!' And it was always in her prayers that the perfect lovers of whom she dreamed made their appearance. Always when she reached a certain point in her petitions they appeared. 'God bless father and mother . . . and all my little cousins . . . and make me a good girl—' She had a vision of herself as a good girl, a charitable Princess giving alms to footsore men, and one of them saying, out of parched and swollen lips, 'She is more radiant than the sun, and blesses what she looks on. It is she that the King my father sent me to seek.' As she grew older, *make me a good girl* changed its wording, but the sentiment remained and so did the vision, changed also. Her prayers had long footnotes, in which she had visions of herself in all the splendid roles she pleaded with Heaven to let her play; and always a hero came, whose comment on herself she heard, and whom she answered. She was a missionary in a dangerous land, and a ferocious chieftain knelt sobbing at her feet. 'You are more wonderful than all the gods of my people. Your God will be my God, and you shall be my queen.' She was a nurse in hospital, and the sick and wounded blessed her name. A great surgeon saw her pass, noted her touch. An emergency operation must be performed. The man's life hangs on it, he is delirious, fights, will not take the anaesthetic. 'You will come, hold him.' He is calm in a moment, his life is saved. 'Yes, the first time I saw my wife she helped me with a critical case. Saved the man. She has a wonderful touch.' Or perhaps the hero was diffident and would not speak. 'I'm on the Fetter-Rothnie Committee—may I introduce myself?' 'Ah, beloved, had you not had the courage to speak to me that fateful day, how drab life would have been.'

The immediate words that broke upon her prayer, however, were not these; were not, indeed, intelligible. Aware merely of voices, she opened her eyes; then rose and faced the two intruders, flushing with satisfaction. She had always wanted to be discovered at prayer in the woods. *Into the woods my Master went.* She composed the face one must remember, and heard Lindsay and Captain Forbes think, 'Her face is shining. It is by such devotion that the world is saved.'

Louie lifted her eyes from her subconscious play-acting to look at Captain Forbes.

'How ugly he is! It must be years since I've seen him.' Her satisfaction was marred. Garry's face was working. He was still thinking, 'That creature there.' She felt an antagonism. Was it not a waste of effect? 'The wrong sort of man to appreciate me. Life's like that—never the right people.' Distinctly, the wrong sort of man. Louie decided to have nothing to do with Captain Forbes; but immediately she tilted her head a little sideways and held out a hand. 'I am so glad. And what was doing at the Front? Oh, Captain Forbes, now that we have you here; you must say a few words at our concert. Next week. Comforts for the troops, you know.'

'Comforts? Oh yes, you protect yourselves against us with comforts, I believe.'

'Protect—?'

'Parcel us up your comforts, and then feel free to forget all about us.'

'But, Captain Forbes! Linny, do tell him he is absurd.'

'He always is. Garry, you'd better go to her concert and *tell* them about the comforts.'

'Tell them—Good Lord, I will! But it won't be a happy concert. You'd better not ask me, Miss Morgan. No, on the whole better not. Let's get on, Linny. Good afternoon.'

'So you won't come?' she called after them.

'No, no. Lin, where did that gossip get a start? I hope it hasn't spread far. What you told me, I mean. Who could have spread such a story? About David Grey.'

'But it isn't a story.'

'Isn't a story?'

'Not a story. It's true.'

'No.'

'Yes.'

'It'll need a jolly lot of comforts to protect me against that. Where did you get the tale?'

'But, Garry—don't you believe it?'

'Comforts. Believe it? Did you know David Grey?'

'No.'

'Well, I did.'

'But—'

'David was the cleanest thing on God's earth. And not killed, you know. Not a clean, sharp death. Rotted off. Diseased. To die like that! It's an insult. A stupid, senseless, dirty joke. I wish they hadn't added this to it. These scandalmongers. They must always be at something. This tale about an engagement. Another dirty joke. Senseless and dirty. Accusing him of moral disease, as though the physical were not enough.'

'But she told me—'

Lindsay compelled him to understand that the story was no mere rumour. Louie herself asserted it.

'Of all the brazen— Clawed him up from the dead and devoured him. I wish her joy of the meal.'

'I can't understand you, Garry. Why should you disbelieve her?'

'Did you know David Grey?'

'You know I—'

'Well, I did. David was utterly incapable of fooling around with a woman he didn't mean to marry. And utterly incapable of marrying a woman like that thing there. It's obscene. See that tree there, Linny? It's like phosphorescence on decaying fish. Evil look, hasn't it?'

'Why, it's just the sun.'

It was the naked rowan they had seen before. Garry felt a poison in the air. He strode to and fro.

'But your precious Louie shall disgorge. I'll see to that. Give him back his character. In public, too.'

In their restless turning they came face to face again with Louie.

'Captain Forbes, I am sure you will reconsider. It would be such an attraction for our concert.'

Garry stood swaying upon his parted feet. A hand rumpled his forehead. He glared down. Like an ogre, Louie said. One did not fling liar at a woman: still, the thing had to stop.

'I thought perhaps a short address. Some aspect of life at the Front. Of course we want to know the truth.'

The truth, did they? That was easy. David was not cheap. He said aloud, 'Sorry. Been ill, you know. Really don't feel fit for that sort of business. And look here, by the way, this story that's going the rounds. About Grey. Couldn't we do something—fizzle it out somehow? They've got you mixed up in it too, I understand.'

He did not look at her. Louie's eyes melted into Lindsay's. She drew a long breath, then spoke with a guarded frailness in her speech. A mere trickle of sound.

'I don't quite follow, Captain Forbes.'

Lindsay was standing watchfully. A great unhappiness surged within her. Misery, she thought, had ended yesterday, when Garry's letter came at last, when he had said, meet me on the moor. Today had been so perfect that she had thought unhappiness was done with for ever. Why should it begin again? And when Louie's eyes melted into hers, she could have cried for the strangeness of life, its pain, its mystery. She, who had thrilled to her lover's denunciation (in the abstract) of injustice and hypocrisy, stood now aghast while he exposed one hypocrite. But Louie was true, that was the trouble. There was some hideous mistake.

'I don't quite follow, Captain Forbes.'

And then that Garry should say straight out the hideous thing! Now Louie was weeping, talking swiftly. 'But why should I say these things to a stranger? Oh, I know you were my dear David's friend, but some things are too sacred even for a friend's ear. Too secret. How could you know the secret sacred things I shared with David?'

It wasn't Garry's voice she heard. 'I'm sorry, Miss Morgan, I simply don't believe the story.' And Louie still weeping. Garry was going away. What! He could insult a woman like that and then march off and leave her! Louie's sad eyes were watching her.

'Men,' said Louie, 'never begin to understand what we

women have to suffer. The loneliness. The awful emptiness.'

'Oh, I know,' Lindsay cried, remembering her own anxiety. 'Tell me, tell me, Louie. He's quite wrong, isn't he? Oh, I don't know what he means by it. It's horrible. I'm so sorry, so sorry.' She began to sob.

Louie put her arms round the child. 'Ah, we women. We understand one another, don't we?' Lindsay let herself be comforted. There was a subtle flattery in Louie's accepting her as a grown woman, meet for a woman's suffering. She couldn't know all this if she hadn't been through it, thought the girl. Louie was like a priestess divulging mysteries.

'You *were* engaged, weren't you?' she whispered.

'I *am* engaged. As you call it. Betrothed, I prefer to say. My troth plighted unto eternity.'

'Forgive me for asking. Forgive me for asking.' In some deep fashion she felt that it was forgiveness for Garry that she requested.

To Garry the problem thus set seemed on the first evening simple, if a trifle disgusting. He had always disliked Louie Morgan. When he had first come to Knapperley, she, doubly entrenched as daughter of the manse and a young lady five or six years older than the boys, had administered reproof to David and Garry for their behaviour on the way to church. To Garry: 'Even though you do come from a godless house—' To David: 'And you should be all the more ashamed, a saintly man for your father.' The boys lay in wait for my young miss. On the day she wore her first long skirt they walked behind her, whispering and laughing. They sang in chorus, then in antiphon:

O wot ye what our maid Mary's gotten?
A braw new goon an' the tail o't rotten.
O wot ye—O wot ye—A braw new goon—
The tail o't—the tail o't rot-ten—

Louie could hardly wait till they desisted before ducking round to see that the tail of her skirt was in its place. A shout of laughter came from the ambushed boys.

Later they bribed a small girl to be their victim. In full view of the minister's daughter, they pulled her hair and punched her arms. The victim expiated all the sins of her sex in the way she wailed. Miss Louie was scarlet with indignation. She read the boys a homily they would remember. But suddenly all three had joined hands and danced round Her Indignation, whooping. The daughter of the manse spluttered with disgust. Assailing the victim: 'Are you not ashamed, you who come from a Christian home, to play deceitful tricks with these boys?' The victim (who was Kate Falconer) being sturdy and stolid, made a face. That night the boys took Kate to the harrying of a bike.

In the years of their apprenticeship the boys ceased to see each other. They served their time in different towns, and holidays were spent in camp. But with their Technical College Course they were again together. In the last of their student years David chanced to remark, 'Old Morgan's gone. Decent old soul.' 'And what's come of Miss Hullabaloo?' 'Oh, husband-hunting still, I suppose.' Garry could not remember that they had ever talked of her again.

He was therefore sure that the story, wherever it originated, was false. At first it had seemed a simple matter of gossip. That Louie herself asserted its truth made it hardly less simple, though more unpleasant. The claim was a lie, and must be exposed as such. Here was a small but definite engagement in the war against evil, and Garry's heart, on the first evening of the engagement, rose pleasurably to the fray. It was not often one could deliver so clear a blow against falsehood.

SIX

Tea at The Weatherhouse

In the course of the following morning Miss Theresa Craigmyle ran out of cornflour. Theresa made no objections to running out of necessaries. It provided an excuse for running out herself. Theresa's slogan—*A ga'in foot's aye gettin'*—embraced more than what she purchased at a roup. She would come home with all the gossip of the neighbourhood.

This morning she brought in the cornflour and said, 'Mrs Hunter tells me that Bawbie Paterson's nephew is come. Sick leave, she says. And a terrible sight. Influenza and not got over it. All nonsense too thin. "Bawbie won't fatten him sore," I says. "Oh, there's aye a bite and a sup for him here," says she. "Mr Garry kens where to come whan he's teem. He'll aye get what's goin'. The tail o' a fish and the tap o' an egg, if it's nae mair." O aye, he would. He had a crap for a' corn and a baggie for orrels, yon lad. He could fair go his meat. You would have thought he was yoking a pair of horse.'

'Well, well,' said Miss Annie, 'what would you expect? A great growing loon. He needed his meat.'

Kate, who had come home that day with a week's leave from hospital, heard and said, 'Better ask him to tea. Well, why not? You ask all the young men home on leave, don't you? Even if you do object to his aunt—well, even to himself, then—but I daresay he's sobered down by now. We haven't seen him for donkey's years.'

Miss Theresa conceded the tea. It was one of her ways of helping on the war. For every young man of the district home on leave she baked her famous scones and gingerbread, while Miss Annie and Mrs Falconer asked the same series of questions about the Front.

'I'll tell you what,' said Kate. 'Linny and I will walk round by Knapperley. She's never seen the place.'

'She's seen Bawbie. That should be enough. Well, Lindsay, don't you take her tea if she should offer you any. Spoot-ma-gruel.'

'He'll be waiting for me, Katie,' murmured Lindsay when they were outside.

'That's all right. I'll go away.'

'You'd better give the invitation— Or— As you please.'

Garry said, 'You, Kate— Remember the wasp's bike?'

'Why, yes, I do. Will you face my aunts tomorrow?'

'Will you face mine today? Yes, do come, Katie. Linny must see Knapperley. And I want to talk to you. How are we to set to work killing this lie about Davie? That Morgan creature, you know.'

'Is it a lie?'

'Oh, Katie,' cried Lindsay, 'do help me to convince him. He's taken such a dreadful idea into his head—that poor Louie has invented the whole story. He's hurt her so.'

'That sort doesn't hurt. Does it, Kate?'

'Why, yes. Very badly, I should fancy.'

'What! Hullabaloo? No. You thrust, and she closes up round. Unless she's changed a lot.'

'But why a lie?'

'You think David would have married that?'

'I don't know. Why not?'

'Lord, Kate!'

'Well, I don't see what's preposterous in the idea. She's a good woman. Feckless, a bit. Rather conceited. I'm not particularly fond of her. But David Grey may have been, for all I know. I presume he was, since he asked her to marry him.'

'But he didn't.'

'Didn't?'

'Garry, you don't *know*,' cried Lindsay.

'Look here, Kate, you wouldn't dishonour David, would you? You wouldn't think him capable of such meanness?'

'But why should it be meanness to marry a woman? Most men do.'

'But that Louie.'

'Louie's all right, Garry. I don't see why you should be so angry. I don't like her much, as I said, but lots of people do. You haven't seen her for so long. Of course, she was a bit—you know—self-important. Put on airs. But that sort of thing wears off. Or else one gets accustomed to it. She'd make as good a wife as another. I don't see why David shouldn't have chosen her.'

'David, Kate? As good a wife as another, yes. But for the other man—not for David.'

'David is merely the other man for me, Garry. Any man. I hadn't seen him for years. How could I know what he might or might not do? And a lot of men make fools of themselves when they marry, anyhow.'

'So at least you acknowledge that such a marriage would be folly.'

'No. I was talking of a general principle.'

'Katie, can't you see what is at stake? It's a lie. A blasted, damnable lie. She's false as hell. It must be killed. She must be forced to acknowledge there was no engagement.'

'But what an idea! You propose to put it to her?'

'Oh, Katie,' cried Lindsay, 'he isn't only proposing. He's done it.'

'And she acknowledged it, of course?'

'No, she denied.'

'Well, what more do you want? Why do you suppose it's a lie? I didn't know there was any doubt over it.'

'I suppose it's a lie because it can't be true.'

Kate stopped in the road and gave him a long, considering look.

'Because you refuse to believe it's true, you mean. Do you *know*? David ever say anything about it to you? You've no proof? Look here, Garry, you'd better be sure you're not doing this because you hate Miss Louie Morgan. You never used to miss a chance, you know, of tormenting her.'

'Of taking her down a peg, you mean. She needed it.'

'Yes. But it was good fun, taking her down.'

'Well . . . it staled. You never could take her down. Just what I said: you thrust and she closed up round. Oh yes, good fun enough. But you don't suppose there's any fun in this business about Grey, do you?'

'I think you are persuaded by your own dislike.'

'Katie,' Lindsay's clear, sharp voice rang out, 'you have no right to speak to Garry like that.'

'You don't want him to make a fool of himself in the countryside, do you?'

Garry winced.

'Louie Morgan is too much respected—her father—her mother. People would simply gape. It's your word against hers, isn't it? And they'll all remember the things you used to do to her. Even David Grey thought you went too far. That time you made on to be fighting, and she separated you and you carried her off and shut her in the old Tower.'

'And forgot to let her out.'

'A willing forget.'

'No, I don't think so. No, I'm sure we were doing something else. Queer how hard it is to remember. We did mean to let her out.'

'Do tell me,' said Lindsay.

'Nothing to tell. Horrid rumpus. Dr Morgan purple in the face. And David's father— That was something to remember. Davie said it happened only once before. Davie's father told him off. Six words, no more. No more needed.'

'No one could understand how you got in.'

'We pinched the key.'

'Are you quite sure you are not pinching the key this time? I'll leave you two,' Kate finished abruptly.

'But, Katie—about going home. I came out with you. They'd think it funny.' Lindsay did not wish the old women to understand Garry's identity. They would make uncomfortable remarks.

'Yes,' agreed Kate, 'they do chatter. Very well, I'll wait for you. Behind the spruce trees.'

'But,' Lindsay questioned as she watched Kate melt against the moor, 'need we go to Knapperley?'

Garry had been thinking of Kate: 'How she has altered! She's growing like her aunts. What, not go to Knapperley? But you must see my aunt. She is not fearsome,' he added, smiling.

'But I fear her.'

'Why?' he asked, smiling protectively down upon her.

'No, it's not that—I am not a child.' She could find no way to express her thoughts about Miss Barbara. They were not thoughts—that was it. They were something felt, apprehended in her dumb silent self. The image of Miss Barbara loomed above her, as she had appeared in the winter night, elemental, a mass of the very earth, earthy smelling, with her goat's beard, her rough hairy tweed like the pelt of an animal. She had thought John Grey too like a portion of earth, as he crawled on all fours weeding; but he embodied the kindly and benignant earth; Miss Barbara its coarser, crueller aspect . . . Has no mythology deified a bearded woman as its god of earth? Lindsay, unable to find words to explain her terror, which could not be explained by anything as yet within her experience, blurted, 'It was the lights. They were awful, Garry, truly. Every window blazing, in mid-winter, and it war-time.'

'What's this?' said Garry. 'Good old Barbara! She would win every war that ever was.'

'Win it? Keep it from being won. Defying orders.'

'But that's just it. The spirit of it. We shan't have won this war until we're all defiant. Haven't you understood that yet? My aunt's enormously herself. She'll never alter, except to get more herself. I don't suppose the lights mattered. The police would have seen to it otherwise.'

'But they did. She was fined, I think. Warned, at any rate.'

'Very well. Now come and see her after her warning.'

'You think I am a child, to be afraid.'

But perhaps she was. The warm glad sun danced over her. The earth shimmered away into idle space. And now she had seen a blue tit.

'What is he, what is he? I do so want to know his name. Garry, there are herons in the lower wood. I saw one yesterday with Kate. Flying. A great grey heavy one.'

'They are all like that.'

'Are they?'

'Then it had been herons we were hearing yesterday while we were talking.'

'Yes.'

'And are you satisfied now that you know?'

'Oh, to know makes me so happy . . . You think that strange?'

He took her through the high, bare rooms of Knapperley.

'But these are dreary rooms.'

'Not the kitchen. I don't know where my aunt can be.'

'No matter. Let's go out.'

'I was giving these outer doors and windows a coat of paint. Look how warped they are. The wood's shrunken. Do you mind if I go on?'

'How neatly you work, Garry! Do you hear that bird? I must follow.'

He gave himself to the consideration of Kate. She was wrong to be so sure: he was sure, moreover, that she was wrong. And to bring this ignoble motive in to a clean fight against falsehood! It was petty on Kate's part to suppose that he still harboured these boyish animosities. He fought for greater issues now. And if the victim in each case was the same, was he at fault? It was not as a person that he wanted Louie punished, but as the embodiment of a disgrace. He brought the brush down with neat furious strokes. But Mrs Hunter, when he had called the night before at Craggie, had scorned his suggestion of duplicity in Louie's tale.

'She has the ring, Mr Garry—his mother's ring that she showed me herself, and her dying, and said her laddie's love should wear. That's nae ca'ed story, Mr Garry. Louie fairly has the ring.'

'His mother's ring,' muttered Garry.

'I'm nae saying but it's a queer whirliorum, a matter like a marriage to come out in a by-your-leave fashion like that. Miss Craigmyle, now, was of your way of thinking—that she made the story up, But "Na, na," I said to her, "na, na, she has her credentials." And her credentials is more than the ring, Mr Garry. There's the name she has, and her family.'

Miss Theresa Craigmyle? Very well, then, he would go to their tea.

Lindsay came bounding back.

'Garry, your aunt knows—why didn't you tell me? Your aunt knows all kinds of things. There's a heronry in Kingcausie woods, my heron must have come from there. They have to shut the doors and windows at breeding time. Against the clamour. And there are oyster-catchers' eggs on that bit of shingle. Lying in the stones. You stumble on them. Oh, Garry, I like your paint. You have made a difference.'

'So you found my aunt.'

'I was watching a bird. I didn't know what it was, I am so ignorant. I crept in, under the trees there, following. She found me. I thought it was something wonderful. It was only a chaffinch. But even a chaffinch is very wonderful, if you know just nothing at all, like me.'

'Wonder what Aunt Barbara thinks of this Louie Morgan affair?'

'What does it matter, now? It's ended, isn't it?'

'Ended?'

'Surely Kate convinced you? Do you still think Louie made the story up?'

At the Weatherhouse, after tea that evening, Mrs Falconer followed Kate to the garden. How still the air, how shining pure the sky! Waiting—all waiting for the revelation of spring. But it was so hard to talk confidentially to Kate. Her mother stumbled, came in broken rushes against the girl's tranquillity.

'Garry is coming? I thought, I used to imagine—long ago—you were such friendly you two. I wondered sometimes—but then he went away. I used to think you cared.'

Kate knit her brows, considering the implications of her mother's insight; decided that the secret was not hers to divulge.

'Why, yes,' she said, unbending her frown. 'But there was no need for you to know.'

'And now? It hasn't altered?'

'No. No, I think not.' She thought, 'As good a way as any to cover Lindsay.'

Mother and daughter parted.

'Stop your bumming, Ellen,' sharply said Mrs Craigmyle. Leeb was accustomed to say, 'Not one of my daughters has tune in her, and there's Ellen would bum away half the time, if I would let her.'

Ellen laughed and forebore. She went out to the long brown Weatherhill, where no one would resent her bumming. It was that hour of waning light when colours take on their most magical values. The clumps and thickets of whin, that had turned golden in the few days of sun, glowed with a live intensity, as though light were within them. The colours of life had for Ellen the same bright magical intensity. She was more excited than she knew. Had Kate a hidden life her mother had not suspected? She was so placid, so contained; Ellen had schooled herself for so long to the disappointment of believing that her daughter was thus contained because there was nothing to spill over. Had she misjudged her Kate? Ellen's thoughts turned back to Kate's girlhood, and she remembered how the girl had run about the moor with this Garry Forbes—a great awkward lad, she had never seen much in him. Wild ruffian, Theresa said. Yes, they had all condemned his madcap ways, and Kate had suffered in silence. But Ellen had woven a whole romance around the two and hidden it in her heart, hardly believing it had more foundation than the hundred other romances that she wove. But it had, it had. Foundation, and a new miraculous lustre. Kate took on a new dignity in her mother's eyes—perhaps the grandeur of a tragic destiny. But no, that must not be—unless he were slaughtered. No, no, I must not fancy things like that. Kate's love would reach its consummation. They would be wedded. He would call her mother. The boy had had no mother—and now he would tell her the things that a son keeps for a mother's ear. 'Mother, it is so easy to tell this to you. You have a way of listening—' No, no. I must not fancy things like that.

But on the morrow, when Garry came to the Weatherhouse, Mrs Falconer tingled with her excitement. She pressed herself upon the guest, eager to know him. 'For Kate's sake, I must get to understand him.'

'You've no knives on your table, Nell,' scolded Theresa.

'No, no. No.' She *scuttered* at the open drawer, sat down again by Garry, smiling.

'See that your mother has those knives put down,' said Theresa to Kate. 'When my back's about I can't know what she'll do. She's been the deed of two or three queer things this day. I've got two or three angers with her.'

'She's tired today, I fancy.'

'Tired! Your granny in a band-box.'

Kate returned from the kitchen and set the knives herself. Mrs Falconer was smiling, looking up in Garry's face, asking senseless unimportant questions.

'You might have the wit to know *that*,' Lindsay was thinking, impatient at the trivial turns the conversation took.

'Mother, don't giggle,' said Kate, aside, passing her.

'Why shouldn't she giggle?' Garry thought, watching for the first time the elderly lady with interest. 'So, Miss Kate, you are growing like your aunt Theresa. You put people right.' He gave Mrs Falconer's questions a serious attention.

Theresa brought in the tea.

'There', slapping down her pancakes before the guest, 'you don't get the like of that at Knapperley. It's aye the same thing with Bawbie, a stovie or a sup kail.'

Garry drawled, 'A soo's snoot stewed on Sunday and on Monday a stewed soo's snoot.' And he did not look at Miss Theresa, whom he hated, with her air of triumph, her determination to show him that man must live by bread alone.

Miss Annie laughed delightedly. 'When did I hear that last? And whiles it'll be as tough's the woodie, I'm thinking, your soo's snoot.'

Lindsay cried, 'Garry, do you know them too, all these funny picturesque phrases? You must teach them to me.'

But Theresa muttered, 'Sarcastic deevil.'

'I would have you know'—he addressed himself mentally to Theresa—'I can't stand people who humiliate me. The pancakes are excellent, Miss Craigmyle,' he said aloud. 'And now please tell me, why do you suppose Miss Louie Morgan was not engaged to David Grey?'

'Did ever you suppose such a thing, Aunt Tris?' asked Kate.

'Garry has taken a dreadful idea into his head,' cried Lindsay, 'that Louie made the story up.'

'There!' cried Theresa triumphantly. 'Didn't I tell you that long ago, but you weren't hearing me. I was right, you see. I'm not often wrong.'

But was she right? Now, where did the tale begin? Let's trace it out. But nothing came of that, except to disturb everyone's sense of security. No, not a whisper before his death: that was plain. But shortly after, 'I haven't the right to wear mourning,' she had said to Mrs Hunter. And she had the ring. And Mr Grey received her often. But counter-balance that with her character: well, a good character, a moral character. But they all knew she was out after a man. Oh yes, a flighty thing, always ogling the men. 'Though there's lots that's taken in with her airs and her graces.' Would a man like Grey be taken in? His character against her known assertiveness, her pretty dangling. But where does all this lead? Since the man is dead, it can't be known for certain.

'Since he is dead, I must put it to the proof. His reputation must be cleared. And publicly.'

'Be wary, Garry,' said Kate. 'If you are wrong—no, accept the possibility for a moment—if you are wrong, you will have pilloried your friend.'

'Publicly,' Miss Annie cried. 'You wouldn't do the like of that. She's a harmless craiturie that nobody seeks to mind.'

'And it would hurt her. Garry, you don't understand—it will hurt her horribly,' Lindsay pleaded. 'Suppose he did love her, after all.'

'And David Grey,' said Miss Theresa, 'is hardly of the place now, as you might say. Since he went away to go to the college we've hardly seen or heard of him. Except his medals, to be sure, and prizes. But he might marry anyone you pleased to point at, and who would care? Not a soul would let their kail grow cold with thinking of it.'

'And anyway,' said Kate, 'now that he's dead, does it matter?'

'Captain Forbes matters,' said Mrs Falconer.

Ellen's hands were clasped tight together above her breast, and they shook rapidly from her excitement. They were like a tiny bald nodding head that gave assent to her speech. Her head nodded too, slightly and rapidly.

The gaunt young man looked across the table; and remained looking, his jaw down, as though, having opened his mouth to speak, what he was about to say had become suddenly unimportant.

'I mean,' she continued, 'honour matters. Whether people care or not, and whether she's to be hurt or not, you've to get the truth clear. Because of truth itself. Because of his honour. And it matters to you, because you feel his honour's in your keeping now he's gone.'

'Yes,' he said, 'that's why. Because of truth itself. It's good of you to see that.'

If one had never seen a bird before, never seen a flake of earth, loosened and blown into the air, change shape and rise, and poise, and speed far off, beyond the power of eye to follow; seeing one would understand the sharp delight that Mrs Falconer experienced at hearing the young man's words. She kindled, her face became winsome, like that of a young girl. She laughed—a low, sweet laughter. When he talked to her, words bubbled on her lips.

'But must you go so soon?' she pleaded. '—Yes, yes, a pack of women, we can't entertain you very hard.'

Indeed, as he walked away the man felt relief from the pack of women. On the other side of the dyke Francie Ferguson, slicing turnips, droned a song. Garry leaned his arms on the dyke and looked over.

'Ay, ay, you're having a song to yourself.'

Francie straightened his shoulders, pushed his cap farther back on his head, answered, 'Imphm,' scratched himself a little, added, 'Just that,' and returned to the turnips.

'Decent fellow,' thought Garry. Yes, that Morgan creature had to be corrected. Beside the honesty of Francie she showed unclean.

In the Weatherhouse: 'Stop your bumming, Ellen,' commanded Mrs Craigmyle.

'Mother, don't giggle,' said Kate apart.

As on the evening before, Mrs Falconer left them and walked alone on the Weatherhill. Again the sky was shining pure. Again the wide land waited. Annunciation of spring was in the brown ploughed fields, the swollen buds, the blackbird's sudden late cascade of song, the smell of earth. A wood of naked birches hung on the hillside like a cloud of heather, so deep a glow of purple was in their boughs. And a bird had gone up out of Ellen's heart, pursuing its unaccountable way into the distance. A flake from her earth had risen. Life had a second spring, and it was opening for this woman of sixty who had lived so long among her dreams. The earnest young man, his brows drawn in that anxious pucker, his eyes unsatisfied, roving from face to face, burdened with the pain and ugliness of life—yes, she was sure that that was it, that haunted look of his betrayed a soul unhappy over the torment and mystery of life, its unreason and its evil—this young man had brought her suddenly back into its throng and business. She who had been content to dream must now do.

And her fancy was off. She saw that it was she who was to help the young man (she called him mentally her son-in-law) to establish the truth, to rout Louie.

'How can I have lived among trivial matters for so long?' she thought. 'This is real, and good. I feel alive.'

She wandered back slowly to the house. Light still lingered in the sky; the hills, that had been dissolved in its splendour, like floating shapes of light themselves, grew dark again. Ellen too, emerged from the transfiguring glory of light in which she had been walking. What did her happiness mean? Why, of course, she was happy because of Katie. This mysterious and tranquil glow that had irradiated life had its source in a mother's satisfaction. Kate loved, Kate would be loved, Kate's mother would be satisfied.

But in the house there was no satisfaction. They were all talking together. Lindsay tossed back her disordered hair, angry tears were in her eyes. The leaping firelight gleamed on her face, her agitated movements, and on Theresa's fingers as she put away the knives and silver, and on Leeb's busy knitting needles and the glittering points her eyes made in the gloom.

'Cousin Ellen,' cried the girl, 'Cousin Ellen, Louie is true. Oh, she is! Garry is wrong, wrong, wrong.'

'It's not worth the to-do, Lindsay,' said Miss Theresa.

Ellen flamed magnificently from the exaltation with which she had been suffused. 'But yes. Always worth, always worth to follow truth. The young man is doing the right.'

'To hurt her? Even if it wasn't an engagement. If she just loved him—and never told?'

'She never did. She just couldn't stand being unimportant.'

Ellen said it suddenly. She had not known it herself till that moment. 'There's all the girls round about, they all had their lads, and some of them killed and some wounded, and everybody making much of them and them on everyone's lips. And Louie had nobody. She had a lot of talk one time about *missing*, *missing*, as though she wanted us to believe she had someone and him lost.'

'What an idea, Mother!' said Kate.

'But she had. "It's cruel, this *Missing, Presumed Dead*," she would say. "It keeps one from starting fresh." '

'Yes, she said that to me.' Lindsay stared across at Mrs Falconer. 'She said, "It's the faithfulness that is unto death. It deadens you. Keeps you from beginning life anew." What a curious thing to say!'

'Always what we couldn't disprove, you see. And then she hit on David Grey. And so she paraded her tragedy. It made her important. They may say what they like about Louie looking miserable—she's never looked so *filled out* as she has of late. She was a starved sort of thing before.'

'But, Cousin Ellen, I can't believe that it's all a lie. If you had heard Louie talk about it. So tenderly. You can't imagine. A lie couldn't be lovely like that.'

'There's lots you can't believe in life, Linny. Angels of darkness masquerading as angels of light. I'm some afraid she's lived so much with her lie that she can't feel it a lie any longer. Her head must know, but her heart is persuaded.'

Lindsay's eyes, mournful and still, were fixed on her. 'Why, the child herself had some affair,' Ellen remembered. Surely it was over. This eager Lindsay, following bird song, catching at country ways and sights, gathering windflowers, was quite changed from the pallid girl who had come to them at Christmas. 'Yes, yes, she was too young. It must be over.' But the girl's eyes burned in the dusk; not eyes of light forgetfulness.

Theresa put the last of the knives away, and stood scratching the side of her nose.

'Such a to-do about a dead man,' she said, 'that can't come back to set the matter right. I've had an itchy nose all day—itchy nose, you'll hear of fey folk. It's to be hoped no more of you are doomed, the way you're carrying on. I always told you Louie made the story up. But to hold this parliament about it—'

'Cousin Theresa, don't you dare to mention it to anyone. Not anyone. That Louie made it up, I mean. Not till it's proved, if Garry ever does prove it. To disgrace her publicly— If *you* begin to talk, she'll have publicity enough.'

Mrs Craigmyle chuckled from her corner. 'Take you that to butter your skate.' Without lifting her eyes or altering a muscle of her face, she began to hum a little tune.

'You're turning as rude as that young man, Miss Lindsay,' retorted Theresa. 'But you will note that he enjoyed his tea. You needn't be in such a taking over Louie, bairn,' she added, more kindly. 'Grows there skate on Clochnaben? She was born with a want—you'll get no sense yonder. But *you* needn't turn your head about it. You greetin' like a leaky pot, and Nell with a great baby's face on her—I never saw the like. Worse than you's useless.'

The face that Ellen turned towards the fire was indeed strangely child-like. A soft smile played on it, pleased and innocent. She was still thinking, 'I shall help him to proclaim the truth.' But the sharpness of truth was not visible on her countenance. She had the look of the dreamer who has not yet tried to shape his dream from intractable matter.

In the firelit room Mrs Craigmyle's hum grew more audible. The words became clear:

Duncan Forb's cam here to woo,

sang Mrs Craigmyle, with a subtle emphasis upon the altered word:

Ha, ha, the wooin' o't.

Ellen looked up. Her face quivered. She began to talk loud and quickly.

'Hateful,' she thought, 'making it uncomfortable for Kate.'

Later she found her mother alone. Mrs Craigmyle raised her voice (but not her eyes) at her daughter's approach:

Duncan Forb's cam here to woo.

She sang gaily, her foot tapping the time, and her snow-white head, crowned with its mist of fine black lace, nodding to the leap of the flames. And her face was innocent of any intention. She was singing an old song.

'Mother,' said Ellen, with burning cheeks, 'you shouldn't do that. Hinting. In your song. It isn't nice.'

Mrs Craigmyle turned an amused, appraising eye upon her widowed daughter.

'You're right, bairn,' she answered blandly. 'The young man has a good Scots name that won't fit into the metre. You're right. I shouldn't spoil an old name as though I had an English tongue on me—feared to speak two syllables when one will do. I'll not offend again.'

She watched her daughter with a fine regard that had malice in it. Mrs Craigmyle, through her apparent unconcern, had noted Ellen, habitually so quiet and reserved, kindle and crackle, and it amused her.

'Well,' said Ellen, 'but if Kate doesn't like it.'

'That's right my lass, study you to please your family.'

Ellen went away, her cheeks still hot; and a mocking laughter followed her, faint, that seemed to echo from very far off, centuries away, in ancient story.

Lindsay was leaning from her open window. The spring night, hushed and dim, yet held a tumult. Out there, in every field, in boughs of the secret wood, life moved. Kate slept, but Lindsay could not sleep. Everything—the promise of spring in the air, an owl's call up the valley, the tranquil radiance that the young moon had left above the hills, water tumbling with a thin clear note, the shame and trouble of her nature—all conspired to keep her exquisitely awake. And Lindsay thought, 'I want everyone to be happy. It shouldn't hurt like this—all that beauty.'

She could not tell herself what the hurt was. All was vague and confused in her mind. Garry was different from what she had supposed him. But she had known him so little—only his kisses and those amazing talks, far into the night, until her father came and sent them all to bed. This Garry with the worried frown and haggard eyes was someone else. Worrying because he wanted to do a wicked thing—Lindsay was still convinced by Louie's phrases. Or—were her confusion and trouble because she was no longer quite convinced? Was Louie, whom she had set admiringly in her temple, no god at all, but brittle clay?

'I don't understand,' she cried, leaning to the night. 'Life's so strange. It isn't what you want.'

One grew and things altered, people altered, just being alive was somehow not the same. Spring was like that, changing the world, taking away the shapes and colours to which one was accustomed. Were seeds afraid, she wondered, and buds? Afraid to grow, afraid of life as she was afraid of it. Evil, and wrong—one knew there were such things in the world, but to find them in people, that was different. In people that one knew. Garry cruel, and Louie false; and all the while earth and sky brimmed with beauty. And she leaned farther into the tranquil night.

Below her on the grass someone was moving. Who should be in the garden so late? If it were Garry! How good to have him seek her presence in the dark, in the still, sweet April glamour! A very night for lovers.

But the figure on the lawn moved farther off. Now it was against the sky, and she saw that it was a woman's. Her eyeballs were stinging. 'I only want to be happy,' she cried. The sound of her own voice, breaking unexpectedly upon the silence, affrighted her. But Katie did not stir, and in a moment another voice was borne to her upon the air. She recognised it for Theresa's. 'Come in to your bed, Ellen.' The voice floated from the next window. 'Walking there like a ghost.' There was no answer, but the figure in the garden moved back towards the house; and Lindsay heard a stair creak. Cousin Ellen! Why should she walk in the night? Why should anyone walk in the night but the young and the untranquil and the lovers who cannot wait for morning?

SEVEN

Why Classroom Doors should be Kept Locked

Morning changed the temper of the spring. Plainly the lady had no more mind for honeyed promises. Her suave and gracious mood was done, and those who would win her favours must wrestle a fall with the insolent young Amazon. Sleet blattered against the ploughman's side as he followed the team; or, standing in a blink of sun, he saw the striding showers cross the corner of the field like sheeted ghosts. Never tell me, ghosts took to sheets for the first time in a Deeside ploughman's story, who, bewildered in an April dusk, saw white showers walk the land, larger than human, driven on the wind.

'Where are my birds today?' asked Lindsay. 'And oh, the poor thin petals! Look, Garry, on the whin.'

But Garry answered, 'I'm going to take you home.'

At the Weatherhouse door Mrs Falconer met them, running.

'Come in, come in. You must be wet.'

She did not pause to question why they were together.

'They never seem to guess,' Lindsay thought. 'Old people don't see.'

Doors flapped, sleet scurried along the lobby.

'Come in, come in,' Mrs Falconer cried. 'She will be angry at this mess.'

She drew them in and, stooping, plucked with her fingers at the melting flakes of sleet, and dabbed at the runnels with a corner of her skirt. 'There, she'll be none the wiser.'

'Not a whit,' Garry said. He had taken out his handkerchief and wiped a smeared wet patch from the hat stand.

But Theresa was safely in the kitchen, so they sat and talked by the living-room fire, with old Aunt Leeb spider-quiet in her corner, and Paradise in a happy doze. She opened her eyes and smiled at them. 'I'm dozened,' she said, and slid away again.

Garry began to talk of after the war. 'It will be a very different Britain before we're done with it.' He told them all that was to be accomplished to make life worthier. Lindsay glowed. This was the talk she loved to hear. Her young untried enthusiasms delighted in the noble. Above all she wanted her lover to be good. These splendid generalities were like the fulfilment of all her own vague adolescent aspirations.

Ellen also glowed. 'Why, what a barren useless life I have lived!' She felt a smoulder of shame run through her at the thought of the evanescent fancies in which her inner life had passed. 'But *this* is real. How I hate these shams and unrealities!' And, without noticing what she did, she began to form a new fancy. 'Katie loves him. If they should ever marry—when they marry I trust they will let me live with them.' How good that would be—to live in daily touch with men's enterprises, to know what was done and thought in the world. Hearing the young man speak, she would never slide again into these wicked imaginings. And she remembered how he had taken out his handkerchief and wiped away the smear of sleet. 'But when I live with them, I shan't need to go in terror of Tris.' She could open the door then, without fear of what came in, to strength and manhood and new ideas, and even to brave young folly that laughed in the sleet when it might sit warm at home.

All this she fancied at the very moment that Lindsay, lifting her eyes to smile into her lover's, was thinking, 'I thought if he came here there would be all their stupid jokes to face, but not one of them seems to notice.' Then she saw Miss Annie's eye upon her. But Miss Annie only said, 'I think I'm taking a cold. Lindsay, you've no clothes on.'

Lindsay ran behind the old woman's chair and put her arms round her neck. 'Girls don't wear clothes nowadays, Paradise, you dear.' And she wanted to tell Paradise that Garry was her lover. 'Because I'm sure you saw,' she thought. And, after all, it was pleasant that Paradise had seen. 'It's the others who would talk. Paradise, your hair's so soft behind. Paradisal hair.'

'It's got most terrible grey.'

'Silver, you mean. Silver of Paradise. Apples of gold and silver of Paradise.'

'You're a wheedling thing—what are you wanting now?'

'Only a kiss.'

She dropped a kiss in the nape of Miss Annie's neck and danced round the back of Garry's chair, running her fingers across his shoulders as she passed; but Cousin Ellen she did not touch. Even grand-aunt Leeb she had breathed upon, blowing a kiss so light upon her ancient head that the gossamer of her lace hardly trembled.

'How strange!' she thought. 'Last night I was miserable. And now today I'm glad. I don't know what to make of life.'

And Mrs Falconer, whom she had not touched, was unaware of the omission. A warm glow suffused her body. She was thinking, 'This false betrothal, that is something true. To expose the falsehood is something real that I can take my part in.'

Garry went away. The sleet eased off, but the roads were like mortar and the land looked bleak. An empty land—he remembered his vision of it as taking form from the primordial dark. Some human endeavour there must be: like Lindsay unaccustomed to a country year, he had hardly realised before today how much endeavour, skill and endurance went to the fashioning of food from earth in weathers such as these. His midsummer holidays had not told him of wet seed-times, of furious winds blowing the turnip seed across the moors, of snow blackening the stooks of corn. He saw a man lead home his beasts through mire, fields not yet sown were sodden wet again. He had never thought before of these things. There must be grit and strength in the men who sowed their turnips thrice and ploughed land that ran up into the encroaching heather. A tough race, strong in fibre. Yet since he came how little he had seen of them! Women mostly—Lindsay like whin blossom on the cankered stem of her people; his aunt like an antique pine, one side denuded, with gaunt arms flung along the tempest; Mrs Hunter like a bed of thyme . . . pleasant fancies, dehumanising the land.

Across them he felt suddenly as though a teasing tangle

had been flung—nets of spider-web, or some dark stinging noxious weed from under ocean. He had thought of Louie Morgan. He disliked the thought—no question as to that. And how this mean affair had tangled across his vision! Wherever he turned he saw it. Three days ago, when they came on Louie at her base devotions and he had heard the story first, it had seemed a simple thing to dispose of it. Now it was less simple. He had recoiled instinctively from the tale as something false, but his instinct was to be taken as no proof by other people. These women with whom he had discussed it insisted, moreover, after the fashion of women, on treating it as a personal matter, a matter of Louie Morgan, not of truth. His aunt, to be sure, had raised the issue to a matter of principle, but not one that helped him much.

'What's she wanting with a man ava?' was all he got from Miss Barbara.

The others saw it purely on the personal plane; and Kate's assumption that he himself was moved by a personal rancour smote him to wrath. Even Lindsay could not see that truth and justice were beyond a personal hurt—Lindsay, who had looked so sublimely lovely in her pleading that he resisted her hardly. Her eyes had been fixed on him, mournful and limpid. She was lovelier than herself. She had identified herself with Louie. She too, was hurt and was transfigured in her acceptance of another's suffering.

He had thought, 'But you can't ask other people to pay the price. You can't ask Lindsay.' Was truth, after all, more important than the pain you inflict on others for its sake? It was only that long, lean, nice Mrs Falconer who understood that truth and honour were at stake. A curious champion of truth. He remembered her furtive ducking in the lobby to dab the runlets of sleet with her petticoat. Well, he supposed, one could tilt at error even in petticoats and in spite of an abounding fear of one's sister in her domestic cogencies.

He had as yet, in these three days, had no man's opinion upon his problem. Not, for instance, John Grey's. But to visit John Grey, as he knew he must, David's father, was of necessity to find some expression for what he felt over David's death; and he could find none.

At that moment, through the darkening light, he saw Miss Morgan approach.

'The deil has lang lugs to hear when he's talked about,' muttered Garry.

Miss Morgan picked her way towards him along the puddled road, and her face was as puddled as the road itself. She was weeping. She stood with downcast eyes in front of the astonished young man and said, 'Oh, Captain Forbes, what shall I do? I've been a wicked woman. Help me, Garry—I may call you Garry? We are such old friends, we used to play together.'

A man stumped past and regarded them with curiosity.

'Well, we can't talk here,' Garry said.

'No, no. The school. I was going there. I have the key.' And she led the way, looking back at him over her shoulder with eyes that languished and saying, 'The concert, you know. For those comforts. Garry, I understand what you meant about comforts. We think our responsibility is over, and it isn't. Our responsibility is never over. We are our brother's keeper all the time. You must be my keeper.'

She unlocked the school door. 'I have a key. I am in charge, you see. A little sketch they are doing—there are so few hereabouts that understand these things.'

The school was a two-roomed building, built close upon the church. The church having no hall, and a vestry like a cupboard, the adjoining school was used for many parochial purposes. Miss Morgan went in. 'I have to measure something—curtains, you know.'

Garry followed in spite of a remarkable distaste. To chatter of curtains amid tears of contrition argued, to him, a blameworthy lightness. But were the tears of contrition? He waited.

'No, I think in here,' Louie was saying. She led him to the inner room, and with some ostentation locked the door. She had an indescribable air of enjoying the situation.

Then she came swiftly at him.

'Help me, help me. What am I to do? I've done such dreadful things. I've lied and I've stolen. I am a miserable sinner, and my transgression is ever before me.'

He stopped her torrent of words with a cold: 'It is easy

to bring such general accusations, Miss Morgan. We are all sinners. If I understood what you referred to—'

She darted him a glance of hatred.

'Of course you understand. But you will make it as hard for me as you are able. Oh, what shall I do? What shall I do? People must never know what I have done. Promise me that—they mustn't know. Promise me.'

'When I know myself—'

'Yes, yes, make it as hard for me as you can. It's right, it's just. I want to confess to the uttermost. Abjectly. I will tell you—I want to tell you everything. You. But no one else. Oh, do not make it public! My name, my mother, afterwards.—Yes, yes, I will tell you all.'

Garry stood in the dark schoolroom and marvelled. He had never seen an emotional abandonment so extreme, and it seemed to him as ignoble as her perfidious clutch on his friend. He would not have helped her out in the confession, determined that she should taste its dregs by telling all; but disgust drove him to shorten the affair.

'You mean that there was no engagement.'

'No, no, it's not like that.'

'You made it up.'

'No, no, I did not make it up.'

'What then?'

'It wasn't like that. Yes, yes, I made it up. Oh, how wicked I have been! Quite, quite wrong. Evil. I see that now.'

Suddenly she raised her head, listening.

'Yes, there's someone there,' said Garry.

He had heard before she did a sound of voices outside and of feet. Now the outer door of the school was pushed open and men came in. They heard their tramp and the noise of speech.

Louie's whole expression altered. She snatched her companion by the arm and whispered, 'Caught. It's a session meeting. I had forgotten it was tonight. What shall we do?'

He shook her off. 'There's nothing to make a fuss about. You have the right to be here, I suppose, since you have the key.'

At that moment someone tried the door of the inner room. The voices rose.

'But you,' said Louie, weeping. 'And alone here. And it's dark. Oh, what shall I do?'

'Do what you please. I should imagine you could invent a sufficient story.' He flung the window up and leaped out on to the ground. 'Better shut that window again,' he called back. Then he strode off.

Louie wiped her eyes and opened the door.

An oil lamp, new-lit and smoky, hung in the outer room. Louie blinked. Her eyes, bleared and tender, smarted in the smoky atmosphere; she stood shaking, thus ruthlessly thrust back from her attempt at truth to the service of appearances. To these men she was still Miss Morgan, daughter of their late minister. She put her head to the side and apologised, and in a minute speech came freely to her and with it relief: she had escaped from the terror of her attempted encounter with her naked self.

'I really didn't remember—that concert, you know. I was measuring. I didn't remember your meeting. But I'll go— Well, if you don't mind. I could get on with those curtains.' Aided by one of the elders, she took her measurements, which were in the outer room, and went.

Outside Garry stood in the gloom. It was lighter here than in the school. It was lighter than he had expected. Forms of men passed him and entered at the school door: elders of the kirk, on their way to deliberate. An odd idea seized him—to walk in upon their deliberations and state his problem. He remembered the old kirk session records: *Compeared before the Session, John Smith and Mary Taylor*—the public accusation and punishment. If he were to go now: *Compeared before the Session, David Grey and Louisa Morgan.* She was still there. Why should she not answer for her guilt, her moral delinquency? But to drag the dead man there—

He put the idea from him and walked on; but, considering that he had better have the interrupted matter out with Miss Morgan, returned towards the school.

Jonathan Bannochie the cobbler came from the school door as he hesitated.

'The birdie's flown, ma lad,' said Jonathan. 'Ay, she's awa'.'

Garry stared, but turned and walked on.

Jonathan kept step beside him. 'I'm for the same way mysel'. I've a pair o' boots for Jake Hunter's missus. They can just cogitate awa' wantin' me or I win back. Yon was a gey grand jump you took out at the windock. The laddies wouldna need to ken yon, or the missy'll hae her ain adae to haud them in. Ye're nae takin' us on? Man, it was a grand notion to get the door locked on the pair o' you. Ye're nae takin's on, I'm sayin'. Well, well, and what was the door locked for, my lad?'

'On a point of honour.'

'Eh? What's that? O ay, it's a gey honorable business, a kiss.' And he bellowed:

> Some say kissin's a sin
> But I say it's nane ava.

'Is the construction your own?' said Garry, stopping short. 'Or the finding of the Session?'

In the grey half-light he eyed his man. Jonathan Bannochie was a power to reckon with in Fetter-Rothnie. That the man had character was very evident: his mouth was gripped, a sardonic and destructive light glimmered in his eye. The man was baleful, yet not in action, but in speech. To have one's reputation on the souter's tongue did not make for comfort. If the souter's thumb was broad, in accordance with the rhyme:

> The hecher grows the plum-tree
> The sweeter grows the plums,
> And the harder that the souter works
> The broader grows his thumbs—

(and Jonathan was a smart and capable workman), the souter's tongue was sharp as the thumb was broad. He could destroy in a phrase, spread ruin with a jest. It was he who, in a few days' time, with a twist of mockery, was to make the name of Garry Forbes the common possession of Fetter-Rothnie speech.

Of this Garry could have no foreknowledge; but he saw in front of him a man of parts whose life's achievement had narrowed itself to a point of tongue. Undoubted that Jonathan had made his shoemaking a success, and Garry's philosophy set high the man whose common labour was achieved with skill and honesty; but that Jonathan's gifts would have been adequate to more than the cobbling of country boots he was very sure. The man had been dissipated, though by no overt system of dissipation. He did not even drink: in Mrs Hunter's eyes a downward step. 'I dinna ken what's come over him,' she said, 'he doesna even drink now. And a kinder man you needna have wished to meet when he had a dram in him.' His domestic life had come to grief. The wife whom Mrs Hunter could never understand his having chosen ('I dinna ken what gar't him tak her. A woman with a mouth like yon. The teeth that sair gone that the very jaws was rottin'. And nae even a tongue in it to haud her ain wi'.') moved early from the scene, and left him two daughters, both spiced with their father's temper. Both decamped. A few years later the elder girl, choosing her time with a knowledge of her father's habits, descended on the homestead, 'and up and awa' wi' the dresser under one arm and the best bed under the other.' Jonathan found the house stripped. In compensation a puny child was left on the kitchen bed. But Kitty did not prove another Eppie. She grew up scared and neglected, the butt of her grandfather's scorn, with rotting teeth like those of her grandmother, and her grandmother's lack of tongue.

In addition Jonathan Bannochie was an elder of the kirk, feared but hardly respected, a shrewd and efficient critic of other men's business and bosoms.

'Is the construction your own?' Garry asked, watching his man. 'Or the finding of the Session?'

'Ach, haud your tongue, Mr Forbes. A bonny lassie in ahin a door—we're nae the lads to blame you.'

There flashed across Garry's mind: *Compeared before the Session, Louisa Morgan and John Dalgarno Forbes*. Apparently, the finding was acquittal. He laughed.

'You've the wrong soo by the lug this time. Mrs Hunter, did you say? I'll hand over the boots. But as I've a matter to lay before the Session, I'll take it kindly if you'll step back with me now and hear it.' He stowed Jonathan's parcel away in his pocket.

EIGHT

Compeared before the Session

'Gentlemen,' said Garry, facing the assembled Session, 'forgive this interruption, but I see you have not yet begun your business. And I've some business of my own—yours too—I want to make it yours.'

He looked earnestly round the men. Some he knew, others were mere faces; one lined and puckered like a chimpanzee's, one spare and shrewd; one fat, without distinction, one keen and cultured; enormous brows; black beards; an oppression of watching eyes. He felt the impact of them like a mob; but as he talked, he scanned the countenances, swiftly computing how each would answer to his challenge. At his shoulder he was aware of the sardonic semi-grin of Jonathan Bannochie, that haunted him like an echo of all that grinned within himself, his contempt of his own sensitiveness to ridicule, his fear of the humiliation of failure. In front was the long, serious face of Jake Hunter, a crofter on his aunt's estate, husband to the jolly woman who was his aunt's old servant and faithful friend. Jake, too, was a faithful soul; a stern fighter against the odds of poverty, sour soil, bad harvests and uncertain prices. His bit of land was seamed with outcrops of rock and heather. He cut laboriously with the scythe, both because the land was too steep and uneven for the reaping machine he did not possess, and also because the scythe cut closer to the ground and no inch of loss on stubble could be afforded. Jake had fought his slow, obscure way upwards, quenching errant enthusiasms. Books had been one such enthusiasm. He was already a man over forty, toughened and worn by exposure and labour from his earliest childhood, when he wedded Barbara Paterson, Miss Bawbie's servant girl, and her uncle settled them on the meagre croft. Then for the first time Jake hoped to satisfy his craving for knowledge. He bought some books, a miscellaneous lot picked up from a second-hand bookstall, and settled it with Barbara that he would read for an hour each night. Barbara put the book for him and took her shank to sit and watch. But the reading did not thrive. A day's work is a day's work, and a man must stretch himself.

'I'm nae nane swacker o' anither day's wark, 'umman,' he would say; and then he would *ficher* with the pages awhile and nod a little. By and by it would be up to have a look at the weather.

'I'll just rax mysel' to be mair soople for the book,' he would tell Barbara, and coming back, dropped to sleep again. Not as you would say a real sleep. Still less of course, a feigned one. A sample, rather—three-four grains between finger and thumb for earnest of the wide fields of slumber that would be his at night. Waking from one of these offhand naps, he would stretch himself largely, move to the door again, and restore the book to the shelf before sitting down.

'I'll just be puttin' it by for the night,' he would say, smothering a mighty yawn. 'It's as you might say a habit, the readin', it beats you at the start. It'll come mair natural-like come time.'

Vain expectation. These habits do not grow on one. They have none of your fine Biblical ease in pushing, a man going to sleep and rising night and day while they adjust themselves to the requirements of the universe. Each year that made the rent queerer to come by and the stomachs of his hungry bairns harder to find a bottom to, made Jake swacker neither in the muscles nor in the wits. He stiffened by living. But his fervour for book learning passed to his eldest son Dave, who united the serious humour of his father with the drive of his mother's vitality. Dave, serving his time as a joiner, read far into the night, and fired by his new experiences at the Front, wrote home, as Mrs Hunter had told Lindsay, that he would put the younger boys through the University. As it happened, Dave, returning from the war with a single arm, went through the University himself on his pension and an ex-service grant, and turned schoolmaster, to his parents' great content.

Garry, in the rapid glance by which we can review at times many years' knowledge of a personality, saw the long, grave anxious face of Jake Hunter as that of a good man, a man upright in all his dealings, but too limited in the reach of his experience to understand the matter on which Garry desired a judgment.

His next door neighbour, John Grey, David's father, was not in the company. Garry felt freer to speak, but regretted not to meet him for the first time since David's death among other people.

The minister, who watched the young man curiously, was a latecomer to the district, not very old, pale and shrunken. To him, Garry felt, he was not speaking, but to these elder men who knew both Louie and David and had some pretensions to knowledge of himself.

'Gentlemen,' he said, addressing the pale young minister, 'I had a friend, a man you all knew and I believe respected—as you respect his father, Mr John Grey. He's dead. I lived with him—that tells you what a man is like. Well, I believe in David's honour with all my soul. I come here and I find—we make honourable images of our dead, don't we?—I find the image left of him in your memories defaced. By a woman. The woman who came out of that room there just now. I am given to understand you knew that I was in there too. Well, I was. In the dark. Locked in and all the rest of it. And I jumped out of the window, as I gather you also know. Because, gentlemen, I wanted to prove—I have every reason to believe'—he spoke very slowly, measuring his words— 'that her claim to be engaged to David Grey was an impudent forgery. She is a woman whose word is not to be trusted—'

'Tell her that, and seek a saxpence,' said Jonathan at his ear.

'I am convinced there was no engagement. The thing–the thing's immoral.' He began to talk wildly, blurring his words. Jonathan's interpolation angered him. 'It's an insult to my friend. Tell me—that's what I want you to do, once it was the duty of the Session to regulate the morals of the community, it doesn't seem to be so any longer—tell me what I am to do now.'

The men were embarrassed. The affair at issue was curious. But the man with the keen face, whom Garry did not know, and who was a petty landowner not always resident in the parish, said, 'There would seem to be the man to answer your question.' And turning, Garry saw John Grey, who had come quietly in while he was speaking.

It was a number of years since he had seen Mr Grey, and he was aghast at the change he saw. He was now an old man. His shoulders were bent, what was left of his hair had gone white; but the receding of the hair served only to expose still further the noble and lofty forehead and give his figure a serene dignity, a majesty even, that his smallness of stature hardly led one to expect. He had come in late. Weariness was in his bearing. He had lifted shells all day. But as he stood listening to Garry, his face was alert, and a deep still glow burned in his eyes. He came forward now, a pleasant briskness in his spare figure, and taking Garry by the hand, very courteously gave him welcome, neither mentioning what he had overheard nor inquiring the young man's business among the elders; but the former speaker pressed his point, saying, 'Mr Forbes has a matter here for your attention.'

'Let the matter rest.'

There was a stern authority in John Grey's tone. Without raising his voice, which was habitually soft, he yet conveyed in its intonation a settled finality that caused Garry to tremble. He had heard that note in his voice only once before, when David and he as boys had locked Louie in the tower.

'I know no more than you do,' John Grey said, 'the truth of this engagement. My son never mentioned it to me. The boy is dead. Let there be no more said about it.'

No more could be said. Garry felt a fool. He got himself out of that room and stood fuming on the road, having distinguished nothing in what was afterwards said to him but Jonathan Bannochie's whisper, 'Try her in the Tower, Mr Forbes.'

Inside the schoolroom there was an awkward moment. Most of the men resented vaguely this intrusion into the ordinariness of living. The landowner with the keen face said, 'A curious affair. Has the young man any grounds for his suspicion?'

Another man answered, 'Now here's a funny thing. Just yesterday my lassie had a letter from a friend, a boy in Captain Forbes's Company. Went queer, they said. Left out in a shell-hole and brought back clean off—raving mad. A corpse bumping at his heels that he insisted was himself. Wouldn't leave go of it. Touched, I'm afraid.'

'Is that the way of it? Poor chap! The war has much to answer for. He certainly looked raised.'

Garry, indeed, hollow-eyed, taut with the terrible earnestness of his purpose, breaking upon the Session to propound his riddle, looked hardly sane.

The pallid young minister wiped the sweat from his brow. A bookworm, he liked life plain. The promise of confusion among his people smote him to a sort of panic. Now, wiping his brow, he breathed deep in his relief. The threatened confusion to his peace was no worse than this, the meanderings of a poor fellow not quite responsible for what he said. He had never before seen Garry, but was ready to believe in any mental aberration in a nephew of Miss Barbara Paterson. John Grey interrupted his thoughts.

In his quiet, courteous fashion Mr Grey asked leave, if nothing demanded his presence in the meeting, to follow Garry.

'Yes do, do go,' the minister said. Sweat broke again upon his brow. He had come to this country parish to escape the impact of life, but there were moments when he recognised himself a coward. The sweat breaking on his brow bore witness to such a moment.

'Do go, Mr Grey,' he said.

Garry was still standing on the puddled road. All his boyhood's discomfort in the face of ridicule was working in him. At first he could hardly speak with civil tongue to Mr Grey; but the old man's quiet refusal to note that anything was wrong, as they walked and talked, in time restored him to a sense of deeper hurt than that to his own vanity; and he felt better. He went home with Mr Grey. Garry was unfed, and his host called for food. The room was shabby but gracious. All it contained, if old and worn, was good:

engravings after the Masters, some photographs of hills and of machinery, a Harvest Home, hung in oak frames of Mr Grey's own making. The bookcases, also of his making, were filled with books, like the furniture, good and worn. While Garry ate, the old man, seated by the fire, fell asleep; and awoke in a little to say, 'I'm getting to be a done old chap.' He stooped forward and picked a child's doll from the fender. Garry had observed it there, with china face and blue eyes that stared towards the fire.

'The eyes came out,' said John Grey, as he lifted the toy and examined it with care, 'and her little mistress brought her to me. She believes I can mend everything that breaks, but this was as hard a task as I have tried. I had to work the eyes back into place and fill the head up with cement to keep them fixed. See, it has set.

Garry took the doll and examined the workmanship.

'Jolly neat. I saw a youngster, two evenings ago, as I went past, following you around while you were weeding. Slip of a girl. Her arms were round your neck as you knelt. Once I declare I saw her ride on you, bare leg across your shoulder, and you paying no attention.'

'That is the child.'

'Confident little sparrow, wasn't she just!'

'She was not in my way,' said the old man smiling.

Garry thrust plate and cup from him and buried his head in his hands.

'Perhaps I am not in your way either,' he said at last; and without waiting for an answer he began to talk, pouring out to David's father his bitter distaste at David's betrayal. 'You can't think that ever he meant to marry that woman.'

John Grey talked in his turn; but with reticence. It was plain, however, to Garry that Louie Morgan as a daughter was not a welcome thought. Yet he defended her, even, as it seemed to Garry, to the detriment of his son. He slowly gathered that the old man was unsure of what the brilliant boy, who escaped beyond his father's experience at many points, might not have done. Besides, David and Miss Morgan had certainly met, many times, not long before his death. She had been staying in the south, with friends, very near his lodgings. David's own letters had referred to her presence, even to her quality. 'There's more in her than ever I thought.' They had had long and intimate talks. No, David had never hinted at love, certainly never a betrothal.

'But this confession she was making to me,' stammered Garry. Death was in his heart. To find Mr Grey believing that the thing was possible made Garry face it for the first time, and the thought that David might indeed have kissed that vapid mouth weighed on him like death.

'Think nothing of the confession. Never mind it. She was overwrought. Leave the matter as it is. Let there be no more said.'

Of what was he afraid, pondered Garry. Surely of something. He could not leave the theme, returning to his own contempt of the woman. But the old man silenced his complaint. Garry felt uncomfortably that in his presence one could disparage no human being; not even a woman for whom he had confessed that he did not care.

'You are too good for this world,' thought Garry. 'Or too simple.'

Mr Grey put the theme aside with decision.

'We'll just leave it where it is, lad.'

Garry was profoundly dissatisfied, but drew his chair to the fire and smoked; and they talked for over an hour. Garry would have enjoyed the talk (for he had a deep respect for John Grey, and they had many tastes in common) had his secret uneasiness not kept growing. At last its torment worked through even his interest in shells and fuses, and he rose to go.

The night had cleared. Spring had danced her caper, and sat now dreaming and demure. Under the wide dim sky, where single stars hung soft, the man walked out his torment. He had to face the issue he had evaded: someone he must despise if his convictions were to go unchanged. Was it John Grey, who could believe of a splendid son that he would sully his honour? Or David himself, who had sullied it? Had David loved—no, David could not have loved this woman, but had he perhaps, incredibly, become infatuated with her? Had the ancient madness worked, the old invincible gods snuffed up their reek of sacrifice? David's face rose before him, brooding, strong, ironic as in life, and at the thought that he had lost not only the face but what it meant to him, desolation fell so strongly upon his spirit that David died a second time. His mouth was filled with ashes, loathing took his soul. So it was the Cyprian John Grey had feared, and, prudent man, stayed his eyes from looking lest the goddess smite. It is not well for man to pry into the doings of the gods. But as he paced in his bitter misery the thought returned: what was this incomplete confession that Mr Grey desired him to ignore? It must have had some meaning, and he must know its end.

He had reached the gate of Knapperley when his hand came against the bulge that Mrs Hunter's boots made in his pocket. Jonathan Bannochie had told him they were promised for tonight. He turned, then turned again and took another road that came to Craggie by way of the house inhabited by Mrs Morgan and her daughter.

The house, standing back from the road, was dark, but against the shadowy trees a pale figure moved. Garry leaped the wall and strode across the lawn.

Miss Morgan was as restless as himself. Her mother and the maid had gone to bed, but she had come seeking into the starlight—and found Garry.

'Let's finish that talk we were having,' he said.

She cried indignantly, 'What do you mean, breaking into my garden like this, so late? You are as rude and wild as when you were a boy. Haven't you done me harm enough today already, locked in with me like that?'

'Don't be a fool. Who's to know I'm here?—Listen, Miss Morgan'—he gripped himself and spoke less roughly—'you began tonight to tell me something. Will you finish it?'

He saw, however, that he was dealing with another Louie. Instead of tears he found defiance. Louie's attempted excursion into truth had been too hard. But he was determined this time to hold her fast.

'Yes or no—were you engaged to marry David Grey?'

Louie twisted her hands together.

'What is it all about? Won't you tell me what you meant this evening? Why are you a sinner? You said—'

'Yes, yes, I said! I said! Do you suppose words ever

mean the right thing? I said. And I suppose I meant it then. But you are to blame for what I said. You, by your suspicions and your accusations. I am too sensitive, that's what it is. I see other people's point of view too quickly. I said dreadful things about myself, and they all seemed true then. Because you had moved me and I was seeing with your eyes. Don't you understand? One can accuse oneself of any enormity under the stress of an emotion. You tell me how my conduct looks to you, and I see it. Yes, I see it. I acknowledge my sin and my transgression is before me. But that vision isn't me. When the emotion is over, I recover myself. I realise to what an enormity I have confessed.'

'But you haven't confessed to anything,' said Garry wearily.

'You think I made the story up—that David didn't love me. I will tell you what I meant, what I was trying to confess. But all those tears were quite wrong. I was too humble. It's nothing so very bad, after all. We were not actually engaged—no formal engagement, I mean. I could never bring myself to that—I wouldn't do as David wanted. Because, you see, I was not sure that he was saved. I couldn't say yes until his soul was safe.'

Garry was staring in the chill of horror.

'You think you knew David—you didn't know my David. You think I wasn't good enough for him. Perhaps I was too good. There was a side to him you didn't know. I developed it. I created him. My own part of him. And *you* can't take it from me. You didn't know how much we were to each other in those last months before he died.'

'I heard—something.'

'Oh, something. But no one knew. Do you suppose we blabbed? No, but we talked and talked—six weeks we talked. Oh, just in snatches, when he had the time. He slaved all those weeks. But when he had an hour—how we talked! We threshed out all the religions in the world, I think. You didn't know David cared for that. You thought his machinery and his music were all he thought about. But he did. I made him care. Only—he died so soon I never knew, never was sure that I had saved his soul. And now

I never can be. So, you see, I couldn't enter into a formal engagement, could I? But it would have come to that. Am I so very wrong to claim it before the world? To me it is like a proclamation of my faith in David—that his soul *was* right at the last. It is a mere formality I am assuming. But surely I am justified. The truth that was the truth of our hearts is expressed in it—that is all.'

Garry said slowly and with difficult utterance, 'That is a morality more involved than I am accustomed to.'

'Morality is always involved. Only truth is clear and one. But we never see it. That's why we must live by morality.'

Garry got up from the garden chair on which he had been seated.

'This is too much for me. I don't pretend to understand you. And was this what distressed you in the evening?'

'Yes, yes. You made me feel a cheat, to claim the reality without my formal right. But I do not feel a cheat now.'

'Then I suppose I had better go away?'

'Yes, go; yes, go.'

He went in misery. He could not disbelieve this tale of David. Talk they must have had. More of David—and more of Miss Morgan—than he had known became apparent: new stars slipping from the dusk. He walked bewildered.

In a little he came to Craggie. All was dark and silent. He rattled on the door, and the sound, rolling into the night, roused him to observe that all the countryside was folded. It must be late: he had not thought of time. He made out the figures on his luminous wristwatch—half past eleven. The Hunters were a-bed; he regretted having come and turned to go quietly away.

But shuffling footsteps were approaching, bolts were shot back, and the long knotted figure of Jake Hunter appeared in the doorway, trousers pulled hastily up over his night-shirt. His face was twisted in a look of apprehension.

'What's wrong, ava?'

'Nothing, nothing.' Garry apologised, explaining his errand.

'Man, it's a terrible-like time o'night to tak a body out o' their beds.'

'So it's you that's the death o' them,' cried Mrs Hunter,

coming to the door. 'And me callin' Jonathan Bannochie for a' thing—nae boots for Bill the morn's morn. An' it's nae like Jonathan to be ahin hand wi' his work. He doesna seek nae to put to his hand. And it's you that was poochin' my laddie's boots.'

'Man,' said Jake, 'you feared me, comin' in about at this hour.'

'O ay, now, Mr Garry, sir,' Mrs Hunter interrupted, 'what's this you were up to with Miss Louie? She came by this house with a face begrutten that you couldna tell it was a face, and when I but said "Good evening"—quiet-like and never lettin' on I saw the tears—ran as if she saw reek. Bubblin' an' greetin'—tears enough to make the porridge with.'

'Hoots, wumman,' said Jake, 'let the thing be. Seein' there's naething a-dae, let's to our beds. But man, you fair feared me. Would it be our laddie, I thocht, killed maybe or wounded.'

Garry apologised again.

'Miss Morgan's all right,' he told Mrs Hunter. 'I saw her a little ago. Very cheerful.'

The couple went in and shut their door. But Garry stood on the road, struck dumb. Mrs Hunter's voice had brought to his memory what he had forgotten—the assurance she had given him that Louie had her betrothal ring: the ring that David's mother had reserved for his bride.

Not betrothed to David, yet wearing his mother's ring: now what should that forebode?

NINE

The Andrew Lorimers go to the Country

The sleet had vanished in the night. Airs were soft as summer, and over the last golden clumps of crocus, wide open in the sun, bees droned and buzzed.

'A flinchin' Friday,' warned Miss Annie, who had a farmer's knowledge of the weather signs. 'There'll be storm on the heels of this.'

Storm! thought Ellen, bumming as she cleared the breakfast dishes. Youth was in her heart, she had risen up at the voice of a bird, and the world for her was azure. She could not understand this flood of new life that welled up within her.

The postman came, bringing the letters, and told them the story of Garry before the Session.

'He had no call to shame her like that,' said Miss Annie.

'Pity for her in her snuffy condition,' scoffed Theresa. 'The lad's as thrawn as cats' guts, he'll do as he pleases.'

'But it's not to laugh at,' said Ellen, with an unexpected heat. 'It was a noble thing to do.'

'Locking her in a schoolroom, the same as he locked her in the old Tower—where's your nobility in that? Well, well, Louie'll be having him next, wait till you see. The cow dies waiting the green grass, and if she can't get one to her mind, she's well advised to take what she can get.'

Lindsay thrust her thumb into the envelope of a letter and ripped it savagely open, and glared at Theresa above a trembling lip.

Ellen said, 'Tris, you're an old fool. As if the boy would mind her.'

'If he can't get a better, where's the odds?
 Are ye hungry?
 Lick the mills o' Bungrie,

Are ye thirsty?
Kiss Kirsty.

'What stite you talk!' said Miss Annie. 'The lad was scunnered at her.'

'There was once a lad that took a scunner at butter, and after that he could never eat it thicker than the bread.'

'Oh, they're coming here,' cried Lindsay, reading from her letter. 'The children—for a picnic.' She began to read aloud, hastily, to hide the trembling of her mouth, and even she was less indignant than Ellen at the monstrous suggestion that Theresa had made. The sisters were still bickering, and Theresa had just said, 'Oh, no, to be sure I know nothing. What should a silly tailor do but sit and sew a clout? It was me that had the right of it in the other affair, I would have you remember. I told you she wasn't engaged to him'—and was making for the kitchen, but paused to hear Lindsay read her mother's letter.

Mrs Andrew Lorimer wrote that as the holidays had begun the children were eager for a picnic. They were taking lunch out, and would the Weatherhouse ladies give them tea?

'And there's them turning in at the foot of the brae,' said Theresa. 'What a congregation! We'll need our time to tea all that.' She went to the kitchen and began to bake. Theresa liked nothing better than to provide a tea. Lindsay ran flying down the brae to meet the children, and as she ran the words spurted from her lips, 'Brute, brute, brute. I hate her. Brute.'

'She's never away in these thin shoes,' said Miss Annie, following Theresa to the kitchen. 'She'll be ill.'

'Fient an ill. She's that excited you would think she was a bairn herself. That's her that was so dead set on marrying. There's no more word of that affair, it seems. And she doesn't get letters from any at the Front but Frank.'

About the same hour Garry Forbes was walking up to Mrs Morgan's door. He was stern and ill at ease, but determined to go through with the task that he had set himself. Louie, too, was ill at ease. When she saw him her face crumpled up, puckering as though she were to cry, and she lowered her eyes and would not meet his. He was sure she had already been weeping.

'Forgive me,' he said, 'I haven't slept. I must know this: that ring you wear—it's David's mother's. How do you come to have it if you were not betrothed?'

'Why do you pursue me like this?' She sat down with a gesture of despair and motioned him to a seat. He saw the tears trickle between the hands with which she covered her face.

'I did try to tell the truth yesterday,' she said at last, looking up. 'Perhaps if they hadn't come in—and yet I don't know. Oh, must I tell you? Can't you understand how it is? I am so covered with shame—will you let me try to show you how it was? Will you let me try?'

He assented gravely.

'I think sometimes I can't tell the truth—can you understand that?'

He was embarrassed, not knowing what to answer.

'Yes,' she continued, 'truth to me is terribly hard. I am made like that. I live all the time—oh, I am going to scourge myself—in what I want other people to be thinking about me, until often I don't know—indeed, indeed I don't—what I really am and what I have thought they are thinking I am. I understand myself, you see. But I can't give it up, I can't. I've nothing to put in its place.'

Garry was looking in amazement.

'I should have thought the difference between truth and a lie was clear enough,' he said as she paused.

'Oh, no, it's not—not clear at all. Things are true and right in one relationship, and quite false in another. It's false, as a mere statement of fact, that I was betrothed to David, but true as an expression of—an expression of—' She faltered and burst into tears.

'I was going to say, an expression of feeling—our feeling. But it's my feeling. David—I am to tell you the truth now—David never mentioned love to me, or marriage. We had those talks—yes, yes, you must not think those were invented. We talked—all sorts of things, deep, intimate things. And I was always thinking: I am making an impression, I am altering his ideas. I wanted to save his soul. I think—I think I wanted it to be *me* that would save his soul, not just that his soul would be saved. I am trying to be honest, you see. And then I thought: he will recognise how much I have done for him, I shall become needful to him, and in time—in time—yes, I hoped that in time he might marry me. Don't you understand? I think that about every man. There have been so few—just none, just none. No one ever before with whom I even had an intimate conversation, like this with David. It was luscious, it was so good! I wanted to be at the heart of life instead of on its margins.'

'Yes, yes, I can see that. But I don't see that it justifies you in grabbing David.'

'Grabbing! But I didn't grab. Oh, you haven't understood at all! That part of him is mine. I created it. No one can touch it but me.'

'But you said he never—'

'No, no, he never did. I suppose it was all a tiny thing to him—just some occasional talk. He liked it at the time. But between times he was absorbed, he forgot. And I thought and thought until that was all that was alive for me. And yet he liked the talks. He would say, "Now there, what you said last week—I've been thinking about that." He made me feel, somehow, as though what I said was tremendously important, as though I were tremendously important to him. And then I came to believe I *was* important. You see how well I understand myself.'

Garry was at a loss. He felt as though a roof had blown away and he was looking in amazement at a hive of populous rooms where things were done that he had never imagined.

'So when he died it was myself I felt for, that my hope would never come to be.' Garry made a motion of disgust. 'Yes, yes, it was hideous. But don't you see my desperation? "What are the men thinking about?" they said. "Not about me"—I couldn't answer that. Don't you understand? I had to save my self-respect. Confess no man had ever wanted me? "What are the men thinking about, that *you* are still unmarried?" "Ah, I could tell you that an I would." You needn't tell a lie, you see. A hint is all. But it saves you from humiliation—from yourself. Yes, I know it is in your own eyes that you are saved. The others forget, but you keep on remembering that they know.'

'So David had to suffer that people might think—the right thing about you.'

'To suffer! But I forgot. You think it is a degradation for David to be thought in love with me. That is why you have wormed all this out of me.'

He could not deny, and so was silent.

'But why should it be a degradation? I'm not wicked. I'm not ugly. I have charm. I'm thirty five—you wouldn't dream. I've kept astonishingly youthful.'

Juvenile, was the word that flashed across his brain.

'I have such girlish ways. Oh, God, what am I doing? Why did you let me go on? You can't expect me to acknowledge that it would have been a degradation. And yet I know it was only—what was the word you used?—*grabbing*. That I grabbed David. But it didn't feel like that to me. It felt like— Oh, I tried to explain it to you. Like the seal and signal of the great belief I had in him. A high and holy thing. I see now that it wasn't—that it was only—was bad and wicked. The human heart is deceitful above all things and desperately wicked. That doesn't mean that you tell lies. Self-deceitful. You think you are doing a brave thing, and it turns out mean. And you don't deliberately persuade yourself about it. You really are deceived. Only some people—like me, I'm one of them, you should pity us, we are of all men most miserable—, some people see the deceptive appearance and the deceit both together, as it were, only they can't quite distinguish. Or won't let themselves. Just now, for instance, I am hoping that I am saving your soul. As I hoped with David. I am saying, years after, he will look back on this hour and say, "My life was changed—that was a crucial hour for me. I had a new revelation of life given to me." That's what I meant by saving your soul. But you won't, will you?'

'No. No.'

'No, of course not. I know that. Only you see I go on thinking and acting as though I knew you would. There, I have revealed my innermost being to you. No one has seen it before. But you—you have forced me to see how vile it is. Will you not have mercy? Are you to make of me an outcast in the eyes of men?'

Garry found his thoughts in confusion; but remembered suddenly that she had not yet explained her possession of the ring.

She went very white, threw her head back and breathed deeply. 'I took it. Why don't you say something?' she added after a pause. 'I took it. *You* would say stole, I suppose. But it wasn't really that.'

'No?'

'Oh, you are cruel! You are saying, double meanings again. But I shall tell you how it came about. His mother wore that ring. I used to watch it when I was a girl—the strange old set and chasing of the gold. And I was with my mother when we saw her dying. She said, "It's not of value, it's only a square cairngorm, but the setting is old and rare. My son's bride shall have it." I thought nothing then, but you know how unimportant words like that may stay with you. You forget that you heard them, and then one day back they all come. It was Mr Grey himself that showed me it. I asked him, "Have you nothing for our jumble sale?" And he said there might be some useless odds and ends. He pulled out a drawer, and there was the ring. I knew it at once. He put it aside and some other things, and then he said, "If you find anything there of any use, just you take it." So I rummaged in the drawer. But afterwards I couldn't keep my thoughts off the ring. Nor off his mother's words, "David's bride." I said them over and over, and then I felt: if only I could have the ring a moment on my finger I should feel better. David's bride. It would feel real then. I thought about it till I couldn't keep away, and I went back to the house and opened the drawer and slipped the ring on. I felt so happy then, I can't explain to you. It seemed as though something had come true. I could have danced and sung. I couldn't bear to take it off again, and I went and stood by the window—it opens like a door, I had come in that way—and watched the light shine on it. And then I heard a sound, and there was his old housekeeper coming in at the door. So I slipped it in my pocket, meaning to put it back in the drawer, and I said, "Mr Grey gave me leave to take some things from that drawer for the Jumble Sale. I knocked, but you couldn't have heard. I'm glad you've come in, for I was just wondering if I could take the things away when nobody was here." Then I went into the room again and played about among the things in the drawer, always hoping I'd be able to slip the ring back. But she watched me all the time. So I had to carry it away. And I slept with it on that night. Oh, I can't make you understand—in a few days it felt like a part of me. All I had wanted of David seemed to be concentrated in that little piece of gold. I loved it. I couldn't bear to have it off my finger—though I was prudent, and wore it only when I was alone. He wasn't dead a month by then. Well, one day I had it on, and my glove was off, when I happened to meet Mrs Hunter. It was on my wedding finger, you understand, and she pounced at once, and said, "What, what!" and then she stood staring at the ring and cried, "But I've seen that ring before," and I felt like death and said, "Dear Mrs Hunter, it hasn't to be known. We hadn't made it public, and now—" "You poor bit bairn!" she said, and I began to weep. It was such a relief to weep, I felt so frightened. But then I recollected myself and told her on no account to speak of it. Especially not to Mr Grey. "You know that he never mentions David's name," I said. "And at any rate, since the betrothal had not been announced, it's better to keep it secret still. I prefer to suffer in silence." But I couldn't, you know. That was just it. I wanted everyone to know that I was suffering. Mrs Hunter promised faithfully to say nothing—'

Garry gave an involuntary exclamation and clapped his mouth shut on it at once.

'I know, I know. You are to say: she spoke to me, she told me. It *was* Mrs Hunter who told you the ring was his mother's, wasn't it? But you see she did not break her promise, it had got known without her, and she was free to speak. Got known, I say. I made it known, was what I mean. I couldn't keep it, you see. I gave other people hints—it was so sweet, oh, if you knew how sweet their pity was! No, not their pity—their admiration. For the way I bore my suffering, I mean.'

Garry sighed profoundly. The whole interview oppressed him. Her speech was an unseemly mockery of human pain. Yet she was terribly in earnest. He could not refuse to listen to the end. In some tortured and labyrinthine way she was revealing a soul. All was not sham. He sighed and listened.

But the door was opened, and Mrs Morgan came in, cordial but inquisitive. Louie's demeanour changed. She jumped to her feet, laughing, and said, 'Mother, I'm defeated. I've tried to persuade Captain Forbes to give a brief talk at our concert, and he refuses.'

Mrs Morgan sat down. She took possession of the room.

'Mother dear,' said Louie softly at last, 'Captain Forbes was so good—he called to—to tell me some things about David. Do you mind?'

Mrs Morgan did mind, plainly, but she rose and went. Garry sighed again. She was so enmeshed in falsehood, he supposed, that she hardly noticed when she told a lie.

'Now, where was I?' she was asking. Was it possible that she enjoyed this too, that her tale was one huge ostentation? She would have another invention for her mother's ears, of that he was sure. Mrs Morgan's knowing smile would invite till she received—received what? What had he to 'tell her about David'?

She continued. 'But I didn't dare to wear the ring, so I hung it round my neck and bought another not unlike it. I wore that, and trusted that Mrs Hunter, who was the only person who knew, would never notice the difference. It does sound deceitful, doesn't it?'

He did not reply.

'What are you to do now?' he asked after a pause.

'Do? Does anything need to be done?'

He rose and paced the room impatiently.

'At least I hope you will restore Mr Grey the ring.'

'The trouble is, how am I to get in without attracting notice?'

'Without— Good God, you don't mean that you would put it back and say nothing?'

'What can I say?'

'The truth, of course.'

He saw the sheer pain in her eyes.

'What I've told you?'

'If that is the truth, yes.'

'*If* it is the truth! Oh, do you not believe me yet?'

'Very well, of course you must tell it to him.'

'And then—then you'll proclaim it abroad. You'll tell everyone I am a common thief. That's what you wanted, wasn't it, to tell them all?'

He shook his head. To clear David's honour was one thing, but a very different matter to set the tongues wagging over such a sordid story. He would have felt it an indecency to expose her, and smiled a little soberly as he thought that those who could not see his point when he talked of his friend's dishonour would see quickly enough the point of a stolen ring. A profound sadness invaded him as he saw by what strange ties honour and reputation may be bound.

'No, no,' he said, 'this is not a matter for the public. But you must go by what Mr Grey decides.'

She was weeping now and said, pleading, 'Captain Forbes—Garry. I shall tell him, but need it be now? Listen. Our concert—it's just two days ahead. And I have so much to do in it. I'm playing. And there's that sketch. I've the curtains to finish, and final rehearsals. And if I tell—I'm so, so—I feel so keenly, it will kill me. I know I shall be ill. I feel I might collapse. Perhaps at the concert. I know that I'll be prostrate after I tell. Mayn't I wait? It's—it's a sort of public duty, to keep fit for the concert.'

Garry rose to his feet. Blind blundering emotions had hold on him. To his surprise he felt surges of pity where he had thought to feel only disgust; but it was a pity that it hurt him to give, as though some portion of himself had been rent to make the pity possible; and he was profoundly uncomfortable.

'Yes, yes, tell him when you please.'

'But you will say—'

'Nothing, nothing. Till your concert is over, then.'

She accompanied him to the door, talking loud and laughing. Mrs Morgan reappeared. He supposed she had come to hear what had passed. Louie, of course, would dissemble. He went rapidly out.

He was astonished at the pure sweet morning into which he walked—as though he had come from a murky den where the air oppressed. It was incredible that there could be a world as fresh and unashamed as that he saw around him. For a time he stood, breathing the sweet air, then rapidly climbed to the summit of the ridge. There space encompassed him. Space sang again its primal song, before man was, before the tangle of his shames began. Infinite sky was over him, blue land ran on and on until it seemed itself a ruffled fold of sky, a quivering of light upon the air; the blue sea trembled on the boundaries of space; and the man standing there alone was rapt up into the infinitudes around, lost for awhile the limitations of himself. He came back slowly. Strange how the land could be transfigured! A blue April morning, the shimmer of light, a breath, a passing air, and it was no longer a harsh and stubborn country, its hard-won fields beleaguered by moor and whin, its stones heaped together in dyke and cairn, marking the land like lines upon a weathered countenance, whose past must stay upon it to the end; but a dream, willing men's hearts. In the sun the leafless boughs were gleaming. Birches were like tangles of shining hair; or rather, he thought, insubstantial, floating like shredded light above the soil. Below the hills blue floated in the hollows, all but tangible, like a distillation that light had set free from the earth; and on a rowan tree in early leaf, its boughs blotted against the background, the tender leaves, like flakes of green fire, floated too, the wild burning life of spring loosened from earth's control. On every side earth was transmuted. Scents floated, the subtle life released from earth and assailing the pulses. Song floated. This dour and thankless country, this land that *grat a' winter and girned a' summer* could change before one's eyes to an elfin and enchanted radiance, could look, by some rare miracle of light or moisture, essentialised. A measure of her life this morning had gone up in sacrifice. Her substance had become spirit.

Garry's thought went back upon the evening when he had seen the land emerge and take form slowly from primordial dark. Now its form was on the point of dissolution into light. And the people whom the land had made—they too, had been shaped from a stuff as hard and intractable as their rock, through weathers as rude as stormed upon their heights; they too (he thought) at moments were dissolved in light, had their hours of transfiguration. In his aunt dancing her wilful reel on the kitchen floor, in Lindsay as she had grieved for Louie's hurt, he had seen life essentialised.

A shouting caught his ear. The swarm of young Lorimers, skimming the moor, hummed about him. He gave in gladly to their merriment, lunched with them beside the old tower, and led their games. Lindsay's gaiety, however, was assumed. She was still furious against Miss Theresa for her cynical suggestion of the morning; but though she tried to convince herself that her misery came from that, as the day wore on she was compelled to acknowledge that there was a deeper hurt in what Garry had done the previous evening in the school. After all, he had exposed Louie to public scorn. Her eyes sought his many times, reproachful and sad, but it was only on the homeward way that, lingering by common consent, the two could talk.

'I thought you would have done what I wanted you to do,' she said.

She did herself injustice by her complaint. She had no sense of personal grievance; but she had been quite sure that Garry would be good—that he would do nothing out of accord with her creed and standards. Her rebuke was the grieving of a bewildered child.

Garry kept silence. He could not tell her the collapse of Louie's story. The purloined ring had altered his attitude to the affair, and he almost hoped that Lindsay need never know of it. In any case he could not assert his knowledge of Louie's perfidy without revealing its proof. Constraint fell between them. They made up on the others, and reached the Weatherhouse in a bunch.

'What's *he* seeking here again?' said Miss Theresa, looking from the window.

Mrs Falconer looked from the window too, and saw Garry, as it happened, toss an empty basket laughingly to Kate. The bird sang in Mrs Falconer's heart—that fugitive bird, that flake from Ellen's earth that had escaped, far out into the blue air, across distant seas and islands of romance. She ran to set another cup and plate, thinking, 'How happy they look together!'

'You needn't bother yourself,' said Theresa. 'He's away.'

Ellen turned to the glass door, and saw him passing through the gate. She flung the glass door open and ran across the garden with hasty, unsure steps, her long angular body bent forward from the hips, and she reached the low wall before Garry had passed beyond it.

'Just a cup,' she panted. And when he would not come she continued to talk, leaning upon the stone-crop that covered the wall.

'A pack of old women—I don't wonder. We must seem unreal to you. A picture-book house.'

'Well.' He stood considering. Unreal—he could not know all that she had put into the word, her lifelong battle against those figments of her fancy that had often held her richest life, yet it expressed what he had vaguely felt when he took tea with these women. 'After out there,' he said.

Mrs Falconer had the curious sense of having run, in her stumbling progress through the garden, a very long distance from her home.

'You're a dimension short,' he continued. 'Or no. You have three dimensions right enough, but we've a fourth dimension over there. We've depth. It's not the same thing as height,' he added, looking up. 'It's down in—hollowness and mud and foul water and bad smells and holes and more mud. Not common mud. It's dissolution—a dimension that won't remain stable—and you've to multiply everything by it to get any result at all. You people who live in a three-dimensional world don't know. You can't know. You go on thinking this is the real thing, but we've discovered that we can get off every imaginable plane that the old realities yielded.'

'We can perhaps imagine it a little.' She kept her adoring eyes upon him, and smiled at undergoing this initiation into a soldier's world.

'Imagination's no good. Imagination has to save the world, but the people who haven't it will never believe what the others say. Your sister's beckoning.'

Mrs Falconer turned and saw Theresa signal from the window. Cups clattered, talk and laughter eddied into the garden. Everyone had gone in: except old Mrs Craigmyle, who walked serenely to and fro on the garden path, knitting and carolling. Mrs Falconer looked, and turned back to Garry. She had a certain elation in disregarding Theresa's summons. There were plenty of them there to serve; but she was choosing a better part. She said, 'That's what I've always wanted—to have imagination.'

'You shouldn't. It's too cruel, too austere. You should pray your God of Comforts to keep you from imagination. Lead us not into imagination, but deliver us from understanding.'

Mrs Falconer shook her head, slowly, as though to shake away an idea that bemused her.

'They laugh at you,' Garry continued (he had not talked like this to anyone since his return, not tried to share, even with Lindsay, the thoughts that had haunted his delirium and convalescence), 'they laugh at you as foolish or pity you as not quite sane if you try to get past the appearances of things to their real nature. That's what they said about me: beside himself, cracked. I was in a fever, you see. But I'm convinced I saw clearer then than in my right mind.' He began to tell her of his adventure with the dead man in the hole. 'I wasn't rightly sure which was myself, you understand. And it's like that all the time. You do things, and you're not sure after they're done if it is yourself or someone else you've done them to.'

She was listening absorbed.

'Yes, yes, that Louie Morgan now. She did it just to please herself, but look what she has done to you. You were right to expose her, I think.'

But Garry was thinking (also of Louie) that in unmasking her he had done something to himself regarding which he was not yet quite sure. Nor did he want Louie on the public stage. He stepped back from the wall, said, 'But she's not exposed. Now I am keeping you from your tea,' and walked away.

Not exposed! thought Mrs Falconer, turning back across the garden. But she would be! A fire ran through her veins. Too austere! How could imagination be austere? Your God of Comforts. Another dimension. His words bubbled in her ears. She had run farther than ever from this idle garden, and the air beyond it was sharp and pungent to her nostrils.

The garden was not empty, after all. Lang Leeb still walked the path, serenely singing; and as her second daughter came near with wide unseeing eyes, Leeb raised her voice and sang on a gay and insolent note. She did not look at Mrs Falconer, but kept her fingers on her shank and her eyes straight ahead:

> Auld wife, auld wife, will you go a-shearin'?
> Speak up, speak up, for I'm hard o' hearin'.
> Auld wife, auld wife, will you hae a man?—

The glass door slipped from Mrs Falconer's hand and clashed, and Mrs Falconer did not even apologise. She let Miss Theresa talk.

The children had finished tea. It was time they were off. There was noise and bustle.

'For the love of Pharaoh,' cried Miss Theresa, 'wash your faces. They'll charge you extra in the train for all that dirt.'

Mrs Falconer sat to her solitary tea. The children's voices came ringing up from the road, fading as the distance grew. Lindsay and Kate had gone with them.

'Your God of Comforts,' Mrs Falconer continued to think. The phrase brought Louie to her mind. 'Why, we must go to that concert. But how can she appear in front of them all? Not exposed, he said. Not. But she must be. And playing, they say. Well, if it's like the last concert, I'm sure I shan't care if I don't go. Terrible grand music, she said it was—just a bumming and a going on. But how can she face them? Your God of Comforts.' Her mind came back always to the phrase A comfortable God—what had the young man meant?

Lindsay and Kate returned. Night came. Lindsay leaned again from her window. She was trying to control her thoughts. They were like horses new let out to grass; brutal and beautiful; unbridled energies. She had never before had so many thoughts at once. Life was too intricate. New complications rose upon her. Getting to know Garry was not what she had supposed it would be like. And now the children would go home and tell that Garry was here, and there would be her mother's disapproval to be faced. She should have been more stern that afternoon, but he had kissed her, her throat was burning still where he had pressed it. Oh, where was she venturing? The sea grows more immense as the distance widens between us and the shore.

Kate was asleep. The whole house had withdrawn. Only she, awake and aware, tussled with life. She felt creep over her the desolation of youth, that believes no suffering has ever been like its suffering, no heart has been perplexed like it. 'They're all happy,' she thought, 'and I don't know what I am. They're all asleep, and I can't sleep.'

She did not know that through the wall, kneeling upon the floor, Mrs Falconer endured an agony of prayer. She too, wrestled, and as she wrestled a strange sense of triumph overwhelmed her, exultation filled her soul.

'Help me, O God,' she prayed, 'help me to overcome the evil and expose the wrong, that Thy great cause may be triumphant. Through our Lord Jesus Christ, Amen.'

The words sang to her spirit. No more for her the pallid shadows of her dreams. She would labour now for truth.

'Grant, O Lord, in Thy mercy, that I may be equal to that which Thou wouldst have me do.'

A shudder ran through her frame. The seraph with the live coal from off the altar touched her lips, and as she rose, chill and quiet, from her prayers, the dreamy innocence habitual to her face had changed to a high and rapt enthusiasm.

TEN

Andrew Lorimer does the Same

The following days deepened the furrows that became so characteristic a feature of Garry's countenance. Life had always been to him a serious affair, but, till the delirium of his recent illness, simple. One worked hard, making boilers and bridges as stable as one could, and played equally hard and sure; and men were good fellows. Evil there was, of course, but always in the next street—the condition that gave fighting its vehemence. The complexity of human motive and desire had not come home to him, and he supposed, without thinking much about it, that right and wrong were as separate as the bridges he helped to build and the waters over which he built them. But in what he had been irresistibly impelled to say to Mrs Falconer that afternoon, his discovery in the dissolution of the solid land of a new dimension by which experience must be multiplied, he was only giving articulate expression to thoughts that had for some time been worrying in his brain. Limits had shifted, boundaries been dissolved. Nothing ended in itself, but flowed over into something else; and the obsession of his delirium, that he was himself the dead man whose body he had lugged out of the slime, came back now and haunted him like the key note of a tune. But what a tune! How hard to play—rude and perplexing, with discords unresolved and a tantalising melody that fluted and escaped. His mind sounded the note again and again throughout that night, but always the tune itself eluded him.

The night was like the morning, soft and still. Earth floated in the radiance the young moon had left above the hills; stars, remote and pure, floated in the wide serene of heaven; nothing moved, yet all was moving, eternally sustained by flight; and Garry walked for hours in troubled impotence, angry at a world that would not let him keep his straight and clean-cut standards. To refute what he had thought a false conception of his friend's honour had seemed a simple and straightforward matter, but it had led him into a queer morass; and now, as he tramped in the night, he was filled with panic lest the story of the ring should become public through his agency. It would be a degradation to expose that. He was glad he had resisted the impulse to tell Lindsay, though her disapproval had been difficult to bear. He had longed to justify himself, and the frustrate longing had made him rough. He had caught her to him with violence, clutching at her throat until the mark burned upon her flesh. Her young primrose love had not yet learned to endure such heats.

In time he went to bed, but sleep did not come. Instead came fever and a new throng of disordered visions. He saw the solid granite earth, on which these established houses, the Weatherhouse and Knapperley, were built (less real, as he had said to Mrs Falconer, than the dissolution and mud of the war-swept country), melt and float and change its nature; and the people fashioned out of it, hard-featured, hard-headed, with granite frames and life-bitten faces, rude tongues and gestures, changed too, melted into forms he could not recognise. Then he perceived a boulder, earthy and enormous, a giant block of the unbridled crag, and behold! as he looked the boulder was his aunt. 'You won't touch me,' she seemed to say. 'I won't be cut and shaped and civilised.' But in an instant she began to move, treading ever more quickly and lightly, until he saw that she was dancing as he had caught her dancing on the night of his return. Faster and faster she spun, lighter of foot and more ethereal, and the rhythm of her dance was a phrase in the tune that had eluded him. And now she seemed to spurn the earth and float, and in the swiftness of her motion he could see no form nor substance, only a shining light, and he knew that what he watched was a dancing star.

It was already morning when he fell asleep, and he woke late, heavy-eyed and languid. Miss Barbara brought him a cup of tea—a visiting star, perhaps, but of peculiar magnitude. Thereafter she left him alone, and he lay swamped in lassitude and dozed again.

In the afternoon she went out. The house grew intolerably still. Not even a dog broke the uneasy quiet. He dozed, and struggled awake in a joyous clamour, a merry and tumultuous barking that did him good. Later he heard the stir around the ingle—sticks broken, fire-irons clattering, even, in the stillness of dusk, a sudden explosive crackle from the burning logs. He wanted food and a shave, the warmth and life of fire; speech, and the comfortable feel of paws and noses; and rising, he went downstairs.

To his surprise his aunt was just coming in. He had supposed her in the kitchen, where she, having seen the lamp lit, was supposing him. They pushed open the kitchen door together, and entered.

The fire was roaring on the hearth, the room was light and gay; dogs snuggled to the heat, tobacco smoke eddied on the air, the lid of the kettle danced and chattered and steam rose invitingly and bellied and wavered towards the chimney; and deep in Miss Barbara's favourite chair there sat a little man, as abundantly at home as if the place were his. As Miss Barbara and Garry came in he was in act of rocking back his chair, stretching his arms with a luxurious content, and singing to a merry tune:

He took his pipes and played a spring
And bade the coo consider—

'If it isna Johnnie Rogie!' cried Miss Barbara. 'Man, but you're a sight for sair e'en.'

The little man turned in the chair, nodded gaily to Miss Barbara in time to his music, beat vigorously with his arms and continued to sing:

The coo considered wi' hersel
That music wadna fill her—

Ay, ay, Bawbie, but I've the reek risin' and the kettle on, an' you shall hae your supper, lass:

And you shall hae your supper.

'You'll have a dram first, laddie,' cried Miss Barbara. 'I've aye a drappie o' the real Mackay—none of your wersh war rubbish, dirten orra stuff.'

'We'll have it out, Bawbie.'

Miss Barbara fetched it running. She polished the tumblers and set them before her guest, who poured the whisky with the air of a god. Not more benignly did Zeus confer his benefits upon humanity than Johnnie Rogie the tramp handed Miss Barbara Paterson of Knapperley a share of her own whisky; and Miss Barbara took it with a gratitude that was divine in its acceptance, and called Garry to come forward and have his glass.

Unshaved, with hollow cheeks and sunken eyes from which the sleep was not yet washed, Garry came to the fire.

'Come awa', my lad,' cried Johnnie. 'Sojers need a dram like the lave o's.' He poured the whisky and conferred it upon Garry. 'Take you a' you get an' you'll never want.' And, raising his own glass, he let the golden liquor tremble to his mouth. 'And sojers need to live and sojers need to pray. Live, laddie, live? Ay, sojers need to live mair than the lave o's. Clean caup oot, like the communicants o' Birse'—his head went back as he drained his glass—'that's the way a sojer needs to live. Tak' you a' that life can give you, laddie. Drink you it up, clean caup oot. It's a grand dram as lang's ye're drinkin' it, and ye'll be a lang time deid.' And seeing that Garry had not yet emptied his tumbler, he added, 'But drink clean in, tak it a' at ae gulp. Life's a dram that's better in the mou' than in the belly.'

He poured himself another draught, and drank.

Apparently he found it good; for when he had swallowed it the sun-god himself was not more radiant, and when he spoke the words flowed out like song.

On Garry, too, unfed and over-strung, the golden liquor was having its effect. The shabby, under-sized man with the matted dingy hair and a little finger wanting, pouring the whisky and swaying his whole body to the rhythm of his chant, was hypnotising him, and with his will. He seemed a ministrant of life, bringing for a moment its golden energies within one's grasp, making the visionary gleam look true. Garry thrust his elbows on his knees and leaned forward, talking eagerly. Miss Barbara was moving from room to room upstairs. When she came in again her face was aglow and she slapped Johnnie heartily on the shoulder.

'And where have you been this long weary while?'

'Where you could never follow, Bawbie.'

'Nae to the wars,' she mocked.

'Just that.'

'Eh? And you near sixty, and a cripple muckle tae and but the ae cranny.'

'For a' that, an' a' that, I've been wi' the sojer laddies, Bawbie.' He reeled off into a popular soldier song. 'Ay, ay, the sojers need to live an' the sojers need to sing. An' wha wad sing to them if it wasna Johnnie? There's nae a camp an' nae a barrack but Johnnie's been there. An' whan the sojers are wearied an' whan the sojers are wae, wha but Johnnie wad gar them cantle up, wi' his auld fiddle an' his auld true tongue?'

He quaffed the golden fire again: Medea's fire, it made him young and reckless. He chanted more uproariously.

'An' mebbe whiles whan pay day cam, a sojer here, a sojer there, wad mind on singing Johnnie. Ay, ay, the sojer lads, they're free wi' their siller, the sojer lads, whan they ken the next march is the march to death. They've a lang road ahead o' them, a lang road an' few toons, the road to death; an' lads that wadna pairt wi' the dirt aneth their nails, in the ordiner ways of living, 'll gang laughin' doon to death an' toss the siller fae them like a lousy sark. What's the siller, what's the siller, give's a sang, they say.'

'You'll have a bonny penny in your pooch, Johnnie,' commented Miss Barbara. 'You'll have made your fortune.'

'Fient a fortune.' The little man ascended again to prose. He drew himself together, sat up straight and squared his shoulders. The reckless fire died down, the cadence of his voice altered. He talked of supper, and Miss Barbara made haste to prepare it.

Supper over, the dogs set up a barking.

'Did you hear a step?' said Miss Barbara.

She rose and let in Francie Ferguson.

Francie stood sheepishly in the glow of light. 'I didna ken ye had company, Miss Barbara. It was the lights. Yon's a terrible blaze, 'umman. I was feart you would dae us some hurt.'

'Ach!' said Barbara sturdily. 'What's in a puckle candles?'

The soldier and the tramp had tilted back their chairs and with sprawling legs and arms flung easefully abroad, trolled out old tales, recitative and chorus. Johnnie had slid away again from prose. The boom of their laughter ceased when Francie entered. Now Garry rose from his seat, crying, 'But hang it all, you know, aunt—' and thereupon went off again in a round of laughter. Recovering himself he said, 'I give you my compliments. He's worth an illumination. Still, you know, *noblesse oblige*. There are weaker brothers—prime ministers and such-like fry.'

'I'm a Paterson of Knapperley, my lad, a Paterson of Knapperley can please himself. It's only your common bodies that need your laws and regulations, to be hauden in about. The folk of race have your law within themselves. Ay, ay, I'm a Paterson of Knapperley, but you're Donnie Forbes's grandson and seek to make yourself a politician. But go your ways.'

He went through the house, and found candle or oil-lamp burning in every window; and put them out: with a queer contraction of the heart as room after room was left dark and dead behind him. The war was putting this out too—this impetuous leap of exhilaration, this symbol of joy. When he returned to the kitchen Francie had been drawn into the charmed circle. He and Miss Barbara together were making lusty chorus to Johnnie's song:

I saw an eel chase the Deil,
Wha's fou, wha's fou?
I saw an eel chase the Deil
Wha's fou noo, ma jo?
I saw an eel chase the Deil
Roon aboot the spinnin' wheel,
An' we're a' blin' drunk, bousin' jolly fou, ma jo!'

Francie too, had drunk of fire, and was like one that prophesied. Warmed by the whisky, heartened by honest song, he began to talk of what sat closest to his own bosom: what but Bell his wife and her incomprehensible trick of not sitting close, of holding off. 'He doesna seek to kiss me. I canna do with that kind o' sotter,' she had proclaimed abroad. A libel on a man. 'A blazin' lee,' shouted Francie. 'Doesna seek to kiss her. Doesna indeed.' For what but that had he waited twenty years, to be thwarted in the end by a woman's caprice: a woman who had the impudence to say, 'Fingers off the beef, you canna buy,' to her own lawful spouse. 'But she'll be kissed this very night,' he shouted. He banged the table and swaggered home at last in glee. His habitual sheepish good-humour had turned to a more flaming quality. A man greatly resolved.

'He needs all his legs,' said Miss Barbara.

Garry went drunk to bed, but not with whisky. Again he had seen life essentialised. Its pure essence had been in Johnnie as he usurped the rites of hospitality and in Miss Barbara's extravaganza of candles; in Francie too, revolting against a niggard life.

He was interrupted in his soliloquy by the opening of the door. Johnnie shambled in, without apology, and asked for money: which Garry gave, amusedly, too much exalted still to resent this degradation in the golden godling; finding it indeed no degradation, but a glory the more. So few people had the grace to take what they wanted with such unabashed assurance. Oh, if all the world would turn audacious—! He fell asleep at last to the sound of Johnnie's voice on the other side of the wall:

There's twa moons the night
Quo' the auld wife to hersel.

Meanwhile for Lindsay the day had crawled. At every moment she had expected to see her mother arrive, and there would be an awkward moment when the ladies learned that the lover she had been sent here to forget was Garry Forbes. She detested the clandestine, yet merely to have sheltered from distasteful pleasantry was not a sign of guilt. She felt guilty nevertheless, and devised a score of speeches to convince her mother that the secrecy was not deceit. Her mother, however, did not come to be convinced.

Lindsay's feverish anxiety increased. She was ready to defend Garry against anything her mother might say, but as the day wore on she found it increasingly hard to defend Garry against herself. Always her accusation was the same—he had wantonly exposed Louie to the clack of tongues, without any proof that what he alleged was true. If he thought evil so readily of one woman, what might he not think soon of another, of herself? The child tossed upon dark and lashing waters, and was afraid. It had been safe and very beautiful on shore.

As dusk drew down she stole from the house, not unobserved by Kate, and shortly afterwards a car panted up the hill, and Andrew Lorimer himself came in.

Mrs Lorimer, as Lindsay expected, put it down to deliberate deceit on her daughter's part that they had not been told of Garry's arrival. Andrew refused to be annoyed.

'I'll talk to her myself,' he said. 'To the young man, too, if I clap eyes on him.'

Andrew Lorimer was a burly, big-nosed man, more like a farmer to the eye than a lawyer, thrawn and conservative, devoted to his children, but determined that they should have their good things in the shape that he saw fit to give them. He was quite willing that his little linnet should ultimately go to Miss Barbara's rough and rather ugly nephew, for he knew that the fellow had sound worth in spite of his execrable opinions; but the child was far too young. He wanted her for himself a long time yet.

'A nice condition you've cast my wife into,' he grumbled to the Weatherhouse ladies, 'letting that daughter of hers run round the country with her sweetheart at her tails.'

There was consternation and surprise. Andrew liked to hector.

'What,' he cried, 'you didn't know? So she takes you in, does she—cheats her mother on the sly?'

Kate looked up calmly from her sewing.

'There was nothing sly about it,' she said. 'Lindsay was perfectly frank. When she came at Christmas she told all there was to tell. And as we understood your objection was merely her age, what harm should we suppose in their meeting?'

And to Miss Theresa, who was still indignantly exclaiming, she said, with the same unmoved demeanour, 'Perhaps *you* may not have heard, Aunt Tris, but it wasn't because Lindsay didn't tell.'

'To be sure we knew,' put in Miss Annie with a chuckle. She remembered the day Lindsay had dropped kisses in the nape of her neck. 'And blithe we were to see the bairn so glad and bonny.'

Andrew Lorimer was in high feather. Theresa, disconcerted, took the check badly. He remembered how, from their childhood up, Tris had liked to be in the know, and he enjoyed her discomfiture. It was not unlikely that Kate also, calmly as she continued her needlework, with frank and placid eyes lifted to look at her aunt, relished the moment.

Theresa began to give Mr Dalgarno Forbes his character.

'You can just hold by his doors, then,' thundered Andrew.

Mrs Falconer sat stupefied. Her mind registered the incredible fact, but she could not feel it. And Kate, who on her own confession loved the man, sat there collectedly and sewed. She had known, even when she confessed, that Garry was Lindsay's lover. Mrs Falconer's dreams were dust.

Lang Leeb warbled from her corner. The fragile sounds were blown like gossamers about the room and no one heeded them, but Ellen moved her head impatiently as though they teased her face. Leeb sang:

My mother bade me gie him a piece,
　Imphm, ay, but I wunna hae him,
I gied him a piece and he sat like a geese,
　For his auld white beard was newly shaven.

Ellen turned and looked at her mother. The old eyes, bright and sharp, glittered like the reflection from a metal that has no inner illumination of its own. She was subtle and malicious, this old woman for whom life had ended save as a spectacle. Ellen, as she looked, read her mother's mocking thought. Theresa too, had said to her, when she ran across the garden to bid Garry stay for tea, 'Nell, you old fool.' What did they think—that she was running after the boy for her own sake? Dastardly supposition, so vile that she blushed, went hot and cold by turns. But wasn't it true? In a flash she realised it, that this sense of tragedy in which she had foundered came not from any grief for Kate, but for herself, because she loved the youth and wanted him near her. But it was life she wanted, strong current and fresh wind, no ignoble desire.

Theresa continued to sneer at the boy's expense. Leeb changed her song. The mocking voice teased like a gnat round Ellen's consciousness:

She wouldna slack her silken stays,

sang Leeb.

What! Not be generous to this young man who had wakened her out of her unreal dreams? They could call her what kind of fool they liked, she would not be guilty of that cowardice. She would give. She cut across Theresa's denunciation with an incisive thrust.

'He is a very fine young man.'

Andrew turned and looked at his cousin, whose long lean cheek was from him.

'Very fine fiddlesticks. He's a very ordinary decent fellow, with some high-falutin ideas that ought to have worn themselves out by now. Better, I grant you, than the low-falutin that seems to be the fashion nowadays. I've no objection to an idealist, always provided he can keep his own wife when he takes one. And what ails you at Bawbie?' he added, swinging round again to disconcert Theresa. 'Bawbie's folk's as good's your own. A Paterson was settled in Knapperley as long since as the seventeen-thirties, and a Paterson was married on the son of an Earl, if you didn't know it, in 1725. A collateral branch, that would be. Let me see, let me see, it was the same branch—'

The door was opened, and Lindsay thrust unceremoniously in by a little wiry wrinkled man who bounced rapidly after her.

'It's yourself, Mr Lorimer,' said he, too excited even to greet the ladies into whose house he had thus bounded. 'Then pass you judgment, Mr Lorimer.' He rattled a tin pail under their noses. 'Pass you judgment. Here's me sortin' up the shop with the door steekit, and what do I hear but the jingle-jangle of my pail, that was sittin' waitin' me on the step. So out I goes and sees my lady here makin' away pretty sharp. "Ye're nae away wi' my pailie, surely," I says. Bang goes the pail and away goes she. So I puts on a spurt and up wi' her. "Ye needna awa' so fleet, Miss Craigmyle," I says.

"I see you fine. You werena needin' to send my pailie in ower the plantin'." But losh ye! It's nae Miss Craigmyle I've got a haud o', but this bit craiturie. A gey snod bit deemie, I wouldna mind her for a lass.' He turned the crunkled leather of his countenance towards Lindsay, in a wrinkled effort at a smile. 'But she would have been up and off with my pailie, Mr Lorimer, and nyod man, see here, the cloor it's gotten whan she flung it frae her into the plantin'.'

Andrew watched his daughter with amusement. Flushed, panting, near to tears, she stood in the middle of the room and threw defiant glances around.

'Clap it on her head, Mr Gillespie,' he answered to the indignant grocer, 'and up on the faulters' stool with her.'

'She has a gey canty hat there of her own,' said the grocer, whose wrath had fallen now that his grievance was recounted. 'But,' he added, glancing round the assemblage of ladies, 'it was Miss Theresa there I thought I had a haud o'. We a' ken she canna keep her hands off what she sees. She maun be inen the guts o' a'thing.'

Andrew bellowed with delight. Didn't he know the ancient habit of his cousin Tris, to appropriate all she fancied: failing roup, barter or purchase, then by simple annexation! The shades of sundry pocket-knives, pencils and caramels grinned humorously there above her ears. So the habit had not died, but was matter of common talk. To have seen his excellent cousin twice confounded in one evening was luck. He rose in fine fettle.

'Well, well, Gillespie man, but we can't let the lassie connach your goods like that.'

'Na, na, Mr Lorimer, sir,' answered the honest grocer, refusing the proffered money, 'I dinna want your siller. The pailie's nane the waur. It'll serve as well wi' a cloor in the ribs as wantin' it.' Mr Lorimer saw him out and came back to challenge Lindsay.

'Well, my lady, what have you been up to?'

'Daddy, I wasn't going to steal his pail—you know that.'

'What were you going to do, then?'

Lindsay looked round. They all awaited her answer. She wondered if they had been talking of Garry and her. Throwing her head proudly back, she answered, 'It's very silly. I don't know what made me do it. But Knapperley was all blazing with light. I thought—I really thought for a minute it was on fire, and I had a sort of panic. I saw the pail and seized it and began to run. I know it sounds absurd—as though my little pail could have helped any if there really was a fire. There wasn't, you know. The lights were blazing, right enough, but we saw them go out just after.'

'There's your Bawbie for you,' Theresa flung at Andrew Lorimer. Theresa was in a black anger. Her slogan, *A ga'in' foot's aye gettin'*, had covered numerous petty assaults on property, never (as of course one would understand) of magnitude to be called theft; but the grocer's calm recital of her obsession took her by surprise. She glared furiously at Andrew, and pounced triumphantly on Miss Paterson's aberration as a shelter from her own.

'Andrew's wanting a word with Lindsay,' Miss Annie interrupted in her pleasant way. 'We all know Bawbie's gotten a dunt on the riggin', Tris. Leave her alone. Andrew, I'm getting stiffened up like a clothes rope after rain. I'm terrible slow. But we'll all go through and let you talk to your lassie.'

'Indeed no, Paradise. Daddy and I will go through.'

Andrew trolled a song in his deep strong voice as he went to the other room. He had quite enjoyed the little episode. Theresa's exposure was part of the ruthless comicality of life. 'O ay, he's a comical deevil, your cousin Andrew,' Lang Leeb had been wont to say. 'He might laugh less if it was some of his own.'

One of his own was now involved. He had yet to deal with Lindsay's affair.

'Your mother,' he said, 'hasn't made the acquaintance of your proposed aunt-in-law. On the whole, we'd better keep this dark. She doesn't relish eccentricity in the family. What's this about the lights? And fined, was she? Well, you keep that to yourself. Your mother needn't know you were chasing round the countryside with the grocer's pail.'

'You're a dear,' said Lindsay.

'And you'd better tell me what to say about this man of yours. All fair and square, I suppose?'

'You bet.'

'What'll I say, then? Hurry up, I can't stay here all night. What am I to say to your mother? Lord love you, bairn, don't weep. Make up the triggest little tale you can.'

A burning tear splashed down upon his hand. Lindsay's face was against his coat, and he felt the shaking of her sobs.

'Daddy, daddy, I'm so miserable.'

'Here, here, cheer up. It's war-time, after all. Do you want to marry him?'

Lindsay raised her head and stared with blank eyes at her father.

'We'll bring your mother round,' continued Andrew.

Lindsay wept the harder.

'Well, well, that's settled,' said her father, drying her tears with his handkerchief, and he plunged exuberantly into talk of Theresa and the pail.

'But daddy, what could Mr Gillespie have meant?'

'Just what he said—your Cousin Theresa can't go past a thing she wants.'

'But taking things—? She's perhaps beginning to get old. Old people do things like that.'

'Don't you suggest it. Tris won't be thought old. No, no, it's not a sign of her decrepitude. Tris wasn't to be trusted with property at any time. If it was movable property that was concerned, she lee'd like a fishwife and thieved like Auld Nick.' He began to entertain his daughter with tales from his youth. 'But this won't do. What am I to say to your mother?'

'Why, daddy,' said Lindsay, with very bright eyes, 'it's your business to make up explanations for people.'

'What am I to say to your mother?'

'Don't eat me up! Are you to be everyone's advocate but mine?'

'What—'

'Well, say then—oh, say that he's a gruff old bear and you can't get a word in edgeways and it wouldn't have been safe to let her know that he was here. Say that he's a terror to the neighbourhood, that he has enormous ears, the better to hear you with, my dear, and perfectly enormous teeth, the better to eat you up. Oh, say what you like, daddy, I leave it to you.'

She clung about her father's neck, convulsively kissing the roughness of his coat.

Andrew fondled her.

'Well, if we let you marry him—you're not very old yet. Sure that you know your own mind? Quite sure you love the bear enough to spend your life with him? Eh?'

'Quite.'

Andrew enjoyed the arrogant lift of her head.

But later, hunched on her pillow, she queried in the dark of Kate, 'And you told daddy I was out with him, Katie?'

'And weren't you?'

'I said no, didn't I?'

'But I supposed—'

'You shouldn't suppose.'

'Oh, I'm sorry if I was wrong. But your father wasn't very angry, was he?'

'Oh, not particularly. It's mother that thinks he is not good enough for us. We're so grand, aren't we? Daddy only says I mustn't be turned into a woman too soon.'

'Well, neither you must, Linny.'

'Oh, you're all the same. As if age—Louie's the only one—'

'What about Louie?'

'Oh, nothing.'

'But it will be all right, Linny, when you're older? Your father won't make objections?'

'Oh, quite all right. It's perfectly all right, isn't it, not to make objections to an engagement that doesn't exist?'

'That doesn't— But it will exist when they give their permission.'

'I've broken it off.'

'But whatever—'

'Tonight. I wrote it. I was posting it when I was out, if you want to know.'

'But Lindsay, this is terrible. Whatever for?'

'Oh, for everything.' She slipped under the bedclothes and lay rigid, her face hidden. 'Don't speak to me, please, Kate.'

Kate held her peace.

'Katie.'

'Yes.'

'Life's so terribly strange, isn't it?'

'Is it? I don't know.'

'Don't *you* think it strange, Katie?'

'No, not particularly.'

Lindsay sat up again.

'But truly, Katie? Have you never thought life was tremendously queer? One day one thing, and the next day all changed. Don't you find yourself wanting one thing at one moment, and then in a trice you know that wasn't what you wanted at all, but something different? Don't you?'

'No, I can't say that I do.'

'Then is it only me that's unlike everyone else? How could I be anyone's wife, Kate, if I'm like that?'

'But—'

'Oh, it wasn't for that I broke it off. At least, partly that. He's—he's not what I thought quite, Katie, and I'm not what I thought, and I don't know what to do. I wish I had been like other people, but I don't know what to make of life. I don't know what I want. It's all so queer.'

'Lindsay, you're hysterical. Lie down and sleep. It'll all be right in the morning.'

'No, it won't. You don't understand. I don't seem to be like other people, Katie. I'm queer. It must run in the blood.' Kate smiled to herself at the thought of queerness running in the respectable Craigmyle-Lorimer veins. 'Look at Cousin Theresa,' continued the girl's impatient voice. 'That's her that cavils at Miss Barbara for being queer. I was never so ashamed in my life as when that grocer man shouted, "You hold your hand, Miss Craigmyle, we know you like to nab a thing fine." '

'In the house–I know she claims all she wants as hers. But outside— And so Miss Barbara's lights were up again, Lindsay? The police will be on her. She's been fined already, you know. Crazy old thing. A public nuisance.' Kate chatted on, in hope of distracting Lindsay's mind and persuading her to sleep. But the girl flared out, 'I don't see why you're all so bitter about it. I think she's splendid. She knows what she wants, and wants it enough to have it, too. She's magnificent. She's herself. She can burn her house up if she likes.'

'And it doesn't matter if other people suffer?'

'Not in the slightest. Oh, don't let's talk any more, Katie.'

Kate was silent as she was bid.

The night air grew colder. Lindsay tossed restlessly. The wind rose. A sough ran through the pines. Blinds shook, and somewhere in the house a door rattled. Lindsay shivered. How cold the night was now!

'Don't tell them I've broken it off, Katie. You see—we don't know yet what he may say.'

'Very well. Now sleep. It will be all right tomorrow.'

In the next room, preparing for bed, Theresa rapped out, 'Sleekit bessy she's been. And such a bairn to look at. Butter wouldn't melt in her mouth. And Kate's no better, Ellen, let me tell you that. To think of the two of them, and them up to such a cantrip.'

'They've done no wrong.'

'Ask Mrs Andrew as to that.'

'I can decide for myself without any Mrs Andrew.'

'Well, if you don't think it wrong, I'm sure—! Sleekit, I call it. And raking about with him like yon after dark—you never know what harm she might take.'

'Oh, pails are easy to come by,' said Ellen.

Theresa held her tongue and got into bed.

'Hist ye and get that light out,' she commanded in a while. Ellen raised her eyes from her Bible and said nothing. 'Your chapter's lasting you long tonight.'

Ellen dropped her eyes, but did not speak. She had read no chapter. One uncompleted sentence only: the sentence with which she had been wont, in her hours of abasement, to scourge her fleeing fancy. 'Casting down imaginations and every high thing that exalteth itself against the knowledge of the Lord.'

Imaginations! It mattered nothing to her what the commentators said, the word for her summed up those sweet excursions into the unreal that had punctuated all her life. She thought she had forsworn them, fired as she was by the glimpses that Garry had provided of man's real travail and endeavour. But all she had achieved was a still more presumptuous imagination; and as she saw the ruins of her palace lie around her, she realised how presumptuous, and at the same time how desirable it had been. Now she would never open the door of her dwelling to youth and arrogant active life. Desolation came upon her. The cold wind searched her and made her shudder. Her prayer was a long and moaning cry, 'Me miseram. I have sinned. I have sinned.'

ELEVEN

Garry and his Two Fools on the Housetop

Mrs Falconer awoke suddenly and could not remember what had occurred.

She knew that she had been hurt. Her mind was aware of its own suffering, but could not find the cause. She lay very still, grappling with memory. This impotence was horrible. It gave one a sense of calamity too huge for the mind to master. Her eyes went straying, and across the window she saw the passage of a falling star; then another, and another. 'That's someone dead,' she thought; but instantly came recollection. Her mind cleared and the weight of disaster lifted. Stars did not fall from heaven in the course of ordinary living; one's pain had other sources. Kate loved a man she would not marry: that was all. Kate— But Kate remained unmoved. The blackness of desolation was not for that, but was born of shame and of despair. There was no escape for her from unrealities to the busy world of men, and when she sought to break away she did shameful and presumptuous things. The gnat-bites of her mother's song had swollen now, poisonous and hateful seats of pain.

Outside, the shooting stars were still falling across the window. They could not be stars—so many, so continual. They eddied and fluttered. Mrs Falconer raised herself and stared. Sparks! Something must be on fire. She was fully awake now and her mind was alert and vigorous; as she got out of bed and crossed to the window she reviewed in a flash the whole story of the preceding days. 'There's no good not confessing it,' she thought. 'I do love that boy. I want to live the kind of life he would approve, to fight with real opponents for a real cause. I want to find the dimension that he said was lacking in our lives.' And then she thought, 'I can at least help him to expose the falsehood about that betrothal. That is something real I can help to do.'

Even if her fond dreams of his saying to her, 'Mother, no one understands what I mean like you,' could meet with no fulfilment, she must still do all she could to fight the evils he detested.

All this passed through her mind as she hastened to the window, at the same time as she was thinking, 'Can the fire be in this house?'

When she reached the window she saw that the air was full of large, floating flakes of snow. A shaft of light lay across them and made them glow like tongues of fire. And now a voice rose from the garden. Mrs Falconer leaned out, and saw Francie Ferguson standing in the whirl of snowflakes, moving a lantern.

'Ay, ye're there, are you? Ye're grand sleepers, the lot of you, nae to hear a body bawlin' at your lug.'

'But what's the matter, Francie?'

'A dispensation of Providence, Mistress Falconer. Ay, I tell't you whan a' that lights was bleezin' to the heaven, I tell't you the Lord would visit it upon her heid. Knapperley's up in a lowe, Mistress Falconer—'

'What! But are you sure?'

'As sure's a cat's a hairy beast. Ay, ay, I've twa e'en to glower wi' an' I'm gey good at glowerin'. And thinks I, Miss Craigmyle'll never ca' ower it if there's a spectacle and she's nae there to see. So I e'en in about to let you know.'

'But surely, in that snow—surely it won't burn.'

'The snaw's new on.'

Mrs Falconer roused Miss Theresa.

'What's that? Knapperley? It's just the price of her.'

Theresa was out of bed on the instant. As Francie knew, she would have counted it a personal affront to be left out from a nocturnal fire. Mrs Falconer too, put on her garments, with trembling and uneasy fingers.

'What can we do, Tris? We'll only be in the way.'

But though she offered a remonstrance, she was drawn by some force beyond herself to complete her hasty dressing and follow Theresa to the garden.

As they went out the snow ceased falling and they could see that dawn had come. The sky cleared. Francie put out his lantern, and in a while the sun rose in splendour, touching the leafless tangles of twigs, filigreed with snow, to a shining radiance. Snow coated the ground and the shadows cast along it by the sun glowed burning blue. Francie and Miss Theresa talked, but Mrs Falconer walked on through the sharp vivid morning, and the thoughts she was thinking were pungent like the morning air. 'All is not lost,' cried a voice within her heart. 'If I have been a fool in my imaginings, why, to be a fool may be the highest wisdom. If I have been a fool it was because I loved. To love is to pass out beyond yourself. If I pass beyond myself into the service of a cause, surely I can bear the stigma of fool.' And she was elated, walking rapidly over the melting snow. 'The thing,' she thought, 'is to find how I can help him to prove that Louie affair.'

At Knapperley there was shouting and confusion: but, thanks to the fall of snow, the flames had been mastered. A part of the roof had fallen in. Miss Barbara stood with her legs planted apart, hands in her jacket pockets, contemplating the destruction with an infinite calm. Garry emerged from the building, half-clad, pale and weary, the gauntness of his face emphasised by the black streaks and grime that smoke and charred wood had left on it. He came out brushing ash from his clothing with his hands and spoke in an anxious tone to Miss Barbara.

'Can't find a sign of him. Looks as though it began in that room, too. The bed's destroyed. But not a sign of the man.'

'Ach,' said Miss Barbara, unperturbed. 'He's been smoking in his bed again. He'll be far enough by now, once he saw what he had done. Many's the time I've said to Johnnie, "Smoke you in my beds again and we'll see." '

Garry gave vent to a whistling laugh. 'Well, we've seen.' He returned to his labour among the debris. The little crowd that had collected ran hither and thither, talking and making suggestions. Miss Barbara stalked upstairs. Garry thrust his head from the gap where an upper window had been. From beneath, with his blackened face and protuberant ears, he had the appearance of a gargoyle.

'Friends,' he shouted, 'my aunt is obliged to you all. There's not much harm done, but without your help it would have been much more.'

'You'll need to hap up that holie in the roof, lad,' interrupted one of the men.

'I'll do more than hap it up—I'll mend it. I've been talking to Morrison here, the joiner. He can't take on the job, he's short of men and too much in hand as it is. But he says I'll get the wood.'

'Ay, ay, Mr Forbes, fairly that,' said Morrison. 'But for working, na man, I'm promised this gey while ahead.'

'Well,' said Garry, 'my leave will soon be up. I mean to start myself this very day.'

At these words, 'My leave will soon be up,' Mrs Falconer felt a queer constriction of the heart. The folk began to move away, but Miss Barbara, thrusting her head in its turn from the blackened hole, cried, 'Step in-by, the lot o' you there, and get a nip afore you go.' Miss Craigmyle and Mrs Falconer, looking round a moment later for their escort Francie, and failing to find him, it was clear that he had been enticed by Miss Barbara's offer. Had he not drunk the golden fire the previous night? 'A cappie o' auld man's milk,' Miss Barbara said, pouring the whisky. The two ladies made their way indoors.

'I'll just be bidin', then,' Francie was saying.

Garry talked to him with earnest and eager gestures.

Francie had offered himself as a labourer in the rebuilding of the fallen portion of roof.

'You'll never take him on,' cried Miss Theresa. 'The body has no hands. His fingers are all thumbs.'

'His father, he tells me, helped to build your own house. And his brother was a noted craftsman.'

'You've a bit to go to fetch his brother and his father to your house. The fellow's never been a mile from a cow's tail, he'll never do your work. He's a timmer knife. I don't like to hear of you taking him.'

'You can like it or loup it. I've engaged him.'

'You're a dour billie to deal wi',' said Miss Theresa. 'There's no convincing you. But you'll be cheated. Wait till you see if I'm not right. Your fine fat cash will be gey lean work. But I see you don't care a craw's caw for anything I may say.'

Francie's foolish, happy face remained unmoved throughout her diatribe; but when she added, 'We'll go in-by and tell your wife where you are,' he bounded to his feet, thumping the table till the dishes rang.

'Na!' he roared. 'That's what you wunna do. She can just sit and cogitate. She can milk the kye there and try how that suits her and muck the byre out an' a'. Such a behaviour as she's behaved to me! Past redemption and ower the leaf. Dinna you go near, Miss Craigmyle. She'll maybe sing sma' and look peetifu' yet.'

Mrs Falconer said in a low, hurrying voice to Garry, 'If there is anything that we could do—'

'Nonsense, Nell,' came brusquely from her sister. 'Keep your senses right side up. What could you do?'

The sisters went away.

At the Weatherhouse Lindsay came disconsolate to breakfast. She hardly heeded the excited talk about the fire. 'It's no affair of mine,' she thought impatiently, and going to the window she gazed into the chilly garden.

'It's like winter come back. At this time of year, to have snow.'

'Hoots, bairn, it's only April. Did you never hear of the lassie that was smored in June, up by the Cabrach way?'

The sun had not reached the garden. The grass was covered with a carpeting of snow, except for dark circular patches underneath the trees; but the carpet was too meagre to have the intensely bright and vivid look that snow in quantity assumes. Birds had hopped over its surface, which was marked by their claws. The delicate crocus petals were bruised and broken, and early daffodils had been flattened, their blooms discoloured by contact with the claggy earth. Only the scilla and grape hyacinths, blue, cold and virginal, stood up unmoved amid the snow.

And how cold it was! Although the sun shone beyond the garden, melting the foam of snow that edged the waves of spruce, yet the air was bitter, searching its way within doors, turning lips and fingers blue.

'The milk's not come,' said Kate. 'Oh, that's the way of it. I always said Francie did the milking. Well, we've enough to last us breakfast.'

When breakfast was over, Miss Theresa put on her outdoor things.

'Now really, Tris, where are you off to? Haven't you had enough of gallivanting for one morning?'

'To see about the milk,' said Theresa, who was agog to discover how Bell was taking her husband's mild desertion.

'Well—I'll come too.'

Mrs Falconer hardly knew why she wished to go any more than she had known why she rose from her bed to see the fire. She seemed to be driven by a force outside herself.

'These things are real life,' she thought. 'That must be it. I ought to pay more heed to what other people are doing, not wrap myself up in my wicked fancies.'

The sisters made their way along the soft, wet cart-road. The first member of the family they came upon was the young boy Sid, who hodged along the road, hands in his pockets, spitting wide, in perfect imitation of Francie's gait and manner.

'Poor brutes, I don't believe they're ever milked,' Theresa said.

Bell greeted them with fine disdain. When Francie had first courted her, twenty years before, she must have had a bold and dashing beauty. Even yet she was handsome, in a generous style, and her black eyes had lost nothing of their boldness. Until Francie had wedded her, after the death of his brother Weelum, she had had a rude appetite for life but no technique in living. The spectacle, however, of her faithful and humble lover, claiming her in steadfast kindness after his long frustration, gave Bell a rich amusement. For the first time she ceased to follow her momentary appetites, and studied in a pretty insolence how best to take her entertainment from her marriage. She was therefore furious at Francie's disappearance.

'You can whistle for your milk,' she said. 'I wasna brought up to touch your kye, dirty greasy swine. Guttin' fish is a treat till't. The greasy feel o' a coo's skin fair scunners me.'

'Stellicky's milkin' the kye,' interrupted the little boy, who was keeking at the visitors round the edge of the door.

'Haud yer wisht, ye randy. Wait you or your da comes back.'

'But where is he?' gravely inquired Theresa.

'Whaur would he be? On the face o' the earth, whaur the wifie sowed her corn. Up and awa and left me and his innocent weans in the deid o' night, that's whaur he is. America, he's been sayin' gey often, I'll awa to America. I'll let him see America whan he wins back. I'll gar him stand yont. If he's to America, I'll to America an' a'.'

It was evident that she had received no hint of Francie's whereabouts, and the absence of the devoted drudge had wrought upon her finely. She was purple with wrath. The sisters went to the byre, where the small Stella, clad in an enormous apron, with a brilliant red kerchief knotted over her black hair, was milking the two cows. Stella saw the ladies, but paid not the slightest attention to their advent, and continued to milk with an important air, manoeuvring her little body, slapping the cows and addressing them in a loud and authoritative voice. Stella was in her glory.

'When you're done, we'll take our pailful,' said Miss Theresa sharply.

The girl looked round in an overdone amazement, kicked her stool from under her, swayed her little hips beneath the trailing apron and shoved the nearest cow aside. 'Haud back, ye—' she commanded, using a word that made the Weatherhouse ladies draw in their breath.

'You can bring that milk as fleet's you like,' said Miss Theresa. 'I'll give you your so-much if I hear you speak like that again.'

Stella tilted her chin and jigged her foot. In the darkness of the byre, clad in the old apron and the turkey-red kerchief, she glowed with an insolent beauty. Miss Theresa returned to the house, but Mrs Falconer remained at the byre door, watching the girl. Stella finished her milking, but instead of carrying the pails to the milk-house and giving the waiting customers their milk, she thrust the cows about, flung her stool at the head of one that refused to budge, and began with frantic haste to clean the byre. Mrs Falconer made no remonstrance. There was something in the impudent assurance of this nine year old child that frightened her and saddened her. When she heard the same wicked word tossed boldly from the childish lips, she thought, 'Well, this is reality, indeed. Why did I never think before of all that this implies?' and she began to talk to the child.

Stella was ready for an audience.

'And do you often milk?' Mrs Falconer had inquired.

'Oh, he learned me, but he never lets me. I did it all myself,' she added, with a gleaming toss of the head. 'She said'—she jerked her elbow towards the house—'she said, "Let the lousy brutes be." And she padlocked the door and wouldna let me in. But I waited till she went out to the yard, and I after her and up with a fine big thumper of a stick. "Give's that key," says I. But losh ye, I had a bonny chase or I got it out of her. Round and round, it was better'n tackie any day. "Deil tak ye, bairn," she said, "you fleggit me out o' a year o' my growth." "If it comes off you broadways," I says, "you needna worry." '

Mrs Falconer did not ask for the milk. She continued to watch the bouncing child.

Stella made the most of her audience. She talked large.

'Ken whaur I got my head-dress?' she asked, flaunting the Turkey cotton. 'I got it frae my Sunday School teacher. I'm in a play. I've got to speak five times. Ay, gospel truth, I hae! Molly Mackie has only four times. Gospel.'

She struck attitudes, strutting about the byre and mouthing her words.

'Ken this, I have that handky on my head in the play. Ay have I. Teacher she says, "Now, girls, fold them all up and we'll put them in this box." ' (Whose voice was she mimicking, thought Mrs Falconer. The little brat had put an intonation into it that was curiously familiar.)

'But Stella, how have you the handkerchief here?'

The girl burst into noisy laughter and went through a rapid but effective dumb show. Mrs Falconer gathered that she had brought the handkerchief away thrust into the neck of her frock.

'But Stella, that was naughty. Your teacher will be disappointed.'

'She hides things herself,' said Stella carelessly. 'Ay does she. Gospel.' When she said *Gospel* Stella breathed noisily and crossed her breath with her forefinger. 'I'll tell you,' she rattled on eagerly. 'Teacher has a ring she keeps hine awa' down her neck. She's another ring that she keeps on her finger, just its marra. Twins!' The girl giggled with delight at recounting her story. 'Ken how I found that out? She aye bides ahin whan we're learnin' the play, a' by hersel. So one night I thought I'd see why, and I leaves my paperie with the words in ahin a desk and then goes marchin' back to look for it. So I sees her standin' there and one ring danglin' on a ribbon kind of thing, and the t'other ring aye on her finger. And she stuffs the ring intil her bosom, and my, but she got red. She's right bonny whan she blushes.'

The girl grasped her little nose with her fist and squinted, laughing, over the top of it to Mrs Falconer, who said severely, 'You are a naughty girl, Stella. You should never spy on people.'

'Tra la la, la la la la,' sang Stella hopping about the byre. 'I wunna tell you any more.' But she could not keep it in. Immediately she began again.

'Ken what it is she does whan she stays ahin? My! She's play-actin'. Just like us in the play. I think she'll be to say her piece at the concert an' a'. It's awful nice. It's just rare. I've found the way to climb up and see in at the window, and I've seen her ilka night, and naebody else has had a keek. They'll get a rare astonisher at the concert the morn, ay will they. Well, she pu's off the ring that's aye on her finger and dirds it down on the floor. "You hateful thing," she cries. Syne she jerks the other one up out of her bosom, louses the string, and puts the ring on her finger. This way.' The child was an astonishing little mimic. Her pantomime was lifelike. She began now to kiss the imaginary ring, holding her head to the side and rubbing the third finger of her left hand to and fro against her lips.

'Syne,' continued Stella, 'she turns the ring round, so that the stone's inside. And then she makes on to shake hands with somebody, and she says, "Do you take this woman to be your wedded wife?" "I do." Whiles after that she starts to greet and whiles to sing. I dinna ken which it really is, but we'll see the morn. I hope she'll be dressed up. She kens it rare. It's auld John Grey's ring,' she added carelessly.

'Whose?'

'Auld John Grey's, him that's head o' the Sunday School.'

'Surely, Stella, you call him Mr Grey.'

'What for? He's just auld John Grey. He's a rare mannie. You can scran anything off him. If you go in about whan he's delvin' he gives you sweeties and newses awa' to you. Ae day I was newsing awa' and the rain cam on. Loshty goshty guide's, it wasna rain, it was hale water. The rain didna take time to come down. So he took me in to his hoosie and the body that makes his drop tea spread a piece to me. And syne he gied me a pencil that goes roun' an' roun' in a cappie kind o' thing. It was in a drawer with preens and pencils and orra bits o' things—some pictur's that he let me see and bits o' stone wi' sheepy silver. And away at the back o' the drawer there was a boxie wi' a window for a lid, and yon ring was in there. I kent it fine whan I saw it again. She had scranned it off him, same's I did a preen wi' a pink top.'

'But when was that, Stella?'

'Oh, a while sin'. I dinna ken. Afore the New Year.'

'Was it before his son died, do you think?'

'The chiel that made the guns? Na, na. A long while after that.'

'And who is your Sunday School teacher?' asked Mrs Falconer.

'Miss Morgan, of course,' Stella answered, with a contemptuous stare for her visitor's ignorance.

The long lean woman positively shook where she stood.

'Stella, my dear,' she said, swallowing hard, 'you know you shouldn't take away Miss Morgan's handkerchief. What will she say when she doesn't find it in the box?'

Stella gave a loud and scornful laugh.

'Bless your bonnet, she'll find it there all right. I'll have it back afore she sees. Though, of course, after the play's done—' She broke off laughing, and leaping about in fantastic figures through the byre, she sang, 'It's half-past hangin'-time, steal whan you like.'

'So young, so shameless and so smart,' thought Mrs Falconer sadly. The warm byre oppressed her and she stepped to the door, opening her collar to the chilly air; but seeing Theresa at the same time step from the door of the house, she went back to the byre and lifted the two pails of milk.

'Is that milk not ready yet?' cried Theresa, appearing in front of the byre.

'Just ready,' Mrs Falconer answered, and balancing her body between the pails she carried the milk to the milk-house.

Miss Theresa had had a good fat gossip.

'It seems Francie's hinting at leaving them,' she told her sister. 'All talk, I fancy. If he goes to America, the wife says, I go too.' Miss Theresa laughed. 'They'll need a good strong boat and a steady sea before they take that carcase across the ocean. She had made the ground dirl, chasing round like that and the lassie after her. I'm glad to hear somebody can keep her in her neuk.'

Mrs Falconer walked home in troubled soliloquy. Reality had pressed too close. Her thoughts swirled and sounded in the narrow channel of her life, crashing in from distant ocean. Lindsay's betrothal, the fire, the young man's imminent return to the war, Francie's revolt, the pitiful spectacle of the child Stella in her vigorous vulgar assault upon life, the mystery of Louie Morgan's play-acting with the rings, her own shame, her mother's cruelty—smote her like thunder. From the hurly-burly of her mind one thought in time detached itself, insisted on attention. What had Louie done? What did the strange story of the rings imply? If the ring that had been David's mother's was indeed lying in the box in John Grey's drawer some time later than David's death, how came Louie to possess it? She turned the theme about in her head, puzzled and afraid. If it was true, as Garry maintained, that Louie had never been betrothed to David Grey, could she have given colour to her story by clandestine appropriation of the ring—in short, by stealing it? Mrs Falconer felt like a country child alone for the first time in the traffic of a city. What am I to do? she thought, what am I to do?

In the afternoon Mrs Falconer went to call on John Grey's housekeeper. This elderly woman, deaf and cankered, had few intimates and knew little of what went on beyond her doors. Gossip passed her by. 'And as for the master himself,' she would say to Mrs Hunter, 'he says neither echie nor ochie. I've seen me sit a whole long winter night and him never open his mouth.' She had therefore heard nothing of the interrupted Session meeting, nor of the speculation that Mr Garry Forbes had set going with regard to Miss Morgan.

Mrs Falconer bundled some wool beneath her arm. 'I can give her a supply for socks,' she thought. It made an excuse for her call. But the mere need to summon excuse put Mrs Falconer to the blush. How mean a thing it was to lurk and spy, in hope of proving ill against one's neighbour! Truth must be served, but if this were her service, surely it was ignoble. She sighed and rang the door bell; rang again; then knocked loudly on the panels. At last a step shuffled to the door.

'I'm that dull,' the old woman said. 'Folk could walk in-by and help themselves or ever I knew they were about.'

'I don't suppose many people would want to do that.' Strange point of departure for the interview!

'You never know, Mrs Falconer. Folk's queer. And Mr Grey, good soul, thinks ill of nobody. There's nothing in this house under lock and key. Forbye the meat-safe, Mrs Falconer, and for that I wouldna take denial. Since ever my dozen eggs went a-missing, that I found a hennie sitting on in the corner of the wood, and them dead rotten—I put them into the bottom of the safe, till Mr Grey would dig a hole and bury them. And in-by there comes a tinkey. "No," I says, "my man, I've nothing." But when I went outside, lo and behold, my eggs were gone. He had had a bonny omelette that night. Unless, as I said often to Mr Grey, he sold them for solid siller to some poor woman in the town. Poor soul, she had had a gey begeck. So after that I says, I'll have a key to my safe. If it's rotten eggs the day, it may be firm flesh the morn.'

She had led her visitor in, and rambled on, paying little heed to interpolations, which had, in any case, to be shouted at her ear. Mrs Falconer therefore gave up the attempt to talk, and sat listening.

'And you think nobody would want to help themselves? I'm not so sure, I'm not so sure. I'll tell you what I found here one day. My fine miss, the old minister's daughter, Miss Louie Morgan, right inside the parlour, if you please, with the master's drawer beneath his bookcase standing open and her having a good ransack. A good ransack, Mrs Falconer, minister's daughter though she be. "The master gave me leave," she says, "and you didn't hear me ring, so I just came in." He gave her leave right enough, I asked him. For the Jumble Sale, she says. "The things are no use to me," he said, "she is very welcome." He would give away his head, would the master, you could lift his very siller in front of him and he would be fine pleased, but don't you touch a flower. Pick a rose or a chrysanthemum and you needna look him in the face again.'

Mrs Falconer's mouth was parched, her lips were shaking. She had asked nothing, but the answer she desired had fallen directly in her ears. She was sure now that Louie had taken the ring. The Jumble Sale took place three months after the death of David Grey. But perhaps Mr Grey himself had given her the ring, to seal a betrothal left incomplete at the young man's death? Mrs Falconer put the thought away. No, no. The concealment of the ring, her stealing to the drawer unseen, Garry's certainty, all convinced her; and she was overwhelmed besides by the thought that she had been led straight that day to the discovery. The sense of urgency that had driven her to Knapperley in the night, and to Francie's croft in the morning, so that Stella's remarkable story came to her knowledge, and now the immediate relation by the housekeeper of Louie's conduct, amazed her like a revelation of supernatural design. 'I have been led to this,' she thought.

She rose to go, shouting at the old housekeeper an excuse for her unusual visit.

'There would be no mistake though you came again, Mrs Falconer.'

'But what must I do next?' she pondered as she went away.

Kate, bringing home the messages that same afternoon, overtook Louie Morgan on the road.

'I'm thinking of applying for a Lonely Soldier,' said Louie. 'To write to, you know. Wouldn't it be splendid?' And without giving Kate time to reply she hurried on, 'We must all do something to help the poor men. Or a war-time orphan to bring up. I've been thinking of that. Two of them, perhaps. Uplands is so much too large for mother and me—we'd easily have room for two. Isn't it a splendid idea for people to take these poor orphans and bring them up?'

'Excellent,' said capable Kate; but privately she thought, 'Heaven pity any child that is brought up by you.'

Louie blurted, 'I suppose you think I am making a fool of myself.'

'No. Why should I think so?'

Without answering, Louie burst suddenly into a side road and walked away.

She had just come from Knapperley.

Garry had laboured hard all day. Knowing that unless he saw the repairs completed before he left, the house would remain as it was and rot, he set to work at once to clear away the damaged material. Miss Barbara, keen for a space, volunteered her aid. She was strong as a man. Francie too, worked manfully. As the morning wore on people came in twos and threes to look at the scene of the fire. Miss Barbara's eccentric ways, above all her curious taste for lighted windows, gave rise to many explanations of the outbreak. Nor did the sight that met the eyes of the inquisitive lull the tales; for through the gap in the roof, moving about among the beams and on what was left of the flooring of a low attic, could be seen three figures, the tall lean soldier, the clumsy crofter and the brawny woman, sawing, scraping and hammering to the rhythm of an uproarious song:

I saw an eel chase the Deil
Roun' about the spinnin' wheel.
And we're a blin' drunk, boozin' jolly fou, ma jo!

Garry, swinging through the work in his enthusiasm, shouted as lustily as the other two:

I saw a pyet haud the pleuch,
Wha's fou, wha's fou?
An' he whussled weel eneugh,
Wha's fou noo, ma jo?

He broke off, however, at the sight of Miss Theresa Craigmyle among the spectators below. Theresa had hastened back, to lose nothing of the excitement, and found herself well rewarded.

'They had had a dram,' she declared later at the Weatherhouse. 'Bawling out of them like that.'

'And what more fitting?' inquired Lang Leeb from her corner. 'My tuneless daughters don't understand that work goes sweetest to a song. Did you never know that they built a pier in the harbour of Aberdeen three hundred years ago to the sound of drum and bagpipes? They don't work so wisely now. Knapperley roof will be a wonder.'

A wonder it bade fair to be. Miss Barbara tired soon and went to the stable. Francie fetched and carried, but the young gaffer having left him alone for a spell, he began to follow his own devices—which were various. Garry returned from attending to some matter on the ground and saw Francie, without plan or instruction, cut gaily into the new wood that he had brought from the carpenter's shop. He had hacked and hewed recklessly, but, like his father in the Weatherhouse parlour, though without his father's justification, was so highly pleased with himself that Garry stood abashed, unwilling to remonstrate. It was part of his creed that a man should take pleasure in the work of his hands, and to quench Francie's pleasure gave him the same sense of constricting life that he had felt in quenching Miss Barbara's candles. He set Francie's haggard boards aside.

He was called to the ground again, and before his return the post came in and he found Lindsay's letter. The note was curt: 'Garry, I can't marry you. I'm sure I'm not the right kind of wife for you. I'm sure I'm not.' Garry pocketed his scrap of paper and climbed to the attic. Francie had mismanaged his tools again. Garry cursed and set to work himself, hoping to prevent further mischief by adroit advice and order. As he worked, however, his heart grew cold. Lindsay's note settled hard upon it like a frost.

He worked dourly on; but nothing prospered. In his first enthusiasm to restore, he had been sure of what he had to do. Now he found checks and miscalculations. He had to stop and realise that he was uncertain how to proceed.

Just then he saw, foreshortened on the ground below him, the figure of Miss Morgan. She beckoned. He turned his back. But she called, 'May I not speak to you? Indeed it is urgent.' He went down.

Miss Theresa Craigmyle came near at the same moment. 'Can't you keep away?' he thought angrily. He knew that her visit was an idle curiosity, and had enough regard for the reputation he wished Miss Morgan to retain to ask Louie to enter the house.

'I want you to understand,' Louie began, 'I'm sure I didn't make it clear: in allowing my possession of the ring to become a symbol, a kind of rite, you realise that I had passed beyond the material vehicle to the spirit. Can I make you see? The material symbol was of no moment. I mean, it's some justification for my keeping the ring. I simply didn't see it as a piece of someone else's property. It was just an agglomeration of matter that symbolised what was unseen. I wonder if you understand?'

'I understand,' he said slowly, 'that you want to talk about yourself. But I am busy.'

'Yes, I want to talk about myself. I know, I know I do. To you. Not to anyone else. I can have no peace until you understand that I am not a common thief. You are doing yourself an injustice if you think that. You degrade yourself by your misjudgment. I have to make you see. I feel that I am needful to you, to open your eyes to new ways of judgment—'

He turned away. 'Excuse me, I am very busy.'

'We are all needful to one another. Even I to you. But you don't think so.'

'Excuse me.' He went away.

Louie went home, and meeting Kate Falconer on the road, proposed to adopt an orphan.

Garry returned grimly to his task. He was inexpressibly weary. The muddled disorder of the garret oppressed him.

Mrs Hunter came in her comfortable way and tried to make him eat.

'You never lippened to yon craitur,' she said, spying out the disorder of the land. 'Pay the body and send him hame.'

Later she recounted the affair to her neighbour John Grey.

'That Francie Ferguson—he wouldna cut butter on a hot stane. What a haggar' he's made. You would be doing a good deed, Mr Grey, to give the laddie a hand. He's dirt dane. I took him a bowlie of broth, but he's never even lippit it.'

John Grey went round to Knapperley and said to Garry in his quiet, unassertive way, 'You'd better let me give you a hand there.' He craned over among the rafters to look at Francie's mismanagement. 'Tchu, tchu, tchu,' he said, and began to work rapidly and surely.

Behind his back Garry paid Francie twice the sum he should have had for the completed work, and dismissed him.

'Your wood's unseasoned,' said Mr Grey. 'It's too dark to work tonight. Tomorrow's Saturday. I'll give you a hand in the afternoon.' He showed the younger man with a quiet tact where he had gone wrong in his work and how to remedy the faults. 'You haven't handled wood very much.' It was impossible to feel resentment. Garry swallowed his pride and set himself to learn.

But when at length he went to bed he was overwhelmed in a sense of failure. He could not mend a roof, nor chose a workman, nor love a woman. He could not now even vindicate his friend. He relit his candle, to read once again Lindsay's letter, which he knew by heart. All the self-distrust of his nature, inherited from a timid father and the grandmother whose utmost remonstrance was a sigh, had risen in him at the reading of her note. In vain, from boyhood up, he had sheltered under a bravado, a noisy clowning or proud assumption of ability where indeed he felt none; nevertheless at moments, suddenly, this ogre of self-distrust rushed out and bludgeoned him. He had never discovered how much he was indebted to the ogre. His later reputation as a man with surprising stores of curious knowledge had its foundations there. The shame he felt at being found at fault or ignorant sent him furiously to learn, and he never forgot what was bludgeoned in; but his sensitive heart, wroth to show a wound, suffered in the process. So now tonight, when Lindsay had found him at fault, he was overcome with shame.

'She thinks I'm all wrong about Louie, and I can't tell her. What a confounded mess everything is in!' He wished he was back at war. This land he had thought so empty was proving unpleasantly full. Wisely he slept on it and woke refreshed in a windy sunrise to think, 'I'm blest if I let Lindsay go like that.' Less than ever in the sanity of morning did he wish to see the mob gaping over Louie's theft; for all the subtlety of her excuses, theft it was. But Lindsay had to know, and should know, well and soon.

In the same wind of sunrise Mrs Falconer lay, very still beside her sleeping sister, and prayed, as she had prayed at intervals throughout the night:

'Help me, O God, in all that I may have to do.'

She was sure that she had been divinely led to her strange discovery, and in spite of her shrinking from the public stare, had made the dedication of herself to Garry's service. Her knowledge must be used to help his cause. She had prayed till she was worn out.

TWELVE

Concert Pitch

Breakfast was just ending when Miss Theresa remarked, 'And a pretty picture they made, the three of them, bawling out of them on the head of the house. He's as daft as Bawbie herself. He had a real raised look, they said, at that session meeting. Oh, I forgot, Lindsay, he's your young man. I haven't got accustomed to that yet.'

'Then you may spare yourself the trouble.' Lindsay's voice was curt.

'Eh? Now, Lindsay, you needn't be so short. You know I always say just what I think. There's no manner of doubt that the young man is strange. They are all saying it. So it's just as well to know what you are taking in hand if you're taking him.'

'Which I don't happen to be doing.'

Kate gave the girl a curious look. Lindsay continued, 'Oh, go ahead, Cousin Tris, tell us all you saw and did. He's not my young man. Say just what you think.'

'What I think,' said Miss Theresa, 'is that he's a young man you'd be better without. That Louie Morgan's setting her cap at him and like to get him, I should say. Not a soul did he pay heed to, and him up there on the roof, but as soon as she came in about, down he comes and goes straight to her. Never even saw that any other body was there. O ay, Louie knows what she's about, gazing at him with all her eyes. He had her into the house right away, and him so busy with his roof. No saying how long they stayed there.'

'Brute!' Lindsay pushed back her chair and walked out.

'What would you make of that?' asked Theresa. 'Is she marrying him, or is she not?'

Kate knit her brows and said nothing.

'Of course she's marrying him,' said Miss Annie. 'You've such an ill will at the boy you can't see the good in him. You scare the bonny birdie with your clapper of a tongue.'

The bonny birdie could be heard upstairs, banging a drawer shut. Kate followed her.

'You mustn't take Aunt Theresa too hard, Linny. It's just her way. She's got into a habit of speaking like that.'

'Damned impudence. And I was a damned ass to tell her what I did.'

'What language, Lindsay!'

'I know it's what language. I've been brought up to use tidy language, haven't I? My mother would be finely shocked if she heard me. But life isn't tidy, you see, Kate, and that's what I'm discovering. Louie making up to him indeed.' She jammed her hat on her head. 'I'm going to Knapperley.'

'But Linny, that was only Aunt Theresa's idea—'

'Idea or not, it's abominable. Making eyes at Garry? Someone will pay for this. I could face the devil naked.'

'My dear, don't be so upset—'

'Do you never feel about anything, Kate? You should fall in love. Then you would understand.'

She banged the door, crashed like a cataract down the stair, collided with Paradise, shouted, 'Sorry, sorry,' as she ran. The house door slammed.

Kate, left alone in the bedroom, pressed her hands upon her breast. Her lips drew together in a line of pain. But in a moment she relaxed and began carefully to make the beds.

Halfway to Knapperley Lindsay met Garry seeking her with the same fury of decision with which she was seeking him.

Later, as they walked towards Knapperley, a mournful Lindsay said, 'I can't believe it yet. She talked so beautifully. Made life seem so strange and big. I can't explain. It wasn't like anyone else's world. But Garry—I like the ordinary world best. Only—listen, that hateful Cousin Tris. Oh, I know I shouldn't hate her, but she's always right, always right. And since that grocer let out about the way she sneaks things, she's been on her high horse—you can't imagine! She's just aching for a chance to be splendidly right in front of everyone. And I was ass enough to say I'd given you up. Idiot! And now she'll crow and say she always knew it wouldn't last. Listen, you must take me to that concert tonight, claim me in front of everyone, let her see if all her havering about you is right or wrong. You will come, now, won't you?'

The afternoon sped by. In aiding John Grey, Garry worked happily and well. At fall of dark, Mr Grey said, 'That will have to do tonight. I've promised to look in at the concert. It's not much in my line, but the children will be acting. They are expecting me to come.'

Garry called in the approved fashion at the Weatherhouse door to convoy Lindsay to the school.

'Going off with him, Lindsay,' said Miss Theresa. 'I thought you said you had given him up.'

'Given him up? Who? Garry? But what an idea, Cousin Tris.'

'What were you saying this morning, then?'

'Oh, that—really, if you can't understand a little quiet irony!' Miss Annie listening remembered the slamming of the doors. 'I don't think much of your sense of humour,' concluded Lindsay gravely, and walked away.

'People should say what they mean,' rapped Miss Theresa. 'I always say what I mean myself.'

She set out for the concert with Mrs Falconer and Kate. Ahead of them on the road skipped Stella Dagmar, accompanied by her mother.

'She's fatter than ever,' commented Theresa.

'It's here's-an-end-and-I'll-be-round-in-five-minutes if you wanted to measure yon. As I live, she's wearing a new scarf.' She whipped round on the road, and saw Francie following with the *loonie*.

'So there's you, Francie. You've been giving your wife a present, my man.'

Francie rubbed the side of his nose and sniffed.

'What other would I do with the siller he gied me?' he asked apologetically; and added, with a happy sheepish grin, 'It sets her grand.'

The play went well. Stella flaunted her scarlet kerchief, Miss Morgan 'managed' both visibly and audibly, there was ample applause. The children scattered to their parents among the audience, and Louie took a curtain to herself, bowing and posturing. She had a charming mien, and her dress of filmy green set off the soft gold of her hair. As she stood in the packed, hot classroom savouring the clapping and the cheers ('Oh, we'll give her a clap, just for fashion's sake,' said Miss Theresa), Louie's spirit floated out into its own paradise. To be admired—she craved it as one of her profoundest needs. She threw back her head and smiled at the noisy crowd. The moment seemed eternal, it was so sweet. Slowly and dreamily she turned away and sat to the piano, striking a chord. Now she would play.

But between the striking of the chord and the first note of her music (which was never sounded), Mrs Falconer stood up in her place. She had not known herself what she was to do. White, erect, stern, she had sat through the entertainment like a woman hewn from stone; but suddenly, at sight of Louie posturing and smiling, her teeth began to chatter. 'False, false, false,' she thought. She was not conscious of getting upon her feet, nor did the voice that cried aloud above the chattering and the laughter seem to come from her throat; but the astonished assemblage saw the rising of the white stern figure, saw the thin lips move, and listened as she cried, 'Friends, there has been a wrong done here amongst you. That woman yonder is a thief. Round her neck you will find a ribbon, and on it she carries a ring. Will you ask her where she got that ring?' Louie's face was ashen. She was conscious of the glare of eyes, but all she could do was to shake her head and smile. 'The ring is Mr Grey's,' cried Mrs Falconer, and sat abruptly down. Her knees had given way.

Into the moment of astonished silence Stella's voice broke shrill. Stella had clambered up and was dancing on the seat in her excitement.

'It's a blue ribbon,' she shrieked. 'Oh, Miss Morgan, say your piece. "Do you take this woman to be your–" '

Her voice was drowned in the hubbub that arose. Someone pulled her off the seat and put a hand across her mouth. Stella battered herself free with two strong and skinny hands.

And then John Grey stood up. He had been seated with both hands laid on the head of his staff, a stout cherrywood staff, short, tough and seasoned like himself. He rose in his place and stretched a hand over the turbulent assembly.

'Now, now. Now, now.' His gentle voice would not carry. He stood with a hand stretched out and made a half-articulate sound of grieved annoyance, then rapped on the ground with his staff. In a moment the noise fell.

'There was no need for this bustle. I knew where the ring had gone to.'

Louie gave a gasping cry and made blindly for the door. A hulking overgrown farm lad, a *halflin* not yet old enough for war, thrust his clumsy boot across the passage to trip her. She stumbled and recovered; but John Grey, leaning from his place, hooked the handle of his staff into her filmy clothing and detained her. He detained her long enough to work his way out from among the people, then took her arm in his and led her from the room in courteous silence.

The hubbub recommenced; but Garry leaped to a form and shouted above the din.

'Friends, I'm sorry this has happened, but Mr Grey is sure to have some explanation. Don't let's spoil the concert, since we're all together. Let's sing something.'

He began to sing a rattling song, then another. The chorus was taken up with a will. That concert was remembered for years in Fetter-Rothnie—Garry Forbes's concert, they called it. They sing his songs and repeat his yarns today.

'I did myself ill with laughin',' declared Mrs Hunter.

As Miss Morgan herself had requested, Garry said a few words about the Front. But such words!—droll, gargantuan, unforeseen. Each tale was greeted with a hurricane of laughter, each chorus shouted in a lusty heat. The folk trooped out at last into the night, laughing and warm.

Garry wiped the pouring sweat from his face.

'That *was* fun,' Lindsay said, linking her arm in his. 'Garry, how can you keep so solemn when you tell those ridiculous stories? You didn't laugh once.'

'Never felt less like laughing in my life.'

She looked at him, and grew suddenly grave.

'You mean—you were doing it to keep them from—'

'From talking about her. Yes, of course. Fill up their heads with something else. It's an off-chance that they won't say quite so much about it as they'd have been sure to say if the concert had gone to bits. Good God, the thing was indecent! Do you realise what I feel like? I began it, of course. But to throw the common theft to the mob was mean. What on earth induced her?'

'She's a horrid old woman, thrusting herself into the limelight, that's what she is,' cried Lindsay, in her hard, clear, indignant voice.

Mrs Falconer, walking behind them, heard.

She had not yet ceased to tremble. From the moment when her knees had given way beneath her and she had sat down, her body had shaken without remission. She was deadly cold. Garry's quips, the laughter and the choruses, had passed over her like winds. They sounded in her ears, but brought no meaning. She was wholly given over to one idea, that at last she had achieved something in the world of real endeavour. Its results, its value, she was incapable of considering. All she could feel was that she had made the thrust, though the mere bodily effect upon herself was beyond belief. Yet, though her flesh was shaken, her mind was not. She felt as an arch-angel might who, returning from an errand on the earth, reports to God that his mission is fulfilled: no angel could be surer of the divine compulsion.

When therefore Lindsay's clear indignant cry, 'She's a horrid old woman, that's what she is,' came upon her ear, she did not at once understand its significance. She was, indeed, still wandering in her own pleasaunce. But instantly Theresa began to talk. Theresa had only a moment before made up on her sister on the road, having had words to exchange with sundry other curious persons. Now she demanded news. Ellen had to speak; and Theresa's impatience would not let her wait until the Weatherhouse was reached: she must needs call the lovers back to hear and to discuss.

So it was that Ellen was forced at last out of her dream, and learned that she had done the very thing that Garry was working to prevent. Standing there on the road, in the chill spring night, she heard him say, 'I'd give a good deal for this not to have happened.' The spring sky was hard and clear as Lindsay's voice.

'I meant to help you,' stammered the old woman. Old was what she felt, she who had been so young, feeling the spring in her coursing blood upon the moor. They talked interminably. Even in bed, Theresa's tongue ran on. But Ellen lay impassive. She had not even prayed that night. She was dumb.

THIRTEEN

Proverbial

The throng that passed out from the schoolroom singing Garry's songs and repeating his stories took away also a lively curiosity over the incident he had striven to make them forget, and inevitably it was linked with the earlier incident of Garry's outbreak before the Session. Matters so strange were worth the breath it cost to thresh them out. The wars had little chance of a hearing in Fetter-Rothnie for the next forty eight hours, by which time, thanks to Jonathan Bannochie, Garry's reputation was established in a phrase.

Out of the cold, clear night a wind came blowing. It gathered strength all day, till in the late afternoon nothing was at peace upon the earth. Trees and bushes swirled. Boughs were wrenched away and tender leaves, half opened, sailed aloft or drifted in huddled bands about the corners. Twigs and sand battered against the windows and struck the faces and necks of those who went outside. One had no sense of light in the world. The smooth, suave things from which light habitually glisters were wrinkled or soiled in the universal restlessness. Blossom was shrivelled. 'I can't hear a single bird,' Lindsay complained. 'Only the crows.'

Lindsay stood by the window, where she had stood the other morning to watch the snow upon the garden. Now the garden was changed anew. But while it had lain sealed and mute beneath the snow it was less hard to believe in the life within it than now, when this frenzy of motion tormented it from end to end. This was not the motion of life. How just, that Dante in his vision of love that has strayed from its own nature should see it punished by the blare and buffeting of such a wind as this. No silence, to hear the myriad voices, no quietude, to contemplate and recollect. No fineness of perception. A wind of death.

But Lindsay felt only that the garden was ugly, and the howl and clatter set her teeth on edge. She could stay no longer in the warm room. She could not stay even in the garden. The fury of the wind within its enclosure, where the daffodil trumpets were flattened like paper bags and the air was full of strippings from the branches, seemed more withering and ruthless than on the open moor. On the moor the blast swept on without obstruction. The whole grey sky tore forwards to the sea. Even from the hill-top one saw the huge white bursts of foam that grew fiercer and more numerous from moment to moment. Lindsay ran all the way to Knapperley. She could not keep herself from running. When she turned aside her head she could hardly breathe, the wind drove her nostril in with such violence. But she wanted to run. She wanted to dance and to shout above the clamour of the hurricane. Nothing could have pleased her better than to fly thus upon the wings of the wind towards her lover—faster and faster, riding the gale like a leaf. She was glad to merge her will in the larger will of the tempest, for she knew now that she had merged it in her lover's will. Since the morning when he had told her of Louie's perfidy and she had recognised that her own judgment had gone astray, she had had no more desire to trust herself. She had wept, indeed, for the revelation she had had of the evil that is in life; but now, how free and glad she felt! Running thus before the wind, she had entered into the peace that is beyond understanding: she was at one with the motion of her universe.

At Knapperley she pushed open the door and ran upstairs. She felt free of the house now. She had accepted Miss Barbara. What a child she had been to fear her! As she had been a child to fear Garry's love. The sea was, after all, not so very wide; and earth, primitive, shapeless, intractable (as exemplified in Miss Barbara), was everywhere about one, and could be ignored. Roots, if one thought of it, must grow somewhere—in the customary earth.

She ran singing up the narrow stairway, and found Miss Barbara shaking with a jolly mirth beside the ruins of the tinker's bed.

'There's wounds,' she said, 'and growths and mutilations, bits rugged off and bits clapped on to the body of man that is made in the image of his Maker. Them and their war up there'—she nodded upwards to where her nephew was at work—'they mutilate their thousands, they chop off heads and hands and fingers, they could take Johnny's cranny from him, but could they make another Johnny? What's the use of your war, tell me that. You're making tinklers right enough, I'll grant you. They'll be all upon the roads, them that wants their legs and them that wants their wits and them that wants a finger and a toe, like Johnny. But ach! For all your shooting and your hacking, Johnny's beyond you. Your war won't make him.'

'But you know,' said Lindsay, who had listened in amazement to this novel point of view upon the war, 'wounding people isn't all that the war does.' She would have proceeded to expound as best she could Garry's gospel of a rejuvenated world, had Miss Barbara not cut her short with a decisive: 'Fient a thing does the war do that I can see but provide you tramps to tramp the roads. Wounds and mutilations—that's what a war's for and that's what it fabricates.'

'O Garry, may I come up?' Lindsay cried, turning her back upon the crass earth without perceptions that she divined Miss Barbara to be. 'May I come up the ladder?' she cried, singing, and climbing, she thrust her head above the attic floor and sang, 'Mayn't I hold something for you? Or hand you up something? O Garry, mayn't I help?'

Already the gap in the roof was covered. Garry had stripped a tumbled shed of its corrugated-iron roofing and fixed the sheet upon the boards he had already nailed in place. In the wild fury of the gale the iron sheeting had worked loose, and kept an intermittent clatter above their heads. The wind too, entering by nooks and holes, shrieked desperately round the empty room. The old house groaned and trembled.

'Garry, have you been at work all day? Garry, won't you stop, one little minute—and kiss me? Now go on. I love to watch you work. And I do love to be here. We're so respectable. I went to church this morning, Garry—just myself and Cousin Tris. Kate's back on duty, you know.

And—Garry, it was so strange. Cousin Ellen—'

She stopped, leaning from the top step of the ladder upon the garret planks, and was silent so long that Garry, dragging boards across the floor, stopped too and looked at her.

'Well, what of Cousin Ellen?'

She raised her eyes to his. Unshed tears were gleaming on her lashes. The tin patch rattled on the roof. The wind roared round the garret, raising the sawdust in whirlpools, and out of grimy corners the cobwebs streamed upon its current. And Lindsay said, 'I'm all afraid of life. I thought I wasn't, but I am. We're so cruel to one another, aren't we?' she continued. 'At least over at the Weatherhouse we are. I don't suppose we mean it, but we are. Cousin Ellen came down all ready dressed for church and Cousin Theresa said, "What! Nell you fool, you can't mean to go to church today. Show yourself off in public, after what you did last night." And Cousin Ellen said, "You would take my very God away from me." And she marched out on to the moor. "But what's worse in me than in your pails?" she turned back to ask. "If I'm not ashamed, why need you be?" They won't leave each other alone. Pails, pails, pails, and, Making yourself a public show, I never saw! It went on all dinner-time. I couldn't stand it any more, I ran away. And old Aunt Leeb sits there and chuckles. Oh, she's cruel! She's worse than they are. She's happy when she can say a thing that hurts. She's like the Snow Queen—she looks at you with those sharp eyes, and it's like splinters of ice that pierce you through. There's only Paradise that you can feel comfortable with.'

'Perhaps that's why you called her Paradise.'

'Oh yes, no one will be uncomfortable in Paradise, do you think? But I used to think no one could be uncomfortable in the Weatherhouse, and now it's all so changed. Garry, won't you marry me soon and let me be always with you? I feel so safe with you.'

But not, thought Garry, when later in the day, having taken her home, he was striding back across the moor: not because he was safe with himself. Her perfect trust was, of course, delightful: but oddly, in just those matters where she had yielded most generously to his opinion, he had himself become unsure. Even with regard to his aunt— 'But I'm not afraid of her any more,' Lindsay had said, 'I think she's splendid'—something of the girl's terror had gripped his own soul. While she, safe in his arms, had recounted her moment of panic, he too, had become afraid of his aunt: as of something monstrous, primitive and untameable, not by any ardours to be wrought into place in the universe of which he dreamed, a living mock to his aspirations. Yet how triumphantly herself! The corrugated iron clattering at that very moment on the roof of Knapperley was witness to that.

And over Louie Morgan also he was unsure. Lindsay was no longer her champion; but, strangely, she had championed herself. There was a queer twisted truth in what she had said. David too, had felt it. More bitterly than ever he regretted having thrown her to the mob.

Reaching Craggie on his homeward journey, spent with labour and thought, he suddenly turned aside and, bursting into Mrs Hunter's kitchen, cried, 'Feed me, for God's sake.'

'Weel-a-wat, laddie, come in-by.' Mrs Hunter thrust him in a chair and spread the cloth.

Food was never out of view in Mrs Hunter's kitchen. Enter when you would, plates were there, heaped high with girdle scones, oat-cake, soft biscuits. Jam was in perpetual relief. Syrup and sugar kept open state.

'A puckle sugar's that handy,' Mrs Hunter would say, throwing a handful on a dowie fire.

'I canna bide a room with nae meat about it,' she added. 'If Dave now came in at the door and him hadna had a bite a' the road frae the trenches, a bonny mother he would think he had gotten. And him sending hame his pay to keep the laddies at the school.'

Seizing the loaf, at Garry's request, and throwing to her youngest boy, seated at the fireside, the hearty hint: 'Will that kettle be boiling the night, Bill, or the morn's morning for breakfast?', she began to cut slice after slice of bread, until the whole loaf lay in pieces on the table. Jake, her husband, shook his head.

'There's nae need for sae mony a' at aince,' he said,

in a low voice. 'You can aye be cuttin' as it's called for.'

'I canna dae wi' a paltry table. If it were Dave now, in another body's house, you wouldna like it yoursel.' And she seized a brown loaf, slicing until it, too, was piled high upon a plate.

'I grudge nae man his meat, but there's nae call for sae mony a' at aince.'

Jake remained with his worried eyes fixed on the table. A lifetime of laborious need was in the look he bent upon the piles of bread.

'Never heed him, Mr Garry. I've a gingerbread here.' She cut that too. 'Are you feelin' like an egg, Mr Garry? There'll be a hotterel o' folks in here afore the night's out, see if there's nae. There's aye a collieshangie here on a Sabbath night. And I'll lay my lugs in pawn but it's you they'll have through hand, my lad. A bonny owerga'un they're givin' the twa o' you, you and Miss Morgan.—What kind's your tea, Mr Garry?—Ay, ay, there's been mair mention of you this day in Fetter-Rothnie than of God Almighty.'

Indeed, before Garry had well eaten Jonathan Bannochie came in, and with him others.

'Here's a young man has a crow to pick with you,' said Jonathan, pushing forward a half-witted lad in the later teens. 'You're terrible smart, a bittie ower smart whiles for us country chaps. What way now did you nae wait last night for the lads and the lasses that were ready with their sangs and suchlike? Here's Willie here had his sang all ready and him just waiting a chance to get it sung. But na, nae chance.'

'Indeed I am sorry,' said Garry, rising in confusion. 'I didn't suppose—I supposed Miss Morgan—well, that she had charge of all the programme, and when she was gone that it would fall to pieces.' He stammered an apology to the half-wit, who stared grinning.

'O ay,' said Jonathan. 'Anything to shield the lady. Ay, ay, the first thing that came handiest.'

Again, as when he stood before the Session, the young man felt a fury of rage against this mocker who could penetrate among his secret thoughts. Stammering a further apology, he went out.

'Try her in the tower, Captain Forbes,' quoth Jonathan, with a stolid face. A mutter of laughter ran about: the old story was remembered, had very lately been revived. Well out into the hurricane of wind, Garry could distinguish a louder laughter and Jonathan's voice clear in the general guffaw.

He walked into the anger of wind with his head down. Jonathan's parting barb was in, and rankled. At the moment he wanted to have Louie in the tower, wanted to have her alone, wanted simply to have her. And apology was not the need. She was in his blood like a disturbing drug. He knew that she had already turned to his pursuit, and his soul had sickened at the knowledge; but suddenly he realised that he wanted to seize her, to give her what she hankered after, make her taste to the dregs the cup she wantoned with. He went straight to the house of Mrs Morgan, and was shown in.

Louie sprang from a stool by the fireside and faced him screaming. Her lips were livid, her eyes blazed.

'How dare you come here?' she screamed. 'How dare you? How dare you? Haven't you done me enough harm already, exposing me like that? They all know now. You've ruined my name. And you promised not to tell, you promised.'

Her voice ran on, high-pitched, terrific in its morbid energy. Scarlet blotches showed upon the greyness of her face. Bags of skin hung under her eyes. The possession went from him. His fury of lust for strange knowledge was dead. He began to explain that his promise had not been broken.

She did not listen. The high-pitched voice screamed on. And now she was beating her hands against a chair and laughing because she had drawn blood.

'Oh, this is terrible! Oh, this is terrible!' moaned Mrs Morgan. The elder lady rocked her body back and fore, staring uneasily from her daughter to her guest. 'I shall never be able to give a hand with the tea again,' she moaned.

Garry shook the house from him and its dark sultry atmosphere, but in the howl of the wind he continued to hear Louie's hysterical screaming. He hated both himself and her. Sounds were swallowed in the gale. Nothing lived in the steady pouring noise but its own insistence. Even thought went numb. He let himself be driven before the blast as Lindsay earlier had done, but for him there was no joy of surrender. All that tormented—the whining shell, the destructive sea, lust, folly and derision, brute and insensate nature's roar—was in the cataract that crashed about his ears. To run before this enormous wind put him to shame, as though he had let himself be routed by unholy forces. Of purpose he overreached Knapperley and battled back, and in the tussle felt some control upon himself return. When therefore in the shelter of the house he distinguished voices, he was able to give them a wary attention.

The April night had almost come, but a drab gleam showed the figures of three or four men, curious like so many others, who were retreating from a survey of the burnt house. Unperceived, Garry heard the story of the fire recounted by a man who had indeed been present, but had rendered hardly the effective aid his boast suggested. The unseen listener smiled; but heard on the instant the voice of Jonathan Bannochie, who said, 'You would need Garry Forbes to you, my lad.'

Laughter greeted the sally. The braggart was known.

Garry remained hidden. The bandying of his name moved him to wrath.

'Well, well,' said another voice, 'he made's sit up over Miss Morgan, anyway.'

'Mrs Falconer did, you mean.'

'Ay, where got she her information, would you say?'

'Where she always bides,' said Jonathan. 'Hine up on the head o' the house, like Garry Forbes and his twa fools.'

Garry strode into the open.

'Good evening, gentlemen, you are having a look around. Rather dark, isn't it? Perhaps you'd like to see inside? Hine up on the head of the house, if you want to.'

And he suddenly began to laugh.

'Do come in,' he said. 'The night's young, and my aunt has a blazer of a fire. You're not so often round by Knapperley that you need to go so soon. Come away in.'

He ushered them suavely to the kitchen, lit a lamp and shepherded the party to the damaged room. A boisterous mirth took hold of him.

'Up you go,' he cried, pointing to the ladder by which Lindsay had climbed. It stretched into shadows, through the gaping hole above them that showed like a blotch of darkness upon the plaster. The wind still shrieked through the broken window and the sheet of iron clattered overhead.

Garry acted with a reckless gaiety. A fortunate mockery came to his aid, to assuage his own pain and bewilderment. He mocked at his aunt and Johnnie, Francie, himself, with a tongue so blithe and impudent that his guests felt its invitation to laughter and joined in his mirth. His laughter was quite unforced. The interlude had been high comedy; even his own part in it he could recount with appreciation of its comic values. He swaggered, sang again the drinking song. 'Garry Forbes and his twa fools,' he cried, laughing, and catching the noise of the sheet of iron that clattered on the slates, 'Hark to yon fellow—hine up on the head of the house, like Garry Forbes and his twa fools. The old house has got a dunt on the rigging, like the folk that bide in it. But you can't deny,' he added, with a persuasive gleam, 'that Francie showed spirit. I loved it in the man. A fine large folly we both showed, he to attack the thing he couldn't do, and I to let him. Ha, ha, we want more of that spirit in the world!'

They returned to the kitchen. Garry heaped wood upon the fire and fetched Miss Barbara's whisky. Only Jonathan refused to drink.

'Drink, man,' said Garry roughly, but turned away from him at once and talked to the other men. The talk flowed rich and warm as the whisky. Garry began to speak of the war, not in the sardonic humour of his overnight stories, but with the natural sincerity he used in speaking to John Grey. His guests gave him back of their best. They told him, in shrewd and racy idiom, how a countryside took war: food, stock, labour, transport.

'There's mair goes on here than the King kens o',' said one.

A very old man sat next the fire. His face was crunkled

and dry; he rarely spoke; but tonight, holding the glass of whisky in a trembling hand, as the liquor slowly warmed his old blood, he too began to talk.

'Your war—your war—surely it's gey near lousin' time. What's come to a' the young men that they must up and to the wars? In my young time we kent the way to bide whaur our business was. I was fee'd for ane-an'-twenty year to sup brose ane-an'-twenty times a week—nae gallivantin' frae toun to toun whan I was a sharger. But there's nae haudin' the young men in aboot the day. My lassie's loon, he's but a bairn, he must be aff an' a'. "Come rattle in his queets wi' the poker," I says to her. "That'll learn him to keep to his work." War—it wunna let a body be. It's lousin' time, I tell you.'

'It won't be lousin' time till we've won the field,' said Garry. And he looked strangely at the very old man. How easy, if one could regulate all life by a single duty: a ploughman his field to plough, a cobbler his boot to patch; a life without glory and without failure, without responsibility for oneself.

'Won!' mocked Jonathan across his thoughts. 'This war will not be won. What's your belligerents? Twa fools, playing Double Dummy and grand pleased with themselves. Both'll think they've won, but there's neither won nor lost. A farce all the ways of it.' He added, in a voice hardly audible, his face to the fire and a smile playing about his mouth, 'Twa fools, hine up on the head o' the house—'

Garry argued hotly. 'I don't know, I can't explain it, but I believe we are in some way fighting the devil. Have you no belief in the sanctity of a cause?'

'None.'

'And the rights of the small nations? National honour?'

Jonathan chanted:

Peter my neebor,
Had a wife an' couldna keep her,
He stappit her in a hole in the dyke an' the mice
eat her.

And at Garry's impatient movement, 'You needna get hot, Captain. You think much the same yourself at bottom. All the mercy a war shows to any is to them that gets their pooches filled. I'm told there's some that way,' he added, 'not that I know of it.'

Garry cried on a reckless inspiration, 'You would need Garry Forbes to *you*.'

The roar of laughter that went up from the others told him that the shaft went home. He watched Jonathan, throwing back his head and laughing too.

'Him!' said Mrs Hunter, when later he questioned her. 'He would skin a louse to get tallow. O ay, I'm told he's made a tidy bit out o' the war. A country cobbler—you would wonder, wouldna ye? But he must have a smart bit o' siller laid by and there's folks in debt to him round and round. There's places up and down that's changed hands since the war, folks bought out and businesses shut down, and some grand anes wi' new-got siller set up in their braw establishments, and Jonathan's got his nieve packed tight, ay has he that. He kens mair than he'll let on, but folk has an inkling. He kens the ins an' the oots o' maist o' the places that's come to the hammer hereaboots.'

Garry sat in Knapperley kitchen and watched the man. He changed countenance not at all, but laughed the matter by, saying idly, 'Garry Forbes would have his own ado.'

The phrase was established.

The following evening Jonathan said, in his own shop before a half dozen witnesses, to Mally Sandison who swore that she had paid the boots when she brought them to have the 'tackets ca'ed in,' 'What's that, mistress?' Jonathan said. 'Paid, said ye? You would need Garry Forbes to you, I'm thinking.'

The joke went round. It penetrated the more surely for being more than joke, or joke not fully understood. It puzzled the consciousness of Fetter-Rothnie, but remained on its tongue. The phrase became the accepted reproof of falsehood.

For the other phrase of Jonathan's coinage, 'Hine up on the head o' the house, like Garry Forbes and his twa fools,' that also passed into current speech, but baldly, a jesting reproach to those who attempted what they could not overtake. Like other phrases debased by popular usage, it lost the first subtle mockery it took from the brain of its originator. The intelligence of its victim alone apprehended it; he knew (as Jonathan did likewise, else he would not have mocked) that his folly on the housetop was a generosity, a gesture of faith in mankind.

Returning by the dark avenue when he had seen his guests to the gate of Knapperley on the Sunday after the concert, Garry heard a noise among the bushes that was not caused by the wind, and immediately a stone hit him on the shin-bone. He thrust his way among the bushes and dragged a captive to the open. His match flared in the wind and went out, but gave him time to see the half-wit whose song had not been sung. He spoke kindly to the lad, who wrenched himself free with evil words and made off.

The wind poured on—a south-wester like an elemental energy. Garry stood awhile in the fury. The shriek of wind brought to his mind the flying shells, and he thought of troop ships and minesweepers riding the storm. Only those without imagination, he felt, could love the wind. A tree crashed. He shuddered, and a longing seized him to have done with sick-leave and be again in battle. The danger that was abroad in the tortured night of wind cooled and braced him. 'I'm fit now,' he thought, 'I must get back. Damn that man and his talk of futility. It's a battle about something and I must get back.'

Jonathan's cynical smile recurred to his mind, and the roar of wind changed in his ear to the roaring of their ridicule as they made phrases of his name. That also seemed an elemental energy, and the screaming of a woman sounded through it, elemental too, destructive as the hurricane.

He slept at last, and the wind fell.

FOURTEEN

April Sunrise

He awoke before the dawn. There was no sound at all, no motion in the house or wood. The silence was unearthly, as though the wind had blown itself out and with it all the accustomed sounds of earth.

Birds brought back the normal world. Sounds began anew. Garry threw himself from bed and went outside.

The morning was like a flute note, single, high and pure, that for the moment of its domination satisfies the ear as though all music were in itself; but hardly has it sounded when the other instruments break in.

Life recommenced. Dogs barked, cocks crew, smoke rose, men shouted, women clattered their milk pails. Soon figures moved upon the empty fields. Somewhere a plough was creaking. Garry turned his head towards the noise and searched the brown earth until he saw the team. Seagulls were crying after it, settling in the black furrow, rising again to wheel around the horses. As he watched, the sun reached the field. The wet new-turned furrow was touched to light as though a line of fire had run along it. The flanks of the horses gleamed. They tossed their manes, lifting their arched necks and bowing again to the pull: brown farm horses, white-nosed, white-footed, stalwart and unhurrying as the earth they trampled or the man who held the share.

From where he watched Garry could see a long stretch of country. Jake Hunter's croft was visible. Jake was bowed above a heap of turnips, slicing in his slow, laborious fashion. Mrs Hunter sailed across the stackyard in a stream of hens. And on his steep, thin field Francie Ferguson walked, casting the seed. It was his moment of dignity. Clumsy, ridiculous, sport of a woman's caprice and a byword in men's jesting, as he cast the seed with the free ample movement of the sower Francie had a grandeur more than natural. The dead reached through him to the future. Continuity was in his gait. His thin upland soil, ending in stony crests of whin and heather, was transfigured by the faith that used it, he himself by the sower's poise that symbolised his faith.

That gesture, of throwing the seed, seemed to the man who watched the most generous of movements; and he was glad to associate it with Francie, whose native generosity he had seen and loved. His blind anger of the previous night flared suddenly anew. 'Garry Forbes and his twa fools,' he muttered. 'I had rather be Francie and capable of a generous folly than these others with all their common sense.' His own wild mockery of both Francie and himself had had last night a harsh wholesome savour; this morning it felt like a disloyalty.

At that moment Mrs Falconer appeared among the trees.

The strong family resemblance among the Craigmyle sisters had never seemed to him so marked as when he saw Mrs Falconer walking towards him from the wood. She had an almost truculent air. Theresa herself could not have put him right with more assurance.

'So you like a sunrise, too,' she said in an abrupt, hard way. 'Well, I wanted to say, I believe I crossed your wishes the other night, letting them know about that Louie. I thought you wanted them to know. But it seems you changed your mind.'

'Oh well, you see—' The accusation in her tone annoyed him. 'A matter of common theft—pretty low down to expose that, don't you think?'

'Well, I'm sorry. But it was for—' She was about to add '—your truth that I did it,' but something in his face made her pause. He was grey and haggard. She left her sentence incomplete. 'I'm sorry,' she repeated humbly.

'Her neck's thrawn now. Much good may it do us all.'

Mrs Falconer found nothing to answer.

'Don't you worry,' he continued. 'It amuses people. One should be glad to add to the gaiety of mankind. They've made a joke of it already. They seem to find me a pretty good joke hereabouts.' With his arms folded on the top of a gate he was leaning forward to watch Francie. 'See that seed-casting machine over yonder?'

'What? Where? Machine—I only see Francie Ferguson.'

'What's he?'

'Mrs Falconer stared.

'Why, he's the crofter at the place by us, just over the field. But you know Francie. It was him you—'

Again she left her sentence incomplete.

'Jerked up like a marionette on the roof at Knapperley, for folk to laugh at. So it was.'

'You spoke of a machine—'

'Men like machines walking. Somewhere in the Bible, I believe. I thought myself he was a man. I'm glad that you agree.'

'Captain Forbes, I'm afraid I don't quite understand you.'

He straightened himself from the gate, stretched his arms, and laughed.

'No, I suppose not. It's quite simple, though. I chose to employ Francie because I liked the spirit of the man. He's ignorant, he's clumsy, but—well, I love him. The men of sense—oh, very decent fellows, I had a drink with some of them last night—have made a laughing-stock of both of us. I could forgive it for myself. I can't forgive it for Francie. And I can't forgive them because I joined the laugh myself. Logical, isn't it? If you're laughed at, always join the laugh. It takes the sting out. But then you see—I laughed at Francie too. They made it seem, if I could put it so, a necessary condition for my entering *their* kingdom.' He ended with passion,'They conspire together to prevent my loving men.'

Mrs Falconer turned away her eyes. His passionate face, dark, unshaven, haggard, moved her with an emotion that she dared not countenance. Gazing intently at the clear blue hills she let fall the words, 'They too are men.'

And suddenly the man at her side, at whom she could not look, burst out laughing. His laughter resounded through the quiet morning. Jake Hunter, several fields away, lifted himself from the turnips and shaded his brows with his hand to search in the direction of the noise.

'It's Mr Garry up there,' said his quicker-eyed wife. 'He has ways real like his aunt. I've seen her rumble out the laughin' an naebody by. Well, a laugh's a thing for twa or for twenty, says I, nae for a man an' him himsel'.' Even her sharp eyes had not made out Mrs Falconer's sombre figure against the trees.

Garry stopped laughing and said to Mrs Falconer, 'It's such an obvious thing to say, isn't it? That's why it is so confoundedly clever of you to say it. Inspired, I ought to say. Clever is a stupid word. Yes, that is the brutal fact: they too are men. As much a part of things as I am. One knows it at the Front, but here—I'm angriest of all, you know, because I mocked at Francie. And yet I suppose I couldn't have mocked at myself without mocking at him too; and it was only when I had laughed at myself, last night, with these men, that I began to feel I was a part of things here.' He interrupted himself to say, 'But all this is boring you. And listen—this Louie business: of course I wanted David cleared. But when I found about the ring—well, any man would have shut up. I felt pretty beastly, I can tell you, when I saw them all agape. Anyhow, it was John Grey's business after that, not mine. I had told her, you see, that I would take no action. But you—I don't want you to—'

'I acted on an impulse,' she said, smiling bravely. 'It was cruel of me. I had just come to know. If I had thought about it longer, I'd have seen it was no business of mine.'

'Please don't blame yourself. Perhaps it's best—'

'Well, I'm glad I met you to apologise,' said Mrs Falconer calmly. 'I'll say goodbye just now.'

Garry went homeward thinking still of her reply: 'They too are men.' It seemed to him the wisest saying he had heard. He looked again at the wide leagues of land. And a curious thing happened. He saw everything he looked at not as substance, but as energy. All was life. Life pulsed in the clods of earth that the ploughshares were breaking, in the shares, the men. Substance, no matter what its form, was rare and fine.

The moment of perception passed. He had learned all that in college. But only now it had become real. Every substance had its own secret nature, exquisite, mysterious. Twice already this country sweeping out before him had ceased to be glomeration of woods, fields, roads, farms; mysterious as a star at dusk, with the same ease and thoroughness, had become visible as an entity: once when he had seen it taking form from the dark, solid, crass, mere bulk; once irradiated by the light until its substance all but vanished. Now, in the cold April dawn, he saw it neither crass nor rare, but both in one.

He looked again at this astonishing earth. And suddenly for the second time he laughed aloud. Mrs Falconer, gone not so far but that she heard him, stopped upon the road. She could not understand why he laughed, and she felt chill and sad.

'Both crass and fine,' he was thinking; but he was thinking no longer of the land, but of the men. Not irradiated by an alien light, but in themselves, through all the roughness of their make what strange and lovely glimpses one could have of their secret nature! 'Each obeying his law,' he thought.

Around him he noted that the woods were flaming. A fine flame was playing over the leafless branches, not gaudy like the fires of autumn, but strong and pure. The trees, not now by accident of light but in themselves, were again etherealised. For a brief space, in spring, before the leaf comes, the life in trees is like a pure and subtle fire in buds and boughs. Willows are like yellow rods of fire, blood-red burns in the sycamore and scales off in floating flakes as the bud unfolds and the sheath is loosened. Beeches and elms, all dull beneath, have webs of golden and purple brown upon their spreading tops. Purple blazes in the birch twigs and smoulders darkly in the blossom of the ash. At no other season are the trees so little earthly. Mere vegetable matter they are not. One understands the dryad myth, both the emergence of the vivid delicate creature and her melting again in her tree; for in a week, a day, the foliage thickens, she is a tree again.

For the first time Garry was in the country at the moment when this very principle of life declared itself in the boughs. 'As fine as that,' he thought, 'from coarse plain earth.' But if one surprised them at their moment, men had the same bright fire.

Mrs Falconer walked home.

Theresa asked, 'Where have you been stravaigin' to at this time of the morning? To get the air! Well, the work stands first, I always say. There's all the windows to clean after that gale. We can't see a thing for dirt.'

Lindsay was coming in from the garden. The grass was quite covered with twigs and torn leaves, with cypress berries, with pine needles and cones. And under one tree, an arm of which had been riven from the trunk, Lindsay had found a nest with an egg and three naked mangled nestlings tumbled on the ground. But saddest of all was the death of the bird she was holding against her body.

'Look, quite dead. I found it lying there. Oh, Paradise, could it be the mother of those gorbals? How pitiful—'

'No, no.' Paradise was touching the soft cold form with her misshapen fingers. 'This one was flying. See, his neck is broken. He had been driven by the wind against a bough. They're frail things, birdies. Many a one the gales bring down.'

'Oh! But can't they fly clear? Can't they see where they are going?'

Paradise shook her head. 'What's a fluff of air and feather against a hurricane? I've seen them rattle down in dozens.'

Lindsay held the dead bird against her breast, smoothing the silken wings and bosom. 'See, see.' She lifted a wing with gentle fingers and displayed a patch of warm bright russet in the hidden hollow.

'Such small, small feathers. Oh, its loveliest part is hid away.'

Mrs Falconer stood apart and watched. She had not offered to show the bird to Cousin Ellen.

'She loves the bird more than me,' thought the woman sadly. And she winced again at the remembrance of Lindsay's scornful words after the exposure of the theft. But as though she had divined a secret chagrin, the girl came softly to her side, holding the bird.

'See, Cousin Ellen.' She displayed the russet pool beneath the wing; and thinking that Ellen was sad because of Theresa's reprimand, she whispered, 'I'm cleaning windows, too—oh yes, I want to help.'

It was afternoon before she went to Knapperley. Garry was on the roof.

'Come down, come down. Have you been there all day?'

He nodded, nails in his mouth, and continued to hammer. Shortly he came down.

'Well, I've discovered a thing I never knew—how slates are put on.'

'Oh, you've slated it. Where's your iron sheet today?'

'Dangling by one tooth this morning. So I gathered what was left of the slates. No, I haven't slated it. Or only a bit. I'll have to get more slates. But I've fixed all that were usable. Come up the ladder and I'll show you. They go on like this—each one overlapping other two.'

'Yes. But stop for a little now, Garry.'

He came down, but almost at once began to clear away the drifts of rubbish that the wind had left.

'Will you be always like this when we are married, Garry? Always at work?'

'Expect so. There's so much to do. I'll tell you what, Linny, the war seems a colossal bit of work to get finished, but ordinary life's going to be a bigger. Coming back here, and finding all the queer individual things people do and think—it's frightened me. To get them all fitted in—I don't see how it can be done.'

The faces came on him in a mob–Francie, Jonathan, Jake, the tramp and the half-wit, Louie, Miss Theresa Craigmyle, Miss Barbara: the substance from which all his fine new kingdoms must be built. He would have liked to repudiate the knowledge he had just gained of human nature: how could one proclaim an ideal future when men and women persisted in being so stubbornly themselves?—And at that moment Miss Barbara rumbled round the corner of the house with a wheelbarrow.

'Build a house,' she said with scorn, as she set down the barrow, which was piled with earthy boulders. 'Build a house, mend a house, that's what your common bodies do. O ay, you're Donnie Forbes's grandson right enough. A Paterson of Knapperley never turned their hand to building houses.'

'And what are the stones for, aunt?'

'I'm putting up a cairn.' She stooped to the barrow handles and continued on her way.

'To commemorate the war?' shouted Garry.

'Deil a war. The fire, my lad, the fire.'

FIFTEEN

Whom the Gods Destroy

For Mrs Falconer, she watched Lindsay, all quick excitement, gather her possessions from the windowed bedroom and drive away, rosy and laughing, by her father's side. Then she climbed the stair and sat down in her empty room. She had never felt so desolate. The past came freely to her memory, and she recalled her dismal marriage, its ending, her humiliation at Theresa's hands on her return. But none of these things had troubled her as she was troubled now. For many weeks she battled against a sense of guilt. But what had she done wrong? Even if she had erred in her public denunciation of the sinner, she had acted in good faith, had meant well. The shame that overwhelmed her was too deep and terrible to have sprung from that. The weeks passed, Lindsay was married, and very slowly Mrs Falconer began to understand. Lindsay's words rang often in her ears—'a horrid old woman, thrusting herself into the limelight'—and at first they made her indignant ('to think that of me, to think that of me'), but after a time she saw that they were true. She had accused Louie so that Garry might be pleased with her.

During these months Mrs Falconer had grown pinched and wan. She sat much alone, with hands interlocked, eyes staring. When spoken to she started and spoke at random. Lang Leeb's appreciation of these phenomena was delicate. Fine barbs went quivering into Ellen's mind. A woman of sixty, pining for a man not half her age, was a spectacle to earn the gratitude of gods and men: so seldom do we let ourselves be frankly ludicrous.

In August Ellen acknowledged to herself that her love for Garry was an egotism. Her sense of shame and guilt grew heavier, not because she had discovered its cause, but because of the revelation she had had of the human heart, its waywardness and its duplicity. She had known quite well what her mother and sister had thought of her infatuation, and had despised them for the vileness of their thoughts. Now for the first time she herself felt evil. 'It was only myself I thought of all the time.' Her sense of escape, of flight into a larger world, was illusion.

She ceased to pray. Prayer, too, was an illusion. 'Your God of Comforts'—she understood it now. Her God had always been a God of Comforts from whose bounty, as she fashioned her petitions, she had taken precisely what she wanted. One could go through a long life like that, thrilled and glowing as one rose from prayer, and all the while be bounded horribly within oneself. The God who had constrained her in her flaming ecstasy of devotion, whose direct commands she had obeyed in denouncing Louie, was created from her imagination: a figment of her own desire.

She continued throughout that winter to go to church, because it did not occur to her to cease the practice; but the services were torture. She looked in horror at the people as they prayed. 'How do they know that there is anything there? Any God at all? I can never trust again what I feel within myself.'

One day in April as she walked alone, a bird flew low, alighted near her, pecked and tugged among the withered grasses, flew up in swift alarm, lit again. She watched, then sharply as though the words were spoken, she heard Lindsay's eager question, 'What is his name? But don't you love birds, Cousin Ellen?'

Yes, yes, I have always loved them, she thought—their grace, their far swift flight, the cadence of their song—as I have loved all beauty, that is a part of my undying self, possessed eternally, the kingdom within my soul. Yet because she could not name the bird that flew up and hopped in front of her, a miserable sense of failure came across her spirit. She went home and found her sister Annie.

'I saw a bird just now,' she began, then choked. She had not spoken all that year to anyone about the things that filled her heart.

'There's lots of them about,' said Miss Annie.

Yes. It flew away and came back again. I wonder what it would have been.'

'What kind of bird?'

But Ellen could not answer. She knew neither its colour, nor shape, nor the length of wing or beak. She rose abruptly and went upstairs. The sense of shame and failure came over her with renewed intensity. It was absurd—because she did not know a bird's name; but as she sat miserably by her window she saw all at once that it was not only the bird's name of which she was ignorant: it was the whole world outside herself.

She had never felt so much abased, so lonely in the multitude of living things. It was spring, they were around her in myriads; but she did not know them. They had their own nature. Even the number of spots upon an egg, the sheen on wing or tail, was part of their identity. And that, she saw, was holy. They were themselves. She could not enter into their life save by respecting their real nature. Not to know was to despise them.

And so with men. One could not be taken into other lives except by learning what they were in themselves. Ellen had never cared to know. In her imaginings other people had been what she decreed, their real selves she ignored. 'I have despised them all.' She felt miserably small, imprisoned wholly in herself.

From that day her new life began; slowly, for she had consumed herself in shame, and at first had neither strength nor faith enough to live on new terms. Moreover, she was sixty one, and, from the monotony with which life in the Weatherhouse had passed, set in her habits. For a time she entertained wild projects: she would go away, work in a slum, learn life. But she had no money. The war was over, Kate was again in a paid situation. One day she drew Kate aside, mumbling.

'I can't make out what you're saying, mother.'

'If you could let me have some pocket money, dear. You know I've none at all.'

'But you never want for anything, mother, I hope?'

'No, no. It was only—just to have it, dear. But it doesn't matter.'

'Of course you shall have money, mother. I should have thought of it before.'

Kate gave her a few shillings.

One day she went to town. Excited, but calm through the magnitude of her purpose, she made her way to the Labour Exchange, and stood, fumbling among words, at the advisory bureau.

'No, that is not what I wanted. No, no.'

The woman who watched her with shrewd and kindly eyes guessed at a tragedy: a gentlewoman fallen on evil days. But when she understood what the worn, haggard old woman wanted, she was silent through astonishment.

'I thought there were so many openings for welfare workers,' stammered Mrs Falconer.

'But you have no training—and your age—but perhaps you must, you have nothing to live on.'

'No, it's not that—I just wanted to get away from home.'

'Oh! Then if you don't need the money, there is voluntary work that you could do.'

Mrs Falconer went bitterly home. Another fine fancy was smoke. She had pictured herself a successful social worker. 'And I wanted to get away from home because I couldn't bear to hear their remarks—to see me humiliated, that's what it is. Confessing that my life's been all amiss till now.'

These essays in sincerity hurt her. 'But it's only through sincerity that I can reach anywhere beyond myself.' She must be sincere even with the birds and the wild flowers she had begun to study, to know their real selves that she might enter their life. Kate's shillings had bought her certain textbooks, but her study halted. Birds moved so swiftly, she forgot so soon, her manuals were poor, and by her untaught efforts it was hard to identify these moving flakes of life and the bright, multitudinous flowers. Identify—discover their identity. She had never valued accurate information, holding that only the spirit signified, externals were an accident; yet when she found that by noting external details she could identify a passing bird or a growing plant, a thrill of joy passed through her heart. She was no longer captive within her single self.

These moments of bliss came rarely in a long, slow time.

That summer she ceased to go to church. God—was there a God? And where could one discover His identity? She had believed all her life in this comfortable God who revealed Himself to her spirit in ecstasy and beauty; but her ecstasies had been a blind self-indulgence. No sincerity in that. 'I can't find God in the forms of a religion that has let me go so terribly astray, that has shut me away from everything but myself.'

Her sisters were aghast when she would not return to church. Annie's was a genuine distress. 'Ah, but you should go to church, you should go. We should all go to church as long's we're able.' Miss Annie herself, crippled and serene, set out each Sunday morning alone, an hour before the time of service, to make her slow, laborious journey.

'You might at least keep it up for appearance sake,' Theresa hectored. 'We've been a kirk-going family all our days. There's no need to be kirk-greedy to do the respectable thing. A pretty story they'll make of it, a Craigmyle and left the kirk.'

Some time after her rupture with the church, Mrs Falconer met the young Stella walking in dignified aloofness on the moor. Stella was in disgrace. Convicted of petty thieving, she had received a reprimand in face of the assembled Sunday School.

'Oh, Stella,' began Mrs Falconer, shocked at the bravado with which the girl flung out her story.

'Oh, yes,' interrupted Stella coolly. 'Tell me, like all the rest of them, that God is watching all I do. I don't believe it. There's not a God, He's just a make-up. So there!'

Mrs Falconer was silent. Stella, who had anticipated good game in the way of shocked remonstrance, inquired impatiently, 'Well, aren't you going to preach a bit to me about it?'

Mrs Falconer answered humbly, with her grieved eyes on the girl's face, 'I can't do that, Stella. I don't know if there is a God.'

Stella stared and cried, 'Well, you're a straight one. I like you for that.'

Perhaps I have done wrong, she thought, saying that

to the child. But no, nothing could be wrong that strove to establish truth. But I was striving to establish truth by exposing Louie. Life was past belief, complicated, huge. The God she had served judged all men by their motives. She had a glimpse now of a darker, more terrible God who judged results. How could it be enough to mean well? One came afterwards to repudiate one's own motives, to see that one was responsible in spite of them. One's true self, which one had not known, had worked. Surely if there was a God, it was one's real self that He judged.

Her mind turned to Louie. They had shut Uplands and gone away for a time. 'She'll get a man and not come back at all—see if she doesn't,' Theresa said. That was the kind of cruel thing that was said of her on all hands now. 'And I delivered her up to it,' thought Ellen. For years to come she was to see Louie degenerate because people knew her for what she was. But did they? She came to her deepest understanding of Louie when she saw that she was like herself, and built rashly on a foundation of her own imaginings. How could people understand that? 'But I understand. I know how it had all seemed to her.' She dwelt on the resemblance till she could hardly distinguish between herself and Louie. 'And people needn't have known her false pretences if it hadn't been for my false pretences.' She remembered Garry's tale of his delirium in the shell-hole. 'I thrust her in, I am rescuing myself.'

'Ah,' she thought, 'here is one person outside myself whom I really know.' And she went to seek Louie.

But some years had passed by then, and Mrs Falconer had made other attempts at knowing people.

It took her many months after the failure of her first grandiose designs to face again her need for entering other lives, and many months more to find a way.

One day she came home from town and said abruptly, 'Well, I'm going to help at the Working Girls' Guild. Tuesday evenings.'

'I'm sure it's a good thing, poor lassies!' said Paradise, who saw nothing incongruous in Ellen, with her old-fashioned dress and ideas, moving in the generation of post-war factory girls.

Nor did Ellen see her incongruity. Tuesday evenings were her excitement. The rude, boisterous life she met provided an experience. She came home too excited to sleep. 'Now, soon, I shall win the confidence of these girls. They will tell me all their lives, their secret thoughts.'

She did not guess that she was herself a problem to the leaders of the Guild. The girls made merciless fun of the hat that perched high above greying coils of hair, of the old-fashioned full skirt and the leather belt drawn tight to a meagre waist; still more of the smile with which she followed them about and the queer questions she put. And she could not do things. Each worker was armed with knowledge: one could guide the dancing, one tell stories, one teach gymnastics or dressmaking. Mrs Falconer had no asset.

'She's such a good soul,' the workers said, 'you don't want to hurt her, but really—she's in the way.'

'Oh, let her keep coming. She enjoys it. There's always something she can do.'

'The girls like her, though they laugh.'

'But she shouldn't be so tall. Old women oughtn't to be tall. They're not so lovable.'

They began to give her hints. She listened humbly, while students and youthful graduates told her how modern psychology decreed that working-girls should be treated. She took her lessons home and brooded over them.

For two years the centre of her life lay here. One evening she found Stella Ferguson in the Guild room, all staring eyes and open ears.

'I'm in a shop,' said Stella contemptuously. 'I'm fourteen. Ay, in the town: *I* wasn't going to your country shoppies, do you suppose.'

Some weeks later a bold girl burst indignantly up to the leader. 'Look here, I'm not going to have that old-clothes wife prying into my affairs. Cheek, I call it.' She let fly a stream of ugly oaths.

The leader was compelled to tell Mrs Falconer that she had been unwise.

'That girl, poor soul—her home and people don't stand

inquiring into. She's ashamed. One has to go very warily.'

Mrs Falconer understood after the conversation she had that evening with the leader that she had been of no great use at the Guild.

'You have been of great use to me,' she said humbly. 'I have been happy—but I won't come again.'

'Oh, please do! Come back sometimes and see us.'

Ruthless to herself, Mrs Falconer saw that her eagerness to know the intimacies of the girls' lives had been for her own sake, to quicken her life.

The following Tuesday she answered Theresa's, 'Isn't it time you were away?' with a proud plain 'I'm not going back. They think I'm too old for that work.'

The shy, baffled soul, entering upon her quest too late, with no key to open other lives, would take no consolation from deceit. It was about this period that she began to brood on Louie Morgan; and one day, though the two women had not spoken since the night of the concert, she set out to visit her.

The door was opened by the Morgans' servant, a middle-aged woman with sleeves pushed up to reveal enormous red elbows.

'It's Miss Louie you're seekin', nae the mistress?'

She led Mrs Falconer to the door of a room, within which someone was speaking.

'There's company—I won't go in.'

'Ach, she's just play-actin', ben you go.' The red-armed woman pushed Mrs Falconer in, but without announcing her, and shut the door.

Mrs Falconer stood amazed.

Louie held a teapot in her hand and was pouring tea. She moved with an elegant air around the table, filling cup after cup, and spoke to each guest in turn: but the guests were not there.

On the empty chairs Mrs Falconer seemed to see dark, menacing figures, guests with suave manners that covered a deadly leer.

A hot fervour took possession of her.

She cried aloud, 'Mr Facing-Both-Ways, Mr Two-

Tongues, My Lady Feigning.'

Louie set the teapot askew upon a chair in her astonishment.

'Oh, go away—my mother is out—what are you wanting?' Her eyes glared, but in a moment she recovered herself and began to posture.

'I'm sorry. I didn't hear you announced, Mrs Falconer. Do sit down.' She waved her hand at the cups of tea. 'I was expecting guests. When I heard the bell ring I thought they had arrived, and I was pouring the tea to be ready. Do have some.' She thrust a cup into Mrs Falconer's hand. The tea was already cold.

She was extravagantly dressed, but the lace at her throat was torn and her fingernails were dirty. Her face, oppressed by powder, and her hair, which had straggled beyond its cut, gave her an air of sloven tawdriness; and she continued to posture and trill.

Mrs Falconer put the cup down and said, in a harsh, loud voice, 'I don't like the guests at your party. Don't pretend not to understand me,' she continued. 'I don't like your party, and I don't like the guests you entertain. You are entertaining ghosts, demons, delusions, snares, principalities and powers. You are entertaining your own destruction.'

The voice hardly seemed her own, but she could not check it. It poured on without intermission, crying a thousand things that she had brooded over, but to which she had given no language.

'Truth, truth—it must be truth. You mustn't compromise. If you would save yourself alive there must be no dallying with the false deities of the imagination. Things as they are. People as they are.'

Scarlet spots burned on Louie's face and throat. She began to retaliate, a fierce and insolent screaming.

'You—you—don't you know that you are to blame? You gave me away. *He* never meant them to know. It was you. And then you come and talk!'

'Yes, yes, I am to blame. We are both to blame. We must help each other to find the truth. No more compromise. But perhaps it's easier for the old not to compromise with life:

the young have so much longer to live. But you mustn't let yourself give in. Let me help you—'

'You fool!' burst from Louie's lips. 'I never want to see your face again.'

Mrs Falconer drew back in paralysed affright.

At that moment the big-boned servant came in to the room carrying a tray.

'Take your tea, the pair of you,' she said, and thrust the tray carelessly among the cups of cold tea upon the table. But Louie, ignoring the interruption, screamed miserably on.

Mrs Morgan's step and voice were heard.

'Not a word,' cried Louie. 'Not a word before my mother. Have you no sense of decency?'

Her whole demeanour altered. She laughed and chattered, a wild roguery possessed her. Gleams of graciousness returned.

Mrs Morgan accompanied Mrs Falconer to the door.

'Dear Louie! You must excuse her. She's so excitable. So natural in the circumstances. He may be arriving any day. Such a delightful man! We met him when we were staying in the south. Of course, we are not saying much, but you may be sure that I shall give my consent.'

The one elderly lady smiled benignly up into the face of the other; and Mrs Falconer, almost without her will, said softly, 'Yes, yes,' and patted the hand her hostess gave her in farewell. The round, pleased little lady smiled up again at her gaunt, tall guest.

'We mothers,' she murmured.

But Mrs Falconer went out on to the road shaking her head and muttering hard. All that evening she could not hold her peace. Words and broken sentences spurted from her lips, until at last Theresa said, 'What ails you, Nell, at all? If you want to say something, speak it out'; and Ellen, as though she had waited for the bidding, rose and spoke.

'I've been frightened of you all my life, Tris—I'm not frightened any longer. But I've seen a thing this afternoon that's frightened me. There's nothing to fear in all the world but deceit. Nothing at all. And I've seen it, I've seen it. I've seen a deluded woman—and he wakened her up from her idle dreams as he wakened me—despising truth, feeding herself on error, pouring her cups of devil's tea—'

'Where were you at all this afternoon?'

'At the Morgans'.'

'Oh, it's Louie you're meaning. Deluded, you may say. Their woman Eppie'll tell you the things she does.' Theresa prepared to expatiate, but Ellen cried, 'It's myself I mean. It was myself I saw. That's what I saw—myself. I'm inside Louie, and I'm a part of her deceit. God's in her, the God I can't get at—'

'You're raving, lass,' said Paradise. 'Feel her hands, Tris, she's in a fever.'

'—and for all my life to come I must proclaim it, that God's shut up inside us all and can't get out. I pushed her in, you see—'

Mrs Craigmyle, half rising in her corner, looked with sudden apprehension at her daughter. Ellen's face was chiselled now, its untouched innocence was gone; and as, for a moment, her mask of careless mockery let fall, Mrs Craigmyle bent forward to look at the raving woman, the old resemblance between the faces became strangely clear, both thin, both shapely and intent, and each significant.

Mrs Falconer's illness, which was tedious and severe, gave rise among the neighbours to such comments as: 'She's breaking up.' 'The poor old soul; they say she's terrible mixed.' 'Auld age doesna come its lane, but better the body to go than the mind, say I.'

Ellen's body in time recovered; but a change had come upon her. Nothing was in her head but the horror and sharpness of truth. She talked of it fiercely and incessantly to any who would listen. Her humble demeanour altered to one of angry pride. She could go to school to life no longer, since what she had learned was already more than her wits could rightly stand.

When her strength had returned she would slip away on Tuesday evenings and visit the Guild.

'Truth, my dear—no, no, I don't mean not telling lies. It's big, it's all one's life, all everyone's life, and no one finds it.'

They saw very quickly that all she wanted was to talk,

and let her be. One evening when she seemed more unsure of herself than usual they hesitated to let her go out upon the street alone; but one girl cried, 'I'll take her home, the craitur. She's real like my old granny. Many's the time I've taken her along. Come on, granny.'

They went off arm in arm.

The next time Mrs Falconer appeared in the Guild room Miss Theresa arrived on her heels, breathless, and apologised with many words; but paused, going, at the door, to indulge her natural inquisitiveness; and Mrs Falconer, stumbling back across the room, her head thrust forward, as she had run across the garden to intercept Garry Forbes, caught hand after hand that was held eagerly towards her, and patting them softly between her own, said, 'A little dottled, my dears, a little dottled. You must just forgive me.'

'Kate,' said Miss Theresa, 'you mustn't give your mother money. She wanders away.'

Kate gave her aunt a shrewd, considering look.

'I suppose she would wander away whether or not, Aunt Tris, and if she does, surely it's better she should have money to fetch her back. In any case, she's not so dottled as you would make out. A fixed idea, if you like, that's all.'

And when Mrs Falconer pulled her daughter aside, Kate gave her, smiling, what she wished.

At times a great bodily weakness came on her. She lay wasted and shrunken, very still, her face no bigger than an ailing child's, but the eyes shone out from it with full intelligence. She spoke seldom, unless her mother were in the room, when beckoning the old lady near, she would speak in a strong, firm voice.

On one such occasion she said, 'There is a God, but I have seen not even the shadow of His passing by. When one has found the secret being of all that lives, that is God. I have hardly begun, I have hardly begun. My life is ending and I have not seen Him.'

Another day she pondered, 'Am I old? I felt so young. I thought I had endless life ahead, and I have not. They say that I am old. I didn't believe that I could die, but I suppose I shall.'

Mrs Craigmyle answered, 'There's no need to get old, my lass. A body can be just the age he wants. For shame on you, get up, get up.'

Later, her strength come again, she would rise and stalk, erect and gaunt, upon the moor; or, gathering flowers, bring them to Paradise to name. 'That's tormentil,' said Paradise; or milkwort it might be, or eyebright; and Paradise would name them to her day after day. Or drawing her chair close in beside her mother's, she would talk with a strange wild clatter, by the hour.

In the last years of her life Mrs Craigmyle ceased to torment her second daughter, and when she died the old lady would not be consoled.

The Epilogue

Lindsay came by chance to the Weatherhouse on the day that Mrs Falconer died.

'Well!" thought Theresa. 'Nine years married and three bairns. Could one believe it?' She looked again at Lindsay's girlish figure and the happy candour of her eyes, veiled for the moment under a profound pity.

'Cousin Ellen,' Lindsay was thinking. 'Dying.' Death was remote and terrible. She had seen no one die; but there flashed back into her mind the recollection of a dead bird she had held against her bosom in this very room. 'I showed it to Cousin Ellen,' she remembered. 'That russet patch beneath its wing.' It comforted her vaguely that she had shown the beauty of the bird she mourned to the woman who was dying now. 'I didn't love her very much,' she thought. 'She interfered.' The gaunt, grey face upon the pillow horrified the watcher. 'I showed her my bird,' she thought, 'I showed her my bird.'

Mrs Falconer lay dazed and blank. 'Jumps out of bed!' thought Lindsay. 'She looks as if she could not move a foot.' But Theresa had explained that they had brought her down from her own high room. She couldn't be left alone a minute—would be up and running on her naked feet to the window. 'We couldn't be trotting up and down that stairs all day.'

'No, indeed,' said Lindsay, in her soft, commiserating voice. 'With Cousin Annie so lame, too—you must have so much to do.'

'Oh, not so much more,' answered Theresa tartly. 'If it's in the house you're meaning, all that Nell did in the house was neither here nor there. She's been about as much use this long while back as her mother, and less. Stravaigin' about on that moor at all hours. "You would need a season ticket, that's what you would need," I said to her. And muttering away to herself, you never heard! As wild as Bawbie Paterson herself, and she's a byword, though she be your husband's aunt, my dear.'

'Oh, you needn't tell me,' said Lindsay, with a glimmer. 'We can't stay in the house now. It's unspeakable. She's beyond everything.'

'It's a marvel to me that you ever stayed.'

'Indeed, yes,' said Miss Annie. ' "You must have taken her up wrong," I said to Tris, that first time after the war, when she came in and told us that Francie's wife had seen you arrive. And never to send us a line.'

'But that was Garry all over,' said Lindsay, laughing again. 'Up and away when he took it into his head. I couldn't have sent you a line.'

'Well,' thought Miss Theresa comfortably, 'I wouldn't be married to a man that's the byword and laughing stock of the place.' And she looked again at Lindsay with amazement. Happy—there was no doubt of it. Now who could have foretold that such a marriage would turn out well? 'It's these modern styles that does it,' she said aloud, with a nip to her tone, surveying the girl's lissome grace.

'I'm glad to see you don't show off your knees, Lindsay,' said Miss Annie.

Miss Annie had said, when the preparations for Lindsay's wedding were toward, 'I would like to hear that she was getting a good white wincey gown, but I don't suppose she will.'

'A byword and a laughing stock,' repeated Miss Theresa to herself. His name in everyone's mouth. *You would need Garry Forbes to you; Hine up on the head o' the house like Garry Forbes and his two fools*; and though *like seeking needles among preens* was an old phrase, *or sane folk among fools* had been added to it locally because of Garry. Mrs Craigmyle herself had made the addition, with a meaning eye upon her daughter Ellen. Theresa remembered the occasion well: an occasion when Ellen had said, unexpectedly, that Garry Forbes was liker a Christ than any other man she knew. A Christ—now what did she mean by *a* Christ? It gave them all a queer shock, coming like that from Ellen's gaunt, pale lips. Annie had said, 'Well, Bawbie now—she's never in the kirk from one year's end to another, and I doubt the young man's much the same.' Theresa remembered that she herself had cried, 'Well, there's no need for blasphemy about it,' and it was later the same evening that Mrs Craigmyle, using the phrase *like seeking needles among preens*, added *or sane folk among fools*.

'And indeed it's real hard whiles to tell the one from the other,' thought Miss Theresa complacently.

But there was no doubt of it, Lindsay was happy. Miss Theresa regarded her again. 'But when you've got your poke', she thought, 'you just have to be doing with the pig that's in it.' Even when the pig was one whose grumphs and squeaks made something of a family scandal. 'Old Garry's just hanging on for the next Coal Strike,' Frank Lorimer had said. 'Wait till you see—he'll come out strong, stronger than this time.' Some of his utterances had even been in the papers. A horrid disgrace. A mere asking for ridicule. Miss Theresa wondered that Lindsay would put up with it, but she didn't seem to care—just laughed and said, 'But that's the kind of thing that Garry does.' Well, she might repent it yet. Nine years was not so very long a time, and the wedding had been hasty enough, in all conscience. Theresa remembered how Mrs Robert Lorimer had come out to give them the news.

There they were, preparing for a marriage in the grand style a fortnight ahead; and that very morning, in the drawing-room at home, Lindsay had become Mrs Dalgarno Forbes; and the bridegroom was returning to the trenches the following day.

'Oh,' Theresa had said. 'Active service again. I thought he wasn't fit.'

Mrs Robert explained that it was his own desire. 'Would get himself sent. And it appears he was able enough all the time. It was just his nerves.'

So it had been a gey hasty affair, Annie supposed. And Mrs Robert told them that even the minister was not to be had in time, and so that old done man, the Reverend Mr Watson, tied the knot. 'And if he didn't forget the ring!—pronounced a benediction on them, and the ring still in the best man's fingers, and him fidgeting about and not knowing what to do. Such an unfortunate affair.'

'Well, well,' Theresa had said. 'Who will to Cupar maun to Cupar. That's her getting married in May. And the service all in a snorl. And no wedding frock and no party.'

'And her father,' continued Mrs Robert, 'he would blurt out anything, would Andrew. He said right out, "You're in a terrible hurry," he said, "come back and pay your loaf." And then they got the ring put on.'

'Sic mannie sic horsie,' old Mrs Craigmyle had said with a chuckle. 'Andrew's his father's son. You'll never see a Lorimer trauchled with overmuch respect for the kirk. And us all to come out of a manse, too.'

'And then,' Mrs Robert had proceeded, 'when he turned to kiss his wife, she actually skipped into his arms. Kicked her heels up—a regular dancing step. The trickiest you ever saw.'

'Oh, well,' Theresa had said, 'she grat sore enough about that wedding not so long ago, and she'll maybe greet again for all her dancing.'

'Yes, that was what I said,' she thought. 'And then mother began with her ballads.' She remembered perfectly what her mother had sung. She had sat aloof, as usual, just listening. One might be sure that in time she would put in her word. A song, most likely. She diddled away at old tunes most of the time. Hitherto, since Mrs Robert had arrived, she had spoken nothing but that chuckling proclamation of Lorimer disrespect. A gey life she and her brother must have led the old Reverend! But with her mind on the walled manse garden she reflected, 'He was real fond of a funnie himself.' Theresa was half a Craigmyle, a dourer folk than the Lorimers—dour, hard of grain, acquisitive; but even Theresa had spent hilarious days in her grandfather's patch of wood. And as she sat watching her sister die, Theresa's mind was a pleasant jumble of apple trees and the ploys of a pack of bairns, through which Lindsay's eager dance step and her mother's nine year old singing recurred like a refrain. The very tune came back and the mocking words:

He bocht an aul horse an' he hired an aul man

An' he sent her safe back to Northumberland.

It was then that Ellen had interfered. Opening her mouth for the first time, 'That's a cruel inference, mother,' she had cried sharply. Neither Theresa nor Annie paid much heed to what their mother sang. She was always singing, though there had been little singing since Ellen took ill. Dowie, the old lady was, peering anxiously. She wasn't in the habit of caring. Theresa thought it strange. 'It's the callow that worry,' she said to herself. A very old woman like her mother was past feeling strongly.

'What did the old ballads signify?' she thought, reverting to the wedding; but Ellen was always finding that her mother meant something—meant more than she should, Ellen intended to say. Well, and if she had meant to hint that the marriage might turn out ill, it was no more than they all thought at the time. 'But we were wrong, and it's a mercy,' she thought, daft Bawbie Paterson's nephew though he was. Would Bawbie have gone to the wedding now, she pondered; and with the black trallop hanging down her back? 'There was nothing amiss with the song, I'm sure,' Theresa said to herself. 'Mother had a rhyme about the ring too, if I could remember it:

a guid gowd ring
Made oot o' the auld brass pan, ay, ay.

But they had all cried out against that one—a sluttish thing, not to be associated with Lindsay. Mrs Craigmyle had let them cry, humming away at her tune, pleasuring herself with the unsavoury words.

The dying woman began to mutter restlessly. Miss Theresa put aside these ancient thoughts and went to the bedroom.

'How she speaks!' Miss Annie said to Lindsay. 'Such conversations as she holds, you never would believe. She's been taking a lot to your husband, my dear.'

'To my—to Garry? But how strange! Why, she hardly knows Garry. Talking to Garry?'

'Talking, my dear, and answering too.' Miss Annie broke off. 'But you never know what a body will say when they're dottled.' She sighed a little, looked towards her mother, and shook her head. The thought had come to her that to speak to Lindsay of Ellen's infatuation was less than kind. 'I remember,' she began again, 'when I was but a little thing, an old, old man—'

Her pleasant voice ran on; but while she told her story she looked again, anxiously and in a puzzled way, at her mother. Lindsay, too, looked at her aged grand-aunt who at ninety four, straight as a pine-bole and with all her faculties unimpaired, was seated on the high-backed sofa, knitting at her shank; but her eyes, Lindsay noticed, never left her daughter's face—Ellen, her second daughter, dottled and dying at sixty nine.

The muttering continued.

'Poor old craitur!' said grand-aunt Craigmyle.

And her voice had still tune to it.

'Yes,' said Miss Annie, reading Lindsay's thought, 'it's the old generation that has the last in it, I say to mother. There's Mrs Morgan now, as blithe and active at her tea-makings as ever you saw, and Louie a poor wasted thing.'

Louie Morgan! thought Lindsay. Strange that she should be mentioned then. Lindsay's thoughts, like Miss Theresa's, had been travelling in the past. And Louie Morgan, as well as Cousin Ellen, had had her part in the singular drama that preceded that hasty marriage service.

She said aloud, 'I haven't seen Louie for—oh, such a long time.'

'And needn't seek to,' said Theresa, returning from the bedroom. 'She's not a sight for self-respecting eyes. The drink. She's drinking hard. Bleared. And her stockings cobbled with a yellow thread. That's you and your religion and no meal in the house.'

'Religion—is she so pious, then? She used to pray—'

'Oh, pray tonight and pray tomorrow. She would pray your head into train oil. But no one minds her—her big words and her grand speeches. They know what to make of *her* declarations.'

Lindsay had a movement of compassion for poor simple Louie, outcast from the love and reverence of the earth.

'But she wasn't saying them that time,' she thought and remembered how she and Garry, when she had stayed at the Weatherhouse before her marriage, had come on

Louie kneeling in the wood as though in audible prayer; but when they came behind her, what she was saying was ludicrous. 'I'm on the Fetter-Rothnie committee—may I introduce myself?' she was saying. And she smirked to an imaginary audience. They had laughed about it often afterwards, though Garry didn't like her to tell the story in public. 'Oh, leave her alone,' he always said. But what harm did it do, Lindsay would ask, with people who didn't know her? Aloud she said, 'Fancy Louie coming to that! Poor soul! I liked Louie,' she added in a moment. 'She used to take me for walks— long ago, when I was a little thing. And tell me stories. She had a dog—Demon, wasn't it? Oh, I remember how he could run. Through the wood. I can see him still.'

'Nonsense!' rapped Miss Theresa. 'Louie had never a dog.'

'But I remember. I can see him. A whippet hound he was.'

'Nonsense! She hadn't a dog. She wanted one—one of the Knapperley whippets, Miss Barbara's dogs. But old Mrs Morgan wouldn't have an animal about the place. Louie kicked up a waup over not getting it, I can tell you. And after a while she used to pretend she had it—made on to be stroking it, spoke to it and all. A palavering craitur.'

Lindsay looked doubtfully.

'Did she? I know she pretended about a lot of things. But Demon—? He seems so real when I look back. Did she only make me think I saw him? He used to go our walks with us. We called to him—*Demon*, *Demon*—loud out, I know that.'

She pondered. The dog, bounding among the pines, had in her memory the compelling insistence of imaginative art. He was a symbol of swiftness, the divine joy of motion. But Lindsay preferred reality to symbol.

'Queer, isn't it?' she said, coming out of her reverie. 'I remembered Demon was a real dog.'

She was unreasonably angry with Louie, as though by her own discovery of Demon's non-existence Louie had defrauded her of a recollected joy. And Garry had proved her a cheat. Lindsay's mind reverted to all that had followed that odd encounter in the wood, and so came back to Cousin Ellen. She shifted a little on her chair, bringing her eye into line with the open door and the muttering old woman who lay on the bed; and suddenly Mrs Falconer began to shout, 'They have despised him and rejected him. Cry aloud, spare not. A stubborn people who will pay no heed.'

Theresa stood over her, saying, 'Now, now. There, lie down again. Weesht ye, weesht. It's all right.' But Annie, who had caught the Biblical cadence of the words, folded her knotted and swollen hands together in her lap; and Ellen continued to shout, harshly and without intermission, tossing her long, fleshless arm above her head.

That evening Lindsay, who was on holiday at her old home, said to her father, 'Daddy, you must go out and see her. No, I don't mean Cousin Ellen. She wouldn't know you, of course. I mean old Aunt Craigmyle. She was always so fond of you. Perhaps you could comfort her a little.'

'Comfort!' grumbled Andrew Lorimer. 'The old lady never needed much comforting that I could see. You don't take things hard at ninety four, bairn.'

'Oh, I know, daddy. I know she never seemed to care about anything. She looked at us all as though she were reading about us in a book. But she is distressed—really she is.'

'Oh, well, we'll see.'

Andrew Lorimer took his car and ran out the nine odd miles that separated the Weatherhouse from the city, and by that time Mrs Falconer was dead.

'Oh, Andrew, I'm right glad to see you,' said Annie, who opened the door to him. 'Come away in. Mother's so dowie. I never saw her so come-at.'

'Eh?' said Andrew.

He remained standing on the doorstep.

'What a brae that is!' he grumbled. 'It's not fit for any car. I've a rheumatic here,' he added, feeling his shoulder. And because he wished to protract the moment before he must go in and talk to his aunt, he asked, 'How's your own rheumatism, Ann?'

Miss Annie looked down at her shapeless lumps of hands. 'It's as much as I could do to open the door for you,' she said. A gleam flickered on her pleasant face. 'I've aye been handless, Andrew, but I'm getting terrible handless among the feet forbye.'

Andrew allowed himself to laugh. He felt less constrained. He disliked heartily the job on which he was engaged; but he had always enjoyed Miss Annie.

'What'll I say to her?' he queried, following her across the threshold. 'You'd better tell me what to say.'

He sat down beside his aged aunt and began to tell her about his rheumatism, wresting his shoulder round to show her where the pain lay; but all the while he spoke his thoughts were on the woman who had just died. He realised that he was thinking of her as an old woman. 'But she can't be old,' he thought. She wasn't so much older than himself when they were all bairns together, the three Lorimer boys and the three Craigmyle lassies, and played in the Manse garden at Inverdrunie, and grandfather Lorimer gave them prizes for climbing the elm trees. 'To keep them out of the apple trees,' he explained to his wife. What a climber Paradise had been, with her long foalie's legs! Tris and he were of an age, and Ellen some three years older. Not yet seventy, then. Pretty near it, though. And he thought, seventy years without event. Oh, to be sure, there had been the episode with that Falconer chap who let her down so badly; but that must have meant four years at the most—long ago. Kate—why, Kate must be going on for forty. And at that moment Kate Falconer entered the room.

An able-looking girl—he had forgotten that she looked so well. Matron in some sort of Children's Home, and exceptionally capable, they said. Looked as though her wits were at her service. She could do well for herself, if she liked—marry well. There couldn't be much money in that Charity Home business, anyway, though he supposed Kate would take what she was offered and make no bones. She wouldn't push for her own advantage. Took that from her father. Couldn't hold off himself. Let any shaver cheat him. And then slipped out of it all and left his wife and child without a copper. Kate wouldn't have a penny but what she earned. Yes, she would marry.

'That's Stella Ferguson gone up the road,' said Miss Theresa, who was adjusting a blind.

A moment later came a sharp ring at the bell. Kate went to the door.

They heard the stranger ask in a loud, challenging voice, 'What are the blinds down for?'

Kate's soft answer was inaudible.

'She's not dead? Her? Lord alive!' The girl broke into noisy blubbering.

'Stella Ferguson?' said Andrew Lorimer. 'Oh, yes, old Jeames's grand-child. No? I remember, I remember.' With a movement of the head towards the noise of her sobbing, he added, 'I suppose that's the etiquette of mourning with that stamp.'

'No,' said Paradise, 'that's not a pose. Stella has a warm heart. A bold bessy but a warm heart. She's done well for herself, Stella has, she's a smartie. She's typist at Duncan Runciman's and making good money, though she's but eighteen. Quite my lady now, and keeps her mother in her place. But she has a warm heart. When Mr John Grey died—they found him dead in bed one May morning, a year past, and all the days he lay, you would have said a lying-in-state—not a cloud, not a breath of wind. Summer in its glory. Halcyon days they were—you would have thought his very garden knew. Well, Stella came and brought her flower. Gean blossom it was—black the next day. And so his cousin, that had come because he had none of his own, she threw away the shrivelled thing. Stella was like a play-actress—ramped and raged. Picked the very branch out of the rubbish heap and put it in his hand again. "I'll not take another," she declared. "I said a prayer over that, I did. I don't say a prayer so often that I want one wasted." So her bit of blossom went to the grave with him,' concluded Paradise. 'Quite right to leave it too, I think.'

Andrew Lorimer had gone only a little way down the hill on his journey home when the girl Stella, leaping from the dyke on which she had been seated, intercepted him.

'Look here,' she said. 'They don't like me much in there. My mother was a bad woman, and they think I'm a bad girl, but I'm not. Gospel.' As she said *Gospel* the girl breathed noisily and crossed her breath with a forefinger. 'But if I'm not a bad girl,' resumed Stella, 'it's to that precious saint lying dead in there that it's due. My eye! They don't none of them know the kind she was. Never goes to church, doesn't she? She was a stunner, I can tell you. Look here, she's got to get my roses in her hand.'

She displayed a cluster of hardy yellow scotch roses.

'Stella,' said Mr Lorimer, stepping from his car, 'if you were the worst sinner that ever was, you'd have the right to pay your tribute to the dead. But you're a good honest girl. Come with me.'

And, quite unconscious of the high scorn in the look that Stella cast on him, he led the way back to the Weatherhouse.

'You can come and put it in her hand yourself, Stella,' Miss Theresa said.

So Mrs Falconer lay that night, white and still, her face, beset so long with pain and darkened by failure, serene at last, and the rose of the girl Stella in her hand.

GLOSSARY

a'thing
everything
begeck
disappointment
begrutten
tear stained
bide bydin
stay, remain; staying
bike
wasps' nest
bit
little, scrap of
blithe
happy
brose
oatmeal and milk or hot water
cantle up
brighten up
cantrip
piece of mischief
canty
lively, cheerful
chiel
lad
cloor
dent
clout
rag
collieshangie
animated talk
connach
devour; spoil
crack
gossip
craiturie
little creature
a crap for a' corn and a baggie for orrels
an appetite for absolutely anything and then some (literally: a bag for leftovers)
deil
devil
delvin
digging
dirds
bangs (vb)
dirl
ring (vb)
dour
stubborn
dunt
a blow
a dunt on the riggin
not all there (dent in the roof)
(neither) echie nor ochie
not the smallest sound
e'en
eyes
fee'd
hired
fey
peculiar, other-worldly
ficher
fiddle, fidget
fient
never! not a! (lit: devil!)
fleggit
startled
flinchin
deceitful promise of better weather

forbye
besides
fyle
soil, make dirty
gar
cause to
gey
rather
a gey snod bit deemie
a rather neat little maid
girned
complained
glower
scowl
grat
cried
greetin
crying
haggar
clumsy hacking
halflin
teenager
hap
cover up
hotterel
a swarm
hine awa'/up
far away/up
ilka
each, every
inen
in among
keek, keeing
peek, peeking
kye
cattle
lift
sky
to lippen to
to trust
loon
boy, lad
lousin time
end of the working day
lowe
blaze
lugs
ears
neuk
corner
newse
chat
nieve
fist
nyod
(an exclamation, lit: God!)
orra
odd, miscellaneous
pi
pious, sanctimonious
pleuch
plough
pooches
pockets
preens
pins
pyet
magpie
queets
ankles
rax
stretch
roup
a sale or public auction
sark
shirt
scran
scrounge
scuttered
fiddled about
shank
stocking being knitted
sharger
half grown creature
sheepy silver
flakes of mica (in a stone)
sic nannie sic horsie
like master, like man
snored
smothered (in snow)
snod
neat

soo's snoot
pig's nose
spoot-ma-gruel
any unappetising food
steekit
shut
stite
nonsense
swacker
more supple
tackie
tig (child's game)
thrawn
stubborn
timmer knife
wooden knife (useless)
tinkey
tinker
trig
neat
wae
woeful
wantin
lacking
waur; nane the waur
worse; none the worse
whiles
at the same time
yon
that
yowies
pine cones